THE ALPHA'S PROMISE
Written by Raven Darkwing

Published by
Darkwing Publications
PO Box 307
Fox River Grove, IL 60021
http://www.darkwingpublications.com/

The Alpha's Promise
Book 1: The Guardian Pack Series
Copyright © 2015 by Raven Darkwing

Cover Design by Kat's Media
Original Artwork by Stephanie Wallace
Book Formatting by Lo Confiado

Edited by LnJs Editing

ISBN: 978-0996488006
Printed in the United States of America
First Edition
June. 2015

eBook edition available
eBook ISBN: 978-0996488013

To all my writing friends who poked, prodded, and encouraged me to venture into the world of publishing my stories.

SUMMARY

It has been fifty years since the Great War between paranormals and the human race. A time when sanctuary packs like the Windy River Pack would seem to be unnecessary. However, the arrival of a wrongly accused rogue and his younger brother will be the beginning of something evil that up to now has been hiding from view.

Grant Walker is the alpha of the Windy River Pack. At one time he had been an undefeated warrior who stood by the former Alpha, his father's side during the Great War. He is in charge of one of the largest packs in the United States and continues to offer sanctuary to any who seek it. But now with a missing pack member and the threat of a rogue coming into his territory, a rogue that he finds out is his mate, Grant will have to fight not only to save his pack and mate, but to also prevent another war.

Ricky Landon and his younger brother Sandy are on the run from their former abusive alpha and pack. Declared rogue for daring to escape from a life of slavery and sexual abuse, Ricky runs toward the only place he feels he and his brother can be safe, a sanctuary called Windy River Pack. Confused by the strange tattoo that was placed on his arm by a Shaman and fueled by the need to protect his younger brother the last thing he wants is a mate.

Can the two be mated or will Ricky's former Alpha be able to reclaim what he considers his property?

TABLE OF CONTENTS

CHAPTER ONE

RICKY CURSED AS HE GLANCED IN THE REARVIEW MIRROR OF the old truck. He sighed and ran a shaky hand through his shoulder length strawberry blonde hair. This just wasn't his day. Actually, it hadn't been his day for as long as he could remember. The twenty-two year old glanced sideways at the young child sleeping in the passenger seat. At six years old, his brother was luckily young enough to be able to fall asleep anywhere. For a moment, he wished he could be the same.

But lack of sleep wasn't the only problem he had at the moment. The stupid bucket of bolts he had 'borrowed' from one of his old pack members had apparently decided to finally give up the ghost. He could tell without even looking that the engine would not be starting again without repair. At one time he had thought about opening up his own shop, but life had intervened and left him stranded with no tools and the nearest auto repair shop still over a hundred miles away.

With a soft groan, Ricky quietly opened the door and exited the vehicle. He grasped the door handle and held it tightly for a moment as the world around him spun out of focus. The young human could feel the sweat beading on his brow as he tried to get his body to obey his commands. It was getting harder as new injuries melded with old to make him feel as if he was in worse shape than the broken down truck. All he wanted to do was find a nice warm bed and sleep for the next century or two.

Unfortunately, he couldn't give into his body's demands. Straightening his shoulders as much as his injured back would allow, he limped slowly towards the front of the truck. The heavy hood wasn't the only groan that filled the quiet night as Ricky propped it open to have a look. It amazed him that the truck had gotten them this far. It only took him a moment to determine that the broken belt signaled the end of their ride.

He tossed the useless rubber towards the side of the road and looked upward. "Great, why don't you just shoot me now and get it over with!"

"Who're yah talkin' to?" Sandy's voice floated on the breeze.

Ricky glanced over and saw a small pale face leaning out of the open passenger window. With a soft sigh, he let the hood fall shut and walked carefully back to the passenger side of the ancient vehicle.

"Just talkin' to the wind, little brother." He tousled his brother's white hair and chuckled when the youngster swatted his hand away.

"Stop it!" Sandy growled, as he ducked back inside and rolled up the window.

Ricky enjoyed the brief respite from his current worries. If it weren't for his sibling, he'd have given up long ago. But he'd made a promise to his stepmother to take care of Sandy if anything ever happened to her. At the time, he never thought things would end up the way they had but he never regretted making the promise. Even though no one else in his life had ever kept one to him, he vowed that he would be different. Ricky closed his eyes and shut out the memories of his life before his stepmother had been killed. He didn't have time to dwell on the past, as their future was what required his attention now.

Ricky gazed over the dark woods that lined the lonely mountain road. It was well past midnight and the wind had the scent of snow. It was late fall in Montana and he knew the weather could get bad quickly in the mountains.

Ricky chuckled as he thought about the name of the mountain range they currently were stranded in. When his one and only friend Jake had told him about a pack of shifters who lived in the Freaky Mountains, he had thought he was yanking his chain. Jake told him the pack was rumored to be a place where those who needed help could go and get it without any questions asked. A quick search on the Internet not only indicated that the mountain range actually existed but also had shown him that it included the town of Sugar Creek where the pack was located. He'd hoped that he could seek asylum with the Windy River Pack but had wanted to check them out before he committed himself. After all, the last time he'd joined a pack it hadn't worked out so well.

The young man shivered as he pulled the collar of his thin coat higher. It was getting colder, but the chill in his bones wasn't just due to the weather. His mind went back to the last conversation he'd had with Clifton, the Alpha of Willow Creek Pack.

"You will bring back my son and face retribution." The echo of the Pack Alpha's cruel voice caused the young human to flinch at the memory.

He'd lost count of how often he'd heard that tone over the past few years. Usually it was just before he'd be punished for some infringement of pack laws or because the Alpha felt like it. When Alpha Clifton had found out that not only was Ricky gay but was also the reason that his stepmother Maria had died, his life had become hell on earth. Apparently, the Alpha had thought Maria would be his and never accepted that she could be the true mate of a lowly human.

Ricky shivered on the side of the road while he remembered that even in a dingy hotel room that was miles from pack land, he had still felt intimidated by the wolf. Yet he had still managed to squeak out a response in challenge: "He's not your son!"

Ricky had felt the whip marks on his back throb even though he had been out of the Alpha's reach at the time he'd gotten the call. His hand had gripped the cell phone, almost crushing it as he tried to get his breathing under control. "You will face retribution boy for taking my son. I have already called the hunt to retrieve what's mine. You know what that means, boy?" The Alpha's voice made him shudder. "You're officially considered rogue. No one will give you safety and when my warriors find you, there will be no mercy this time."

"You can't do that!" Ricky gasped. "I'm human, not a shifter!"

"You agreed to join my pack and to follow my rules boy. When you burned down the Williams' barn, stole a truck and took what was mine, you sealed your fate. Now the question is, will you face it like a man or will you go down screaming like the freak of nature you proved yourself to be?"

Ricky could still hear the sound of the cell phone breaking against the wall just before he heard the sound of howling outside the hotel room. Without thinking about it, Ricky had grabbed his little brother, the duffle bag that held their few belongings and drove into the night.

That had been two days ago and still he knew it was only a matter of time before the Sentries of Willow Creek would find him. He shook his head free of the memories and wished he hadn't been so rash with the cell phone. It would certainly come in handy right now. Instead he currently stood on a lonely road in the middle of nowhere. He had basically two choices: either he stayed here with the broken down truck with the hope that someone would happen by before the Willow Creek Sentries found him, or they had to hike through the mountains and gamble on finding shelter before the storm hit. In the end, Ricky knew he actually only had one option.

He opened the passenger door and grabbed their duffle bag from the floorboard. "Come on short fry, we gotta go on foot from here."

"Where are we goin', Ricky?" Sandy asked quietly as he jumped down from the truck. He was tall for a six year old, probably due to his wolf genes. Ricky smiled as his little brother lifted his face and scented the air before he looked back up at him.

"We're going on an adventure, Sandy," Ricky answered as he closed the door and took a quick look to get his direction before he limped towards the dark woods. "We're going to explore these woods just like Lewis and Clark did hundreds of years ago."

"Cool! Can I shift once we get into the woods?" Sandy asked as he walked beside his older brother.

Ricky smiled as he reached down to pat his brother on the shoulder. He wished his brother didn't have to be so careful. If he were just a normal wolf shifter, there wouldn't be a problem because humans had known about the existence of paranormals since the Great War. Peace had come at a high price, but at least now all the beings on the planet seemed to at least tolerate each other. The issue was not just the unusual color of his brother's fur but the strange birthmark that signified his special status. It brought attention to them, which was something they needed to avoid at all cost.

"Sure thing, short stuff, as long as you promise not to go too far and you remove your clothes this time before you shift. You only have one extra pair of pants."

A short time later the young human grinned as he watched a pale white wolf pup running ahead of him. He couldn't give his brother much, but with luck he'd find a pack that would not only accept them but also help him protect his brother from his destiny.

Ricky rubbed absently at the tattoo on his upper arm. In part, it mirrored the simpler version on his brother's wrist. Maria had taken him to an old shaman, who performed a ceremony he didn't understand, shortly after Sandy's first shift. It was that day that his step-mother explained to him that his little brother was special and asked him to watch out for his younger sibling. He'd agreed and never regretted his decision. As he slowly followed his brother into the wilderness, he just hoped this new pack would be better than the last one they had been in—if not, then Ricky would find a place where his brother would be safe.

• • ❖ • •

Grant Walker sat back in his office chair and steeped his fingers beneath his chin as he gazed at the young wolf pup sitting in front of him. The sixteen year old had been caught skipping out on school again. It was hard to keep a straight face as he watched the young wolf squirm under his dark gaze. Sometimes though, the best way to get to the root of a problem was to remain silent and wait for the other person to speak. He remembered how often his father had used the same technique on him. Even now, he could get Grant to spill his guts with just one look.

"Alpha Grant?" The young boy said softly, as he picked at a loose thread on his jeans.

"Yes, Roger?" It wouldn't be long now before he found out why the boy kept skipping classes.

"I can't go back there, I just can't..." The pup glanced out the window and sucked on his lower lip. Grant leaned forward slightly but remained silent as the boy continued. "It's not that I don't like school, but if I don't stay home and help with the stock my Pa will lose the farm."

"Why would he lose the farm, Roger?" Now they were getting some place.

Grant liked to think that he knew everything that went on in Sugar Creek, but had his limitations being the leader of the largest wolf shifter pack in North America. He wondered if his brothers knew what was happening with the Sanders family. No matter, he'd get his answers from their son and then he'd take care of the problem.

"My Pa's been having trouble finding help since Charlie decided to quit. I can always go back to school later, but if we lose the farm we won't have anywhere to go." Roger straightened his shoulders and looked at Grant.

He'd give the kid credit for having his heart in the right place. However, he and Mr. Sanders would be having a chat about not letting him know of his need. It also angered him that the young pup thought he'd let any member of his pack be homeless.

He closed his eyes and took a deep breath to keep his inner wolf at bay. It wouldn't help matters if he took out his anger on the young pup in front of him. The Alpha sat back in his chair.

"I will find someone to help your dad out. And you will go back to school," Grant stated as he reached for a couple of files on his desk. He'd simply check to see if any members of his pack were available and might be interested in taking the job.

"I don't know, Alpha." Roger hesitated for a moment before he spoke again. "My Pa doesn't like to take charity."

"But he allows his family to help him, correct?" Grant growled softly in warning.

"Well, of course, family is supposed to help. That's why I've been skipping out on school when I can. It's my job to help my family," Roger replied without hesitation. Even though the wolf was standing up to him, the teen still tilted his head in a sign of submission. Again, Grant found himself trying to calm his inner wolf.

"M'sorry," the boy mumbled as he realized how close he was to meeting Grant's wolf.

The Alpha wolf sighed. "You let me worry about talking to your father. In the meantime, I'll make some calls and have a couple of my Sentries help out until we can find a permanent replacement. You need to finish school, Roger, if you want to be able to help your family."

"Yes, Alpha." Roger tilted his head again to the side in a show of submission.

"Good, now that's settled. I'll have someone give you a ride to school while I give your dad a call." Grant could see the uncertainty in the young pup's eyes. "Don't worry, I won't tell him how I found out, this time. But in the future, as part of this pack, I would expect you or anyone else who has a problem to come to me or one of my brothers. After all, pack is family, and as you said, family helps family." He chuckled as Roger quickly stood and exited the room. Grant picked up the phone and began to make his calls. With luck, he'd have time to get some time to relax and work on his current project before dinner.

A short time later, a sharp knock on the door was his only warning before his brother and pack Beta, David, walked into the room.

The wolf bowed with a flourish of his hand. "So how is his royal highness this afternoon? Still listening to the plight of the lowly serfs who live in your kingdom or are you planning the latest battle to take the castle and win the hand of your maiden fair?"

Grant's lips quirked slightly. His brother's chocolate brown eyes were filled with mischief as usual. The Alpha gestured to the chair on the opposite side of his desk. "You do realize that I have a pack to run and unlike you, that doesn't give me much time to play with the latest security toys on the market right?"

"Those 'toys' help make sure this pack stays safe." David started to defend himself before he plopped down into the chair and realized he was being teased. A smirk curled his lips. "Of course, there are other toys you might find more interesting to play with since you obviously don't have time to find someone to help you out. It might make you a little less—intense."

A low growl sounded in the room before Grant stood and walked away from his brother. He knew David worried about his social life, but he above all others should understand that the pack came first. He gazed out over the mountains that could be seen from his office window. He wished he could just let his wolf free and run through the land or be able to spend time doing what he loved, but as his father had pointed out to him at a very young age, that was not to be his role. He had accepted it, but there were times when he could feel the weight and the loneliness of his position eating away at him.

Grant jumped as he felt a hand on his shoulder. "You don't have to do this alone, brother. You have me and Jason as well as a number of friends who could handle things. You just need to learn to let go a little. I mean, how can you find your mate if you don't even look for him or her?"

"Father didn't have to search for Mother did he?" Grant answered as he thought about his parents.

His mother had come to one of the pack runs after her family had relocated to the area. His father told him that it had been love at first sight that night. Fate had brought his mother to his father and he always figured the same would happen for him. If he was lucky, it would be his Semme', his other half and the one that would complete him in ways that not many had the privilege of being. While his parents were deeply in love, neither of them had ever found their Semme'.

In fact, Grant couldn't remember meeting many wolves who had been lucky enough to find the mate that completed them. Of course, as his parent proved, a regular mating could be just as strong. Very few would argue that once his father met his mother that he became a stronger Alpha because of their mating.

"Oh come on, Grant!" David groused. "You honestly think your mate is going to just show up on your doorstep some day? What happens if your Semme' meets someone else in the meantime? You know Semme' mates don't always end up together. You need to start looking for someone who will help you like mother did father."

Grant took a deep breath and faced his brother. He gazed into the brown eyes so much like his own and yet different. His sibling had not only inherited his mother's looks but also her temperament. In fact, he could remember the last conversation he had with his mother being on similar lines. He was glad his father had decided to retire in Arizona rather than stay here after he stepped down five years ago. Dealing with his nosey brother was enough of a challenge. Deciding a change of subject was in order he walked back towards his desk.

"Did you know that Charlie left the pack?" Grant asked, as he settled back in his chair.

"No, when?" David asked, as he sat down.

"According to Mr. Sanders, he left a few weeks before the fall harvest. Charlie didn't even pack his bags. At first they thought he'd just gone for a long run, but now they assume he just moved on." The Alpha looked at the file on his desk. "Do you have any idea where he might have gone?"

"I can have Jason start a computer search to see if we can locate his family. However, it's not likely we'll find anyone. As I recall, he was kicked out of his pack when he refused to marry the Alpha's sister right?" David pulled the file towards him and began to read through it.

8

Grant was always amazed at the details his brother was able to remember. It was one of the many reasons he felt lucky to have David at his side.

"He never did tell us the whole story, but then many that seek sanctuary with us don't." Grant sighed. Hundreds of years ago, his father had started the tradition of helping those who needed a safe place to live, regardless of the situation. In fact, a grateful Shoshone Indian Tribe, who his father had saved from attack, gave them the very land they owned. The tribe had eventually moved on, but the Windy River Pack had remained behind on the land and continued to take in those who needed their help. It was a proud tradition and one that Grant hoped would never end.

"True, but Jason did do a background check and found nothing criminal. It says here that the Alpha didn't even acknowledge that Charlie was part of his pack." David tossed the file on the desk and ran a hand through his close-cropped light brown hair. He still wore it in the military style he'd grown accustomed to during his stint as a Navy Seal. In fact, it was the reason he was so good at what he did.

David ran his own security firm with the help of their younger brother Jason. Between Jason's computer talents and David's knowledge of security and attention to detail, firms all over the world sought after them. Grant respected his brothers' skill and was glad they had agreed to remain with the pack as his Beta's. With their expertise, the security of the pack was strengthened.

"See if Jason can find anything out. I've sent some of our Sentries out to see if they can pick up his trail just in case something happened." Grant glanced once again at the mountains that surrounded the valley they lived in.

Shifters could live for over a thousand years and were difficult to kill. However, even wolf shifters could die at the hands of Mother Nature or by a silver bullet to the heart from a hunter. Even though hunting was not allowed, there were still some humans who defied the law. Usually, they were more interested in the herds of elk and deer. But there were still some humans who thought shifters were unnatural beings. Luckily their numbers were few, but still the shifter community was always on alert.

"You know it would have been easier if Mr. Sanders had told us sooner. Did he say why he waited so long before telling us there was a problem?" David looked up and wrinkled his brow. Grant could tell he was already running various scenarios through his head.

"He honestly thought Charlie just wanted some time off. Since the wolf stayed mostly to himself, it didn't cross his mind that something may have happened," Grant replied gruffly. He was still upset with the fact that neither wolf had asked for his help. What was an Alpha if not to provide what his pack needed? Hopefully the prideful wolf would remember to come to him next time rather than let his son sacrifice his future.

David sighed, his eyes filled with understanding. "And Mr. Sanders didn't think he should bother you with this information. So how did you find out what was going on?"

The Alpha grinned. "A little bird told me…"

"Ah, so you squeezed the information out of young Roger. Honestly, big brother, don't you think your days of playing the big bad wolf are behind you? I bet that poor kid was ready to piss in his pants when you called him in to talk to him." David grinned as he glanced up at Grant.

"For your information, he volunteered the information when I called him here to find out why he was skipping so many of his classes at the high school. The principal called me with his concern over Roger's grades. The boy is at the top of his class and it would be a shame to let him throw it away," Grant replied dryly. One of the many accomplishments he was proud of was that their school system was one of the best in the country. He, like his father was a firm believer that the best way to ensure the future of the pack was to educate its members so they could fit in with society.

David scowled. "I remember you tattling to Dad when Jason and I skipped training one day to go running in the forest. You know ditching school is almost a requirement right?"

"Oh, come on. You know the reason you got in trouble was because you were in the woods alone without any Sentries to watch over you. If you hadn't snuck away from your security detail, Dad wouldn't have been so angry. Like it or not being the son of the Alpha has its risks."

"Gee, thanks, Dad. But I had it under control. You know maybe if you had slipped out once or twice, you wouldn't have that giant stick up your ass now." David smirked as he crossed his legs and sat back in the chair. Grant knew that pose and he didn't feel like spending more time discussing his personal life, or lack of one, with his brother.

Grant pointed toward the door. "Just see what you can find out about Charlie. It may be nothing, but if he is in trouble we need to help him if we can. I won't have a member of my pack hurt or worse if I can help it." He watched as his brother shook his head and sighed.

"Okay, I'll get Jason on it." David stood and bowed at the waist. "Anything else I can do for you, your Royal Ass-ness, or will you be returning to the solitude of your ivory tower?"

A soft growl hid the chuckle that was threatening to escape. Grant sometimes wondered why he put up with his brother's antics, but then he wouldn't want anyone else beside him in a battle. David might be irritating but when it came to protecting the pack or him, he was a fearless warrior. Still, some days.

"There is one more thing, actually. I received a call from Clifton Steward of the Willow Creek Pack."

His brother straightened up quickly and frowned. "I haven't heard about him for a long time."

Grant nodded. "The Alpha didn't even know Dad had retired."

"I bet that was a shock to the old fool. I do remember that Dad didn't like him very much. He thought he was too old school and for Dad that really means something," David added.

Grant's lip twitched, but he refused to let his brother know he was getting to him.

"He's still an Alpha and as such deserves our respect," Grant chastised his brother, but softened it slightly by muttering, "At least until he does something that proves he's a complete asshole." He smiled slightly at his brother's bark of laughter. He might believe in some of the old ways, but he wasn't blind to the shortfalls.

"So what did Alpha asshat want?" David asked as he sat forward.

"It seems he has a pack member who has gone rogue." Grant watched as his brother's expression changed to be more serious.

A rogue was not something any shifter took lightly. It was rogues who had almost caused their entire race to be wiped out when they started the Great War between the humans and shifters over a hundred years ago. Grant had still been young at the time, but he remembered how close they had come to extinction. It was only through cooler heads, and an agreement that the shifters would put down any future rogues, that peace was eventually obtained. For the past fifty years, all beings had lived in relative peace.

"What did the shifter do?" David asked all business now.

Grant sighed. "Apparently he set fire to a barn, and while the pack was busy fighting the fire, he stole a truck and kidnapped the Alpha's six year old son."

His brother's shoulders tensed. "Do you believe him?"

"I have no reason not to believe him. However, I want you and Jason to begin to do some research on the rogue. His name is…" Grant searched for the paper he'd written on during the disturbing phone conversation. He found it and read the name. "Richard Landon. If he is truly a rogue, then the Alpha's son will be in danger."

"Why would he take the pup?" David asked the same question Grant had asked the Alpha of Willow Creek.

"For his own protection apparently; he knew he would be killed and figured the only way to evade his punishment was to take the Alpha's son," Grant said gravely as he looked out the window. "If they come this way, we are to detain and return them both to Willow Creek."

His Beta shook his head slowly. "It doesn't make sense. Rogues normally are beyond thinking rationally. They are more animal than human. Besides, taking a child, not to mention the child of an Alpha? That would only spur the pack on to find him. Even a rogue wouldn't be that stupid."

Grant nodded in agreement. "And that is why I want you and Jason to check the story out. If he comes here, we will get to the truth of it."

Grant growled. He hated rogues for what they had done to their race and he hated that this one had put a young innocent pup at risk.

David took the paper with the name on it and put it in his pocket. "If we find out what Clifton says is true, do we return the rogue to Willow Creek?"

The Alpha stood and growled as he felt his teeth start to lengthen. His claws also began to push through as he fought the change. "If Richard is truly a rogue and guilty of these atrocities, then he will be killed." Grant took a deep breath as he watched his brother tip his head to the side. The Alpha Wolf in him wanted to hunt and kill the threat but the human part knew there could be more to the story. He fought his nature and after a few minutes managed to calm enough that he could speak again. "See what you can find out and report back to me, David."

David stood and nodded before he smirked. "Fine, but don't think our conversation about your lack of social skills is over big brother. I'm onto your diversion tactics. If I have to get Sparky to help me, I will pull that stick from your ass." His brother paused, a mischievous glint in his dark eyes as he finished. "And replace it with a nice vibrating dildo. At least then you'd loosen up a bit."

Grant stood and glared at his brother but realized as usual it didn't faze his sibling. He could hear his brother's laughter as he closed the door and walked down the hall. The Alpha stood and walked toward the window to stare out into the wilderness. It wasn't that he didn't want more, but rather he had no idea how to be both an Alpha for his people and a man who would give anything for someone to fill the hole in his heart. He longed for a lover who could fill the void or better yet be his Semme' mate; the one person who would never leave him and yet, he knew the odds were against it ever happening.

CHAPTER TWO

RICKY STUMBLED FOR WHAT SEEMED THE HUNDREDTH TIME since they had entered the woods. He paused and glanced around. All he could see were trees and more trees. If it weren't for the mountain peak he could see in the distance, he would have been totally lost.

"Sandy!" Ricky called out, surprised by how weak his voice sounded. His body was on fire even though it shivered from the cold. He would be forced to stop soon or fall and not get up. Neither choice seemed like a good idea but his body was past listening to him.

The sound of something running through the brush caused his head to whip around. It was times like this he wished he were a wolf shifter. Then at least he could tell by scent what was coming towards him. Of course, it didn't really matter since he doubted he could even raise his arms to defend himself. Just as he slipped to his knees a white wolf appeared. Ricky sighed with relief as he hugged his younger brother close and petted his fur. Even though his brother was only six years old in human years, in wolf form he was already the size of a large timber wolf.

"I told you not to get too far ahead, Sandy," he chastised lightly as he tapped his brother on the nose.

Sandy squirmed out of his arms and sat back on his haunches. A moment later there was a slight shimmer in the air and a naked young boy now sat where the wolf had been.

"Ricky! I found something!"

Ricky reached into the bag he carried and handed his brother his clothes. He waited patiently until Sandy was fully dressed before he spoke. "Did you find another arrowhead?" The young human smiled as he realized he already carried at least half a dozen in the battered duffle bag. He didn't have the heart to tell his brother they weren't really treasures.

"It's much better." Sandy was excited. If he were still in his wolf form, Ricky could imagine his tail wagging along with his whole hind end. It was clear his brother needed to tell him about his latest discovery.

With a groan, Ricky stood on weak legs and gazed at the slowly setting sun. They would need to stop soon and find some kind of shelter for the night.

"It's a little house, Ricky. I went up and knocked but no one answered, so I don't think anyone lives there. I couldn't smell anyone either. But I bet it would be better than the cave we used last night don't you think?" Sandy barely took a breath as he spoke about his find.

Ricky held up his hand. "Hold on, you went up to the house and knocked? What if there had been someone there?" He hated to make his brother afraid of strangers but with their current situation, he could get them killed if he wasn't careful.

Sandy rolled his eyes. "I told you. I didn't smell no one. I just knocked, 'cause I thought it would be polite. Come on I'll show you!" The young pup turned and began to stalk back in the same direction he'd come from.

For a moment Ricky almost called him back, but then he realized if what Sandy said was true it could be their salvation. He doubted he was going to survive much longer without shelter. Food and water wouldn't hurt either and maybe some aspirin for the fever and pain. All he had left in the medical supplies he'd taken were some bandages. He stopped suddenly as he stepped into a small clearing.

"See, I told you!" Sandy barked out as he pulled Ricky towards the small log cabin.

The porch sagged with age and a few boards were missing from the stairs. But the door was still solid enough and the windows still had glass. If the fireplace worked, maybe their luck had changed. However, first he had to make sure it really was safe.

"I see it, Sandy, now stay here until I check it out okay?" Ricky watched as his brother crossed his arms and stuck out his lower lip.

"I told you, no one has been here for a long time. My nose would know if someone had!" The young pup moved forward, but Ricky pulled on his arm and stopped him. A low growl escaped his brother's throat as he turned to glare at his older brother.

For a moment, Ricky was reminded once again how much stronger his younger brother was than him. It wasn't the first time he wondered why Maria had entrusted him, a mere human, with the care of his sibling.

Ricky took a calming breath. "I believe you, Sandy, but that doesn't mean the building is safe. If we're not careful we could step inside and it could collapse or the boards could be rotted in the floor. Why don't you go and gather some wood while I check it out? That way we can start a fire and get warm as soon as I make sure it's safe for us."

Ricky watched as his younger sibling thought it over for a moment, before he nodded and headed to gather some of the smaller branches and logs scattered around the clearing. He smiled at his brother's willingness to help. For a six year old, he sometimes acted more like he was twice his age. But then their life hadn't been easy and required them both to mature before their time.

Ricky walked carefully up the steps and onto the porch. The boards groaned but held his weight easily enough. He signed with relief as he opened the door and walked inside. He sneezed a few times as he glanced around the one room cabin. There was a rickety table in one corner with two chairs. A cot that had definitely seen better days was shoved up against another wall and then there was the fireplace that took up the third wall. He was willing to bet this had been the home of a shifter or a hunter at one time. The lack of any kind of kitchen or bathroom lead him to believe whoever used this place had probably been an outdoorsman and only used this place to protect them from the fickle weather of the mountains.

The sound of sneakered feet preceded his brother as he entered the one room structure. "I've got the wood and I found a small stream just over the hill for water. It tasted real good and its cold. I could go get you some if you want Ricky." Sandy dropped the wood beside the fireplace and stood waiting for his next instructions.

For a moment, tears threatened to fall down the older sibling's face. He should be the one taking care of his brother, not the other way around. He jumped as he felt a small hand on his arm.

"I can help, Ricky. Please let me help."

The older brother squared his shoulders and smiled as he nodded. "Don't worry, it's going to take both of us to get this place in shape before that snow storm hits."

Ricky glanced around wondering what they could use to gather water. After a moment he opened the duffle bag and pulled out the first aid kit he'd grabbed as an afterthought. The plastic container might be big enough to carry enough water for them to use. He emptied out the rest of the medical supplies back into the duffle bag and handed the box to his brother. "Will this work you think?"

Sandy studied it for a moment with such intent that Ricky almost laughed. But he quickly hid his smile as his little brother grinned and nodded. "I might have to make more than one trip, but that's okay it's not far. Besides, I can drink in my wolf form."

"Good idea!" Ricky praised as he clapped his little brother on the back. He hated to have his sibling out of his sight, but he also knew that even at six years old, Sandy was already stronger than him in many ways. He'd learned quickly once they joined the Willow Creek Pack, that wolf shifters were capable hunters as early as age four. "Just make sure you use your nose and come back here if you smell anyone, do you understand me, Sandy?"

The young boy nodded his understanding before he turned and left the building. Ricky sighed and forced his aching body to remain standing for just a bit longer. He had to at least try to get a fire going and then if possible figure out a way to shake out the bedding on the cot. It would be tight, but both he and Sandy could fit on it. He glanced out the windows and wondered how long they could stay here, how long would they be safe?

It seemed like he had just sat down to rest for a moment when he felt someone pressing something against his lips. Ricky groaned and tried to sit up, but the room spun alarmingly. He noticed the fire was still going, so he couldn't have been asleep for too long.

"Come on, Ricky, you need to drink this and then I got a surprise for you."

Ricky chuckled. "Another surprise?" He smiled as he watched his younger brother's chest puff out before he reached down and pulled up a dead rabbit. For a moment, Ricky pulled back in horror at the bloodied carcass but then his stomach growled. "Well now, that is a good surprise. Just give me a minute and I'll get it ready to be cooked on the fire."

"Drink first, Ricky, please?" His younger brother pushed the plastic container towards him and waited while he drank.

The water was still cool and did taste good on his parched throat. Normally he would have been worried about drinking untreated water, but he knew dehydration was a bigger danger at this point. He drank slowly, savoring the wetness as it slid down his throat. He watched as his brother pulled the old table closer to the cot he was lying on and then went to the duffle to grab the hunting knife. It was the only gift his father had given him. He glanced down at the leather sheaf and remembered the day like it was yesterday.

It had been his seventeenth birthday. Maria had been married to his father for a little over two years and was pregnant with Sandy. It had been a good time for his family. Ricky had never known his own mother as she died when he was only two years old. His father had grieved for the loss of his wife by drowning himself in the bottom of a bottle. His youngest memories were of the smell of alcohol, sickness and the feel of his father's belt. No matter how hard he tried, his father always seemed to find him lacking. Years later, Maria explained to him that it was because he reminded his father of what he'd lost.

However, once his father met Maria his life changed for the better. Suddenly, he had a family with a father who had time to teach him how to hunt and toss a football. His dad had apologized for how he'd treated Ricky and promised it would never happen again. They even started going to church. It was as if Maria had brought the sunshine back into the world. But of course that had only lasted until he turned eighteen and his father found out that he was gay.

"Are you okay, Ricky?" Sandy's soft voice dragged him back to the present. He shook his head slightly and tried to smile. No matter how bad his life had been, Sandy was just like his mother, he brought the sunshine.

"I'm fine. Now, let's see if we can get this rabbit cooked, shall we?" They spent the next hour preparing dinner and then eating what tasted like the best meal he'd had in a long time.

In his former pack, he was lucky to get enough to just get by and meat was something he rarely had. He knew he'd lost weight and muscle but at least during that time Sandy had received decent care, or he thought he had. After overhearing the Alpha's plans for his brother, he knew he had to get him away and someplace safe.

18

"Do you want me to get more wood, Ricky?" Sandy broke into his unpleasant thoughts.

"I think we have enough to get us through the night. Why don't you take part of this and eat? You need to keep up your strength if you're going to go hunting for wood tomorrow." The tired human hated that his brother was being left with all the hard chores, but right now he doubted he had the strength to get to the front door.

Sandy shook his head and grinned. "I'm not that hungry, 'cause I ate the other one before I came back here." Sandy looked down for a moment before he continued. "Is that okay, Ricky?"

The older brother put down the meat he was eating and smiled at his younger brother. "You're a wolf, of course it's okay. Why would you think it's not?" He watched as his brother bit on his lower lip for a moment before he responded in a soft voice.

"Alpha Clifton told me eating cooked meat was for inferior beings like humans. He told me that if I didn't eat my meal raw, I wasn't a shifter. He said shifters are better than humans and that I shouldn't be around them or act like them." Sandy shrugged. "I don't understand why he doesn't like humans but I don't want to be a shifter anyway if it means I can't be with you. Maybe I should have brought back the other rabbit so you could cook it for me, then we could stay together forever."

Ricky saw red for a moment as he tried to get his emotions under control. He had suspected that their old Alpha was filling his brother's head with some kind of crap but could never prove it. He was glad he'd grabbed his brother and left before any more damage could be done. Luckily, his younger brother hadn't accepted what he was being taught.

Ricky took a deep breath and looked at his brother. "What do you think, Sandy? Do you think I'm weaker or less of a being because I'm human or because I don't eat my food the same way you do?"

"NO!" Sandy cried, as he jumped up and wrapped his arms around Ricky's waist. He stifled a groan from the contact on his still healing wounds before he hugged his brother back.

"Look, Sandy. There will always be people who don't like others who are different from them. That doesn't make them right. In fact, they miss out on so much by being limited in their view. When you get bigger you'll travel and see how many wonderful different kinds of people there are in our world." Ricky hugged him tighter for a moment before he pulled back and looked down into the light blue eyes of his sibling. "You're a shifter and more importantly, you're my brother and I love you. It doesn't matter to me if you grow long ears and have a purple tail, I'll still love you because you are a very smart and caring person."

Sandy sniffed for a moment before he stood and picked up the small piece of rabbit. He took a bite and glanced up at his older brother. "Could use a little more seasoning don't you think, Ricky?"

Ricky laughed as he continued to eat. "I'll put that on the grocery list, right next to the sugar cookies okay?"

The two continued to banter back and forth until both were warm, fed and tired.

As the exhausted human put more wood on the fire he stared over at his sleeping brother before he turned to gaze out into the snow filled night. "Please, if anyone is listening, just let us be safe for a little while. Not for me, but for my little brother. He doesn't deserve to suffer." As he looked at the sadness in the hazel eyes reflected back at him, Ricky wondered yet again if there really was anyone out there who truly cared or if he was destined to always be found wanting and to be alone.

As one day turned into another, the two boys had gotten a routine down. The only problem was, even with the food his brother caught and the shelter they had found, he felt himself getting weaker. Ricky glanced from his place on the bed towards the door his brother had gone through when the sun had risen. He wasn't worried yet as sometimes it took his brother awhile to catch the small prey they had been living on. Even with the snow, Sandy still managed to bring back food, water and more dry wood for the fire. It bothered Ricky that his six year old brother was doing the lion share of the work, and yet at the same time he was filled with pride that his sibling was proving to be such a great boy scout.

Of course, he grudgingly had to give Alpha Clifton some credit for making sure Sandy knew how to hunt and use his shifter abilities. Without them, they both would have starved long before now. But he would never forgive the shifter for what he'd done to him and what he intended to do with his younger brother. If he thought his father's abuse had been bad, what Alpha Clifton did to him made him, even now, drop his head in shame. He'd been made into the pack punching bag, household servant and sex slave for those who won favor with the Alpha.

On some level, he felt he actually deserved what had happened to him. Yet, after awhile, he realized that the Alpha was slowly killing him. A part of him was willing to give up and at one time, he almost had. But then his friend Jake pointed out the problem with that solution. If he died, who would be there to protect Sandy, who would keep his promise to Maria to ensure his little brother was safe? As he sat there and waited for his brother to return, he worried what would happen if he didn't get better. His last hope was that the Windy River Pack was truly a sanctuary pack and would at least take his brother in. As much as he hated the idea, he knew what he had to do. If he didn't feel better by tomorrow, he'd have to risk sending his brother on alone.

Perhaps dying in this abandoned shack was his penance for all the harm he'd caused those around him. After all, Alpha Clifton was right on one count. If it hadn't been for him, Maria would be alive and happy today. Sandy would have his mother and Alpha Clifton would not have found out their secret. Hell, even his father might still be alive and happy. His lack of control of his sexual urges had cost too many people their happiness. He closed his eyes and let his mind drift once more to the night all their lives changed.

Ricky had smiled as he and his best friend Robert parked in the driveway of his home. For the past month, the two of them had been experimenting and found they both enjoyed each other more than just as friends. So far it hadn't progressed further than some kissing and getting each other off, but soon Ricky would be leaving home to attend a local trade school and further his mechanic skills. They had talked about renting an apartment together. Ricky had known he was gay since he was sixteen but he still hadn't told his father. Part of him was afraid, because since finding religion again, his father had voiced his feelings loud and clear about how he felt about those who he believed lived in sin.

Robert leaned in and pulled Ricky close. Their lips touched before he opened to allow his lover in. He could feel the blood rushing to his cock and yet a part of him knew they needed to stop. His father would be home from work by now. But it just felt so good. His hand moved to rest on Robert's zipper as he gently rubbed the stiffening cock beneath the cloth. A soft moan sounded in the small confines of the car. Ricky slowly lowered the zipper on Robert's pants as he reached inside to feel the warm silkiness hidden within the folds of cloth.

"I love that you go commando, Robert," Ricky said softly, before he lips were once more claimed. He smiled as Robert began to thrust his hips while deepening their kiss.

Unfortunately for him, his father chose that moment to find out what was taking him so long to come inside. He remembered Robert begging him to just come home with him as his father banged against the windows hard enough to shake the vehicle. But he knew he had to face the man. He squeezed his friend's hand and told him he'd call him later.

Ricky went into the house and sat down on the sofa to wait for his father to come and talk to him. He figured he'd get a beating with his dad's belt, but he'd had them before and survived. Once his father was through, he intended to pack and leave. He was sure he could stay with Robert until the air cleared or until he could find a job and get his own apartment. He heard Maria yell for his father to stop and then he watched in horror as his dad entered the living room with a gun.

Maria grabbed Sandy and ran to put him in one of the bedrooms while Ricky faced his father.

"You're an abomination! How dare you bring that filth into my home!" His father raged at him.

Ricky stood and took it without saying a word. He hoped his father would calm down but instead his silence seemed to fuel his father's rage.

"Your mother would be ashamed of you! Did you know she had cancer and refused treatment so that she could have you?"

"NO!" Ricky shook his head as he listened to his father. He felt his world tilt as he thought about what his dad was saying. Had his mother really died so he could live? His father had always refused to talk about what had happened. With no other relatives to enlighten him, he'd just assumed she'd gotten sick and passed away just after his second birthday.

"That's right! Because of you, she died. If she'd taken the treatment, she would have lived and now you threaten our family with damnation again by being a fucking fag? I won't have it, not again. I won't lose my family because of you!" Arthur Landon raged as he raised the gun and aimed it at Ricky.

At that moment, he saw his death in his father's eyes. He watched as the man's finger tightened on the trigger, heard the sound of the bullet leaving the barrel and then blinked as a form jumped in front of him.

22

"Oh God! NO!" His father cried as he dropped to his knees, the gun hanging loosely in his grip.

Ricky looked down and saw Maria's wolf lying in a pool of blood. He couldn't move, couldn't even breathe as he continued to stare in horror at the unmoving form at his feet. He heard the sound of another shot and looked up to see his father lying on his side. The gun now lay on the floor next to his father's lifeless hand. It seemed like he stood there for hours, but it was probably only minutes before he realized he had to do something.

A slight shimmer in the air caused him to look down at his step-mother's human form. Ricky knelt beside Maria and turned her gently on to her back. Her eyes opened slightly as she coughed up blood.

"Hold still, Maria, I'll get help," Ricky said as he began to stand. He stumbled as a strong hand grabbed his arm and pulled him close.

"Too late for me—bullet was silver. Promise me, Ricky." Maria swallowed and tried to smile before she continued, "Call the Alpha at Willow Creek. Number is on my phone. Have him come. He'll help you." The shifter coughed up more blood and moaned softly before she turned to look at her fallen husband.

Ricky could see the sorrow in her eyes as she looked at him again.

"Not your fault." Her hand grazed the tattoo on his upper arm. "Remember your promise. Take care of Sandy. Promise me…" Maria stared directly into his eyes with such intensity it felt like she was staring directly into his soul.

"I promise. Please, Maria, don't die," Ricky pleaded, but she simply smiled before she took her final breath.

The bullet must have hit her heart. He remembered her telling him that shifters could heal faster than humans, but a silver bullet to the heart or decapitation could still kill them.

"I'm so sorry," Ricky sobbed, as he rocked while holding on to his stepmother.

He didn't remember much after that. Somehow he had managed to call Alpha Clifton. Once he had arrived, the Alpha took charge, leaving Ricky with nothing to do but feel the loss. The house was sold along with all their belongings. Ricky and Sandy moved to the Willow Creek Pack and lived with the Alpha. A couple of months after, Alpha Clifton had come to him to ask if

23

he wanted to be part of his pack. At the time, Ricky thought it was strange, but then he knew his little brother was a shifter and would need a pack to help him as he grew. Besides it was his fault that Sandy no longer had a mother. He had agreed to make sure Sandy was safe and he knew he couldn't do it alone.

Life had been good at first. Alpha Clifton treated both of them like they were his sons. He'd learned that the Alpha had loved Maria but since she had found her Semme' mate and didn't want to leave her family, he had walked away. He could tell the Alpha was sad, but he didn't seem upset about Maria's decision. The Alpha promised Ricky that he would make sure that both he and his little brother would always be safe.

After a few more months, Ricky began to think about finishing his schooling. He had a dream of opening his own mechanic shop. But fate once again intervened. His friend Robert stopped by one day while he'd been gone and talked to the Alpha. His old boyfriend had been concerned about how Ricky was handling what happened. Once again, Ricky returned home, his head filled with dreams only to walk directly into a nightmare. The Alpha threatened to declare both he and Sandy rogue and kill them for the death of his true love.

Ricky remembered begging while the Alpha beat him until he could barely breathe. He was thrown into a room and locked in for two days before the Alpha returned. It seemed he'd calmed down enough to realize that Sandy wasn't responsible and that killing Ricky wouldn't bring Maria back. So the Alpha informed Ricky of his new station in life and warned him that as long as he obeyed, he could live in the pack and Sandy would be cared for. He also made it clear that Sandy would not be allowed to leave with Ricky should he decide to go. Even among shifters it seemed being gay was seen as unnatural. A point that was further pressed home when the Alpha killed his ex-boyfriend to show what happened to any who went against the natural order. Even now, he could still see the dead eyes of his lover begging him to save him.

At that point, Ricky would have agreed to anything just to keep Sandy safe. But as the abuse continued year after year, he began to wonder what his treatment was doing to his little brother. When he witnessed his brother's tears after one of the more serious public beatings he'd endured, he decided that at some point he would escape and take Sandy with him. The final straw was the conversation he overheard between the Alpha and his Beta. They had plans for his brother and were going to use him to ensure that Sandy did what they wanted. It was clear this was not the best place for his brother.

As Ricky continued to wade through his past, time lost all meaning. One scene after another continued to play in his mind until he felt himself beginning to finally release his hold on life. His body hurt, his soul cried out in pain and all he felt was a coldness that seemed to seep into his very bones. He didn't even feel the frantic shaking of his body by the one person he had promised to protect.

CHAPTER THREE

A WEEK HAD PASSED AND STILL THERE WAS NO WORD ON what happened to Charlie. David and Jason had searched but there was no sign of the missing shifter. Grant worried even more about their pack mate. The Sentries hadn't found any sign of him and the Alpha of the shifter's former pack still insisted he had no idea who Charlie was. He hated to admit it, but they may have to just wait to see if the missing shifter would contact them again. Grant just hoped the wolf shifter would be able to.

He glanced down at the folder on his desk and continued to frown. His brothers had been able to find more information on Richard Landon than they had on Charlie. The biggest surprise had been that Richard was not a shifter but a human. When Grant called Alpha Clifton to demand an explanation, he couldn't believe what he was told. The human had agreed to become a member of the Willow Creek Pack and had even accepted the mark of the Alpha. So technically according to the old traditions, Richard was now considered the property of a wolf shifter and a member of the pack.

When he explained to Alpha Clifton that killing the human could cause problems with the peace treaty, the Alpha of Willow Creek had laughed. It was clear he was of the mind that humans should be either used as slave labor or eliminated. It wasn't an unheard of position in the shifter community, but it wasn't as predominant as it had been in the past. Grant huffed as he slammed the folder shut, and his brother thought he was stuck in the past?

Still if Richard did show up, he would present a problem for Grant and his brothers. If he provided sanctuary then he risked war with the Willow Creek

Pack. If he turned Richard over to be killed, he risked war with the humans. Then there was the matter of Sandy. By pack law, once Richard was accepted into the pack, the Alpha had the right to adopt Sandy as his own. Unfortunately, human law would not see it that way as Maria had granted full custody of Sandy to Richard well before her death. Which left another mystery, why would a wolf shifter leave custody of her pup to a human instead of a member of her pack? In a way, he hoped that Richard had kept running and wouldn't show up anytime soon.

The sound of a loud howl pulled Grant from his musings. He quickly ran from his office and headed for the front porch. One of the Sentries had sounded the alarm, which could mean anything from an unidentified shifter to a war party. As he quickly walked down the porch steps he was stunned to see a pure white wolf run directly towards him.

A large mahogany brown wolf and a slightly smaller black wolf jumped in front of Grant and growled at the young pup. Grant watched as the wolf stopped and stared at the two larger wolves for a moment before he dropped on his haunches and looked up at the Alpha. Grant could smell the fear and despair coming from the young pup.

"Shift, no one will hurt you," Grant ordered, while he placed his hands on his brothers' shoulders. "Why don't you two run inside and get dressed. Bring back something that our friend can use to cover himself with, too."

David huffed before he left with Jason to follow his Alpha's orders. It was clear the young pup was no threat. Grant glanced over at the now naked young boy for a moment, noticing his dirty and gaunt appearance. It was obvious the pup was not eating as much as he should. Grant sat on the porch step so that he would be less intimidating to the obviously distressed child.

"What is your name, son?"

The boy shifted from foot to foot for a moment while chewing on his bottom lip. He wrapped his arms around his body and spoke softly. "Ricky told me not to go to strangers but I didn't know what to do. He won't wake up, Alpha."

The boy jumped as the door opened to reveal David and Jason. Jason walked down and quietly knelt by the boy. "Here, why don't we get you into these and then we can go inside and talk, okay?"

27

Grant nodded to the child as he stood and moved to the side. He watched as Jason helped the boy get dressed before taking his hand and leading him into the house. Luckily his mother had insisted they keep their old clothes as they grew. He always thought it was her subtle way of reminding them she wanted grandchildren some day. But he had to admit, having smaller sized clothing had come in handy more than once when a young pup showed up on their doorstep.

He watched as the pup placed his hand in Jason's before following him into the house. His youngest brother had a way with people, especially kids. There had always been a quiet strength to Jason that Grant appreciated, especially at times like this. He couldn't help but notice the birthmark on the young man's wrist when he took his brother's hand. If he wasn't mistaken, the problem he had hoped would stay away had just landed on his doorstep and was even bigger than he had first thought. David stepped beside him and nodded towards the kid.

"You do know who that is, don't you?"

The Alpha nodded. "Yes, that would be a whole lot of trouble heading our way. I need you to gather up Dakota and Sparky. Also, make sure you double up the Sentries, but no one knows about Sandy or his brother until I say so. At least now we know part of the reason the Alpha at Willow Creek is so keen to keep Sandy as his own. We don't need Alpha Clifton on our doorstep before we figure out how we are going to handle this."

"Do you think the young whelp knows anything?" Daniel asked, as he glanced towards the kitchen doorway. "I mean, I've never seen one before, have you?" Obviously his brother had also notice the identifying mark of an Omega wolf.

"No, but Father told me he met one once. I honestly thought they were all extinct since the few who had survived being killed by our own, had been killed during the Great War." Grant shook his head. The problems just kept piling up with the Landon brothers.

Sandy's white fur was one of the traits of an Omega wolf but it was the mark of Gaia on his wrist that confirmed his status. He knew the Omega wouldn't come into his full powers until he turned twenty-one but there was no way to know for sure how much power he currently controlled. Again, his

28

knowledge was more from what he'd heard and he wasn't sure how much was fact and how much was part of a myth told to young wolves to scare them.

However, just the fact that he might be an Omega was enough for Alpha Clifton to want to keep the pup as part of his pack. Omega's were direct decedents of Gaia and were keepers of the old magic. They had been greatly feared by humans and shifters alike due to their unique powers.

Grant sighed. "If he requests sanctuary, we will grant it and he will need to be protected."

A war with the Willow Creek Pack now seemed more likely than not.

His brother nodded and headed towards his office. Meanwhile, Grant could hear Jason talking quietly to the young pup. "You were pretty brave coming here all alone, Sandy."

There was a soft sniffle before the boy's voice answered. "I thought I was helping but he only got worse. My mom and dad both died. All I have left is Ricky. Please, will you help him?"

Grant cleared his throat before he entered the room. He noticed the boy cringed and the smell of fear had returned. He had no idea what the boy had endured, but surely he must know that an Alpha would not harm him. "Can you lead us to your brother, Sandy?" He watched the battle going on with the young boy. It was clear he was torn over what to do. "We can't help him unless you tell us where he is."

"You won't call Alpha Clifton?" Sandy asked, as he glanced fearfully around the room. "Cause if you do, then I may as well leave my brother where he is. At least he won't be hurt no more." Tears began to drip down dirty cheeks as the pup began to cry. "I don't want my brother to be hurt because of me."

Jason's concerned eyes met Grant's as they both wondered what had really happened. The more the Alpha heard, the less he believed that everything was as it seemed when it came to Richard and Sandy. He knelt beside the small boy and placed a hand on his thigh. He could feel the trembling but ignored it as he tried to soothe the youngster's fears. "I promise that I will do what I can for your brother, Sandy. I won't call Alpha Clifton and I promise that I will listen to what you and Richard have to say. This pack is a place for those who need a home and need to feel safe. Can you trust me enough to help you save your brother, Sandy?"

Sandy looked at Jason who smiled and nodded in encouragement. "My brother is right. We don't turn away anyone who needs a safe place to stay. That includes you and your brother. Now, can you lead us to him?" The young wolf pup chewed his lip for another moment before he nodded.

"Good. My two brothers and two of my friends will go with us to get your brother. Can you tell me if there is a road near where he is or will we need to carry him back?" Grant watched, as the pup seemed to think about his question before he answered.

"I didn't see a road. I smelled a shifter come close to where we are staying and just followed his scent back here. I ran straight back to my brother to tell him I found help, but he wouldn't wake up. He keeps crying and there is blood on the blanket but I don't know how to fix it. So, after telling him I was going for help I ran back here and then the two big wolves tried to eat me." Grant smiled. The boy had talked without taking a breath. He had a feeling that once the pup became comfortable he was a real chatterbox.

A soft chuckle came from behind him. "I wasn't going to eat you, pup, and neither was Jason. We prefer our prey to have a little more meat on its bones." David knelt down and tickled the pup as he continued. "Of course, once you plump up a bit, you might make a nice midnight snack." Grant watched as Jason slapped David on the back of the head. "Hey! What did you do that for?"

Jason smiled. "What? I figured something jiggled loose in there and I was just trying to move it back in place."

Sandy giggled and grinned at the two siblings as they continued to banter for a few more minutes. Meanwhile, Grant motioned the other two shifters who were standing quietly outside the door to enter. The small pup tensed up as the two men entered. David turned and smiled. "Sandy, I want you to meet two of our friends. The short one with the spiky, purple?" David paused and turned his head sideways for a moment before he shook it and continued, "The one with no fashion sense is Sparky and the other guy is Dakota."

Sparky put his hand on his hip and hissed. "No fashion sense? I hate to break it to you but that cut you got going on is so 80's. Now this, my friend, is what you call stylin' in the new millennium." The wolf struck a pose to rival any model on a fashion runway.

"Well, at least we won't lose you in the forest. We can just follow the glow!" David yelped as Sparky punched him in the shoulder. Grant stood and moved between the pair before it could get any further out of control.

"Gentlemen, we have more important matters to take care of." He nodded at the now quiet wolf pup sitting at the table.

Sparky smiled and knelt down beside Sandy. "Don't mind us. We actually do like each other." Sparky glanced up and glared at David. "Just some days we like each other a little more than others. Don't worry, though, because once we find your brother and get him fixed up, I'll make sure you are just as stylin' as me in no time."

Grant smiled at the unsure look that crossed Sandy's face before the pup spoke. "Okay, I guess." He turned to look at the Alpha. "Can we go now?"

The Alpha held out his hand to the young boy. "Come on, we have a brother to find and fix before it gets dark."

Before long the rescue party had started following the white wolf pup through the forest. Dakota carried a pack with medical supplies including a collapsible rescue sled. As the Sherriff of Sugar Creek, he also had received basic medical training. He would be able to stabilize the injured man until the pack doctor could get to work. From what Sandy had revealed, it was doubtful that Ricky would be walking out of the wilderness and needed some kind of medical care. The Alpha just hoped the young man didn't require hospitalization, as that would draw unwanted attention and would place him outside the protection of the Windy River Pack's territory.

David carried another pack with spare clothes for them all and other things they might need on their trek. Jason and Sparky had taken up positions of defense to ensure they weren't surprised by uninvited guests. They all knew that a hunt had been called on the injured human and that meant Sentries from Willow Creek Pack would most likely arrive soon.

Grant glanced at the young pup that currently ran slightly ahead of him. It was obvious there was more going on than what the Alpha of Willow Creek had told him. If the Sentries of Willow Creek showed up, he'd deal with them because sending Sandy back wasn't an option. Especially if what the young wolf had hinted at had happened to the brothers. Abuse of any pack member was still considered an offense and could result in the Alpha of Willow Creek losing his position.

31

The wolves all looked up as Sandy yipped excitedly before disappearing over the ridge. They all hurried their pace until the old cabin came into view. As they approached, vague memories of this place surfaced in Grant's mind. He'd forgotten this structure was here. One of his father's old friends had lived here for years before he eventually died six years ago in the wilderness he loved. While shifters lived much longer than humans, they were not immortal. At his death, Hugh had been close to nine hundred years old. The Alpha was surprised that the dwelling still appeared to be in fairly good shape.

Of course, others had probably used it from time to time and he was glad it was sturdy enough to provide the human and his brother respite from the unpredictable weather. This time of year they could get heavy snowstorms that closed many of the mountain passes. Luckily, the snow that currently covered the ground wasn't very deep and actually would make getting Ricky out of here a bit easier with the sled. As they grew closer, Grant scented the air. Along with the smell of the surrounding woods and of burning wood he could detect another scent. He stopped and tilted his head, drawing in a deeper breath.

A surge of excitement had his cock swelling. For a moment he couldn't believe what he smelled on the wind. But the closer they got to the structure, the more sure he was of what it contained. His father had explained it to him of course, but experiencing the scent of his Semme' for the first time had him shaking his head. The fact that his Semme' was human and male didn't bother him, but to find out his mate was the rogue being hunted by another pack had him wondering what the fates were thinking. The situation had just become more complicated than before because there was no way he was going to let anything happen to his Semme' or his little brother.

They all shifted and dressed before entering the cabin. Jason and Sparky remained outside to guard the dwelling while the rest hurried inside. The smell of sickness and death filled the cabin. For a moment Grant held his breath as he got his first glance at his future. Was he too late? But a soft groan assured him the man on the cot was still alive if only barely.

"What have we got, Dakota?" The Alpha barked as he tried to keep his wolf under control. His first inclination was to grab the human and claim him; but luckily his human half was able to reason with his wolf. He realized David was looking at him funny as he paced close to the fireplace but he didn't care. Right now he had to make sure his Semme' was safe.

32

"He's in pretty bad shape, Alpha," Dakota responded softly. "You know, we probably should call in a rescue chopper and send him to the hospital. I'm not sure even Doc Houston will be able to help him." The Sheriff gently turned the young human and sucked in a breath before he gently began to cut away the tattered shirt. Even from across the room Grant could see the extensive damage to the man's back. How was this human even alive?

"What the hell!" David cried out as he also looked at the man.

Dakota sighed as he continued to work. "Not all of these are new injuries. This man has been abused for years. I can't believe that an Alpha would allow this kind of mistreatment to happen to one of his pack members!" the wolf shifter growled as he continued to gently clean the man's back.

"And that is another reason we must keep Richard and his brother a secret for now. You know those humans who want to see another war would use this as proof that we are more animal than man." Grant let out a long breath as he continued to try to control his wolf. His animal was pressing at him to seek revenge on behalf of his Semme', but the human half knew it was not the time. He first had to find out what really happened as the crap Alpha Clifton told him was certainly not the whole story. "Not to mention it would mean that we could not protect him or his brother." Grant paused for a moment before he revealed what his wolf had been whining for since they arrived. "Richard must be protected at all cost because..." The Alpha swallowed and saw the dawning realization in his brother's gaze.

"He's your Semme'?" David whispered as he looked back at the human. Grant nodded as he finally allowed himself to lightly stroke the hair of his mate. Even with the sweat and dirt embedded in the strands, he knew it would be silky and soft once cleaned. He couldn't wait to examine the rest of the man but first they had to get the Landon boys back to his home. A hand on his shoulder brought him back to awareness.

"Well I'll be damned. Your mate actually did show up on your doorstep! Congratulations, big brother." David grinned like a loon as he turned to look at the young boy standing quietly in the corner. He moved slowly and knelt in front of Sandy. "Well, shrimp, it looks like I can't eat you even when you do get some more meat on your bones."

Sandy cocked his head to the side. "Why?"

David laughed as he swung the startled boy up into his arms. "Because you will be my nephew and I'm going to be your awesome uncle. Welcome to the family kid!"

Grant watched with amusement as his brother began to tickle the young boy again. Somehow in less than thirty minutes he not only found himself with a mate, but apparently he was also a father. He dropped his head and sighed. How had his life gotten so complicated?

"We should get moving soon," Jason said, as he entered the dwelling and glanced out the window. "It looks like there is a storm coming in and I don't think the human will survive if it hits while we are getting him home."

"Not just any human, brother. Richard is Grant's Semme'!" David jumped in before Grant could respond. Jason glanced at the injured human for a moment before he glanced up at his older brother. He placed a hand on Grant's shoulder. "Don't worry, big brother, everything will work out just fine," Jason said softly.

A warning howl caused everyone in the room to look out towards the clearing. Sparky was running towards the woods at a fast pace. "Help him while we get Richard ready for travel!" Grant ordered his brothers. Without a word both men shifted and took off after their friend. Dakota had the travois out and was busy getting it ready. Sandy moved closer to the Alpha and looked up worriedly at him.

"Will you be able to help him?" Sandy asked quietly. For a moment Grant hesitated, not quite sure how to handle the young boy's concern. Part of him wanted to hug the boy and yet he wasn't sure if it would be welcomed. He remembered his father had always treated him like an adult when he was the same age as the pup standing next to him. He placed a hand on the pup's shoulder and squeezed gently.

"We will help you both, Sandy. I'm not going to lie to you, though, it won't be easy and you'll have to listen to what I say from now on. Can you do that, son?" Grant watched as Sandy squared his shoulders and glanced at his older brother. He could almost feel the power radiating from the young pup. He had a feeling that some day, this wolf would turn into a powerful shifter.

"Yes, Alpha Grant. I'll do whatever you say…" The boy paused and looked up at him with determination in his eyes. "As long as you don't hurt my brother."

34

Grant knelt down and placed a hand on both of the Landon boys before he looked directly into the solemn light blue eyes of his new son. "You have the Alpha's promise."

CHAPTER FOUR

THEY MADE IT TO THE PACK HOUSE WITHOUT ANY INCIDENTS. There had been a tense moment when Grant almost took Dakota down when he insisted on pulling the sled with his mate on it. But after his friend pointed out that with the other three wolves gone, the Alpha was their best means of protection, Grant had relented. It wasn't that Dakota wasn't good in a fight, but everyone knew Grant was the strongest and largest of their kind. All shifters and humans feared him. During the Great War, he had fought by his father's side making him legendary even after so many years of peace had passed. He had never been defeated and now that he had a mate and a possible Omega to protect, he refused to even contemplate losing the battles that were sure to come their way.

The Alpha stood in his office and glanced out the window. His brothers and Sparky still had not returned which had him worried. He had dispatched more Sentries to catch up with them and help if needed. However, he was pretty sure the reason for their delay was due to the Willow Creek Sentries charged with hunting down his mate. He glanced at the office door willing it to open with news of Richard. As soon as they had returned, Doc Houston had ordered everyone except for Dakota out of the room. That had been over two hours ago.

His gaze moved to the small sleeping form on the sofa in his office. Sandy had tried to stay awake but the days of running and caring for his older brother had worn the pup out. Grant moved quietly towards the youth and gently covered him with the throw that covered the back of the leather sofa. He smiled as the whelp burrowed deeper into the material and settled with a soft sigh. At least one of the Landon boys was getting some much needed rest. He hoped the same was true of the eldest.

A soft knock caused him to move towards the door. As the Doctor entered Grant held a finger to his lips and motioned for them to move into the hallway. Doc Houston glanced at the sleeping pup and smiled softly before he turned to exit the room. They walked in silence until they reached the kitchen. Grant poured a cup of coffee and handed it to the doctor. "You're usual?"

"I think you should have the same, Alpha," Doc Houston said sadly.

He settled at the kitchen table, while Grant reached into the cupboard and added a good dose of whiskey to the coffee. He grabbed a cup of coffee for himself but declined the liquor. Even though it didn't really affect shifters unless they drank a lot of it, he still didn't want to take any chances. The Willow Creek Sentinels could show up at any time and he intended to be ready to meet them.

They both sipped quietly from their coffee cups before the doctor broke the silence. "I've never seen anything this bad, even during the Great War." Doc Houston sighed and glanced back towards the hallway. "That boy has suffered. I don't even know how he has survived this long."

Grant could feel a low rumble in his chest as his wolf pounded at him to be freed. "Tell me," he ordered as he fought his animal.

The Doctor stood and began to pace running his hand through his short graying hair. The man had been the pack doctor before Grant had been born. No one knew for sure how old he was, especially since shifters aged much slower than humans. But Doc Houston looked to be in his late fifties, even though he'd been alive for hundreds of years.

"I was able to clean out the newest damage. The whip marks the boy had received were infected and will probably add to the scars he already carries. His right leg looks like it was broken at one time and healed badly. My guess is he walks with a limp. I also found signs of much earlier abuse, probably at the hands of another. It's hard to tell. But the injuries are older than the time he spent with the Willow Creek Pack." Doc Houston stopped and rubbed his forehead before he continued. "There is also evidence that he's been abused…" the doctor swallowed before he finished, "…sexually. Those injuries are more recent, so I can only assume it happened while he was part of the pack. Of course, we have no way of knowing if it was consensual, but damn, Alpha, a shifter should know better than to handle a human with full force during sex."

Grant growled and stood, his chair falling back with a loud bang as his animal roared. He saw the doctor back away as he felt himself fighting his shift. He hadn't gotten a good look at his mate but from what he could see, the man was on the small side and didn't carry much muscle. To think of him being ravished by a shifter made his blood boil. Alpha Clifton had a lot to answer for beginning with why he didn't make sure Richard had been protected. He paced for a moment, getting his beast under control before he turned to look at the doctor. "Will he live?"

For the first time the pack doctor smiled. "Yes. For a human, he certainly shows the strength of pack. He's dehydrated, malnourished and the infection from his wounds has depleted him. But with medicine, good food and rest he should recover in time. At least physically…"

Grant didn't have to ask what the doctor meant. He wondered what condition his mate would be in mentally. Would he want to bond with him or would he run again? His wolf didn't want to wait, but the Alpha knew he must or he'd be no better than those who had hurt his mate in the past. "Can I see him?"

Doc Houston stood and stretched. "He's sleeping now but I don't see why not. I'll be staying in one of the spare rooms for a few days to look after him." The doctor glanced towards the hallway. "And I probably should check out the pup too just in case."

Grant growled low in his throat at the thought that something similar had happened to Sandy. He nodded at the doctor and left the kitchen. All he could think about was getting to his mate. He stopped briefly outside his office and looked in to make sure the boy still slept. He'd have to fix up the room next to the master bedroom for Sandy but first he had to check on his mate. Grant jumped as a hand landed on his shoulder.

"I'll look after the boy. You go see your mate, Alpha," Doc Houston said softly, as he entered the office with a second cup of coffee in his hand. Grant thanked the wolf before he headed toward his bedroom. His heart was in his throat as he slowly opened the door. He inhaled the special scent that belonged to his other half. The scent calmed his inner wolf as well as made the man feel whole for the first time in his life. If Richard decided he didn't want the mate bond, Grant was afraid his heart would be destroyed.

He glanced at the figure curled on his side and banked in with pillows. The position was probably to keep pressure off the whip marks that cut across the man's pale white skin. The need to soothe the pain those marks had caused ran deep. Grant pulled one of the chairs in the room closer to the bed. As much as he longed to hold his mate, he knew it would only cause the young human pain. Besides, the man had no idea who he was and from what Sandy had told him, he wouldn't trust easily.

For the first time in his life, he cursed the fact that he was the Alpha. If he could have his wish, he'd take Richard and Sandy as far away from here as possible. The fact that his pack was now in danger also caused him pain. How could he reconcile the need to protect his mate with the need to protect his pack when they both conflicted? As he gazed at the face of the man who had become the center of his current problems, he couldn't help thinking how handsome he was. Even now his hand itched to touch while his lips wanted nothing more than to taste every inch of skin on the man's body.

A soft groan caused Grant to sit up straighter. He hoped his obvious excitement was hidden from his mate's view.

"Who are you?" A whispered voice broke the uncomfortable silence.

Grant sat forward and gazed into the prettiest hazel eyes he'd ever seen. Right now they were dulled by pain and if his nose was right, fear. "I'm Alpha Grant Walker of the Windy River Pack. You and your brother are safe here. I already spoke to Sandy, but I wanted you to know as well that you have my solemn promise no one will hurt you while under my care." He watched as his mate's eyebrows scrunched together for a moment before with a defeated sigh Richard seemed to draw inward.

"All I ask is that you give us sanctuary for a few days. Once I'm stronger, we'll leave." Richard swallowed before he closed his eyes once more. "We won't be your problem for long, Alpha."

Grant wanted to shake the man. How could he not accept his pledge? An Alpha's word was sacred and not given lightly. Did he think Alpha Clifton was better or was there more to their relationship than they originally thought? If Richard loved Clifton or someone else, then Grant would back away. It would kill part of his soul, but he would live.

"Get some rest, Richard. We will talk more when you're feeling better."

The Alpha watched as the man who had rejected him close his eyes and fell back to sleep. He slowly stood and walked from the room. Even if Richard didn't want him, he'd still keep his promise. No one should have suffered at the hands of a shifter like this man had. But first he had to prepare for the battle that was sure to come to his doorstep. Then maybe his mate would see he meant what he said.

· · ❖ · ·

Ricky held his breath as he listened for any sounds. After hearing nothing, he slowly opened his eyes and looked around the enormous room he was currently lying in. It was obviously the room of the Alpha. The large mahogany bed was hand carved and big enough to fit ten men easily. But while the wood was warm and enticing, the rest of the room had a cold feel to it. The walls were made of stone and had nothing adorning them. The whole house was probably made from the granite from the surrounding mountains.

In a way, it was a reflection of the man. He remembered the sharp angles of a face that looked as if it had been cut from the same stone. Dark eyes had pinned him and dared him to disobey. Long black hair was gathered back into a ponytail Native American style, which added to the shifter's austere looks. And yet, he couldn't help but wonder what it would feel like to have the man dominate him—to run his hands over the chiseled face and soften those eyes with passion. Would the man allow him to run his fingers through the raven dark hair? He groaned as he realized his cock was hard and leaking. He glanced down and shook his head. How was it possible that he was having these feelings for a man who might be worse than the Alpha he had left?

A glance at the windows showed it was now night outside. He must have slept longer than he thought after the Alpha left. Ricky groaned softly as he tried to move to the edge of the bed. His back screamed in agony and his head spun. After a few more attempts it was clear he was still too weak to get out of bed. The only problem was, he really needed the bathroom. He also needed to check on his little brother. While he hoped the Alpha wouldn't hurt Sandy, his little brother's safety was still his responsibility. Even if he hadn't been doing a good job of it so far, this time he would make sure before agreeing to stay. He couldn't just accept another promise of safety like he had with Alpha Clifton.

40

Ricky tried again to get out of the bed, but only managed to curse as he fell back on his sore back.

"Damn it!" He growled as he fought the tears that threatened to fall.

His head whipped around when the door opened to admit an older looking man. For a moment fear swelled in him as he wondered if it was time for him to provide service in exchange for the care of his brother. That's what Alpha Clifton had called it when he let members of the pack use him to satisfy their itch and order him around like a slave. Well so much for an Alpha's promise. But then what did he expect. He wasn't sure he could do it, but he'd try if it meant Sandy would remain safe and happy.

The injured man watched warily as the man approached the bed with what looked like a cup of something in his hand. "The Alpha told me you were awake earlier. We need to get you in shape and that begins with you eating something. I've brought you some chicken broth. If you can keep that down then we'll see if we can't get you something more substantial tomorrow morning."

"Where's my brother?" Ricky managed as he continued to stare at the shifter in front of him. He didn't get the sense that the man wanted him in that way, but then he'd learned to be on his guard at all times. The shifter tsked before he moved forward and placed the cup on the table by the bed.

"You shouldn't move around too much yet, Mr. Landon. I had to stitch up some of the wounds on your back." Gentle hands turned Ricky slightly to examine the whip marks before he was helped to sit in the bed. Pillows were put behind him to cushion his sore back and the cup was handed to him. "I'll make you a deal. You drink all the broth, take the medicine I prescribed to help you with the fever and infection and I'll bring your brother in here." The man grinned slightly as he cocked his head to the side for a moment. "Actually, the little scamp is outside your door right now instead of sleeping like he was told."

The man stood and walked over to the heavy wooden door. It was barely opened before a familiar figure raced into the room and jumped onto the bed. Ricky couldn't hold back the groan the movement of the bed caused, but he did at least manage not to spill the soup.

"RICKY!" Sandy cried as he scooted a little closer.

The shifter who had brought the soup chuckled as he placed a hand on his brother's shoulder. "Now, Sandy, I told you that we needed to be careful with your brother for a few days until he heals. That means no jumping on the bed

41

young man." He winked at Ricky before he stepped back and fixed a stern expression on his face. Ricky had a hard time stopping the quirking of his lips as Sandy smoothed the blankets before slowly climbing down from the bed.

"I didn't mean to. It's just I had to see him and you said I could as soon as I took a nap. Well I took a nap and I even ate the sandwich you left for me. So can I stay, Doc Houston?"

It amazed Ricky how his brother could talk so much without seeming to take a breath. The doctor rubbed his chin for a moment as if thinking carefully about the request before he smiled and nodded.

"Okay, but I'm putting you in charge of making sure that your brother drinks all the broth. I'll be back shortly to give him his medicine and then I think the Alpha wanted to talk to you about how you wanted your room fixed up."

Ricky watched as Sandy nodded solemnly before climbing up into the chair the Alpha had sat in earlier. Apparently this was the pack doctor. Shame flared briefly as Ricky realized he'd been wrong about his previous assumptions. He wanted to believe things would be better here and so far it looked like they might be, but then things had started out good in Willow Creek too.

"You have to eat, Ricky." His brother's voice pulled him out of his musings. The doctor had obviously left the room, which he appreciated. Maybe his brother could give him some information on what had happened. He took a sip of the broth and almost moaned at how good it tasted. It had been so long since he'd had a decent meal. "That's good. Doc Houston, that's the pack doctor, said you will get better if you do what he says." Sandy swung his legs as he continued to watch Ricky.

"You seem to know a lot about this pack. How long have I been here? Better yet, how did I even get here little brother?" Ricky sat back and watched his brother squirm for a moment before solemn blue eyes looked up at him.

"A couple of days. You scared me, Ricky. I brought back water and you wouldn't wake up to drink it. I touched you and your skin was on fire. So I followed the scent of one of the pack members and asked the Alpha to help you. He's a nice man, but a little scary. His brothers are nice, too, even if they tried to eat me when I first came here. But the Alpha stopped them and now they are my uncles, I guess, so they can't eat me even if I get bigger." Sandy took a breath and continued before Ricky could even open his mouth. "I got my own bedroom and it don't have no lock on it like the old one. The Alpha told me none of the doors have locks here and I can decorate my room any way I want. He said he's gonna buy me new clothes and I can go to school here. Did you know they have schools? I wonder why I didn't get to go in the other pack. Oh and Sparky, he's a guy but he has purple hair and claims he's the bomb when it comes to fashion, although, I'm not sure what that means but he does look cool. He says he'll help me pick out my clothes so I'm as stylin' as he is. I'm not sure I want purple hair, though." Sandy touched his white hair. "But maybe green would be nice. What do you think, Ricky?"

Ricky couldn't help the chuckle that escaped as he watched his little brother come to life right before his eyes. It had been years since he'd seen his brother this excited about anything. For the first time he allowed himself to relax just a little. The fact they had a school and were already talking as if his little brother at least was welcome made him think maybe his friend Jake had been right.

"It sounds to me like you've been busy little brother." Ricky yawned and smiled when his sibling walked over and took the now empty soup mug from his hand. He felt the small hand on his arm as his brother smiled up at him.

"This is a good place, Ricky. I can feel it," Sandy said softly, before he went back to his post in the chair.

"I hope you're right, short fry, I hope you're right." The exhausted man sighed as he settled back down and turned on his side. As he closed his eyes, his mind wandered back to the Alpha who had sat in the chair earlier. He had to admit his brother was right. The man was scary and yet even though the wolf looked like he could eat you for breakfast, Ricky had felt safe for the first time in a long time. Funny, he never thought he would find a larger man attractive, especially after the past five years. But there was just something that drew him to the imposing Alpha.

At least if serving the Alpha was part of the deal for their safety, he wouldn't be as repulsed as he had been in his last pack. In fact he could imagine he might find Alpha Grant someone he might even enjoy having sex with. Unfortunately, that was all he probably would have since there was no way the Alpha could want someone as damaged as him. At least in his dreams, he could imagine how it would be if he were worth being loved by a man like Alpha Grant.

CHAPTER FIVE

GRANT GROANED AS THE HOT WATER CASCADED OVER HIS sore muscles. He thought about the man who was currently sleeping in his bed. The brief look he'd gotten set his blood on fire in a way he'd never felt with anyone else. Sure, he'd had a few one-night stands here and there but he'd always been discreet and upfront with his lovers. There would be no future for them with him. He'd bedded both men and women, but he had to admit he did enjoy a firm muscular body under his to the softer curves of a woman.

His hand trailed lower over his rock hard abs towards his heavy cock. Ever since he'd scented his Semme' he seemed to be in a constant state of arousal. He closed his eyes and imagined his hands holding onto a strawberry blonde head, the plump lips he'd seen on his mate wrapped around the head of his cock as he pushed gently into the warm cavern. His hips pistoned forward, seeking the release only his mate could give him. As the Alpha continued to thrust into his hand, he kept seeing his mate until with a loud cry he painted the wall with his seed.

The shifter sighed as he leaned against the shower wall. One thing he knew for certain. There would be no other lovers from this point on. Even if Richard never let him touch him, he'd never feel like this with anyone else. He knew he had to have patience, but his wolf was howling with the need to claim what fate had decreed was his. If only Gaia had protected his mate better, things might be different. Grabbing a towel, he quickly dried himself off and got dressed. Mate or not, he still needed to get some answers from Richard Landon.

Grant slowly made his way to his bedroom with a tray of food for his mate. He'd spent the last couple of nights in one of the spare rooms to give Richard space. Unfortunately, as much as he wanted to let the man fully recover, time wasn't on their side. David, Jason and Sparky had returned with bad news. The Sentries from Willow Creek had escaped and had probably reported back to Alpha Clifton. He was surprised that his phone hadn't rung with a demand to return the two. Of course, that wasn't going to happen. Even if Richard hadn't been his mate, there was the issue regarding his little brother's future. If what Sandy told him was true, there was no way he could let the Omega return to Alpha Clifton.

He had spent the afternoon yesterday with his brothers and friends working out the best way to keep the Landon brothers safe while avoiding an all out war with the Willow Creek Pack. Sandy had told them some of what had happened to his older brother over the past five years. Luckily the boy hadn't been exposed to the most horrendous acts. Yet for the Alpha to allow the young pup to witness the public beatings of his older brother told him more than he needed to know about how the pack was run.

He and his father before him had run Windy River Pack with a firm hand, but they had always tempered it with fairness. He couldn't remember any member of the pack being publicly whipped; instead they had used the threat of being banned from the pack and in severe cases had administered the ultimate shifter justice, death. Grant wanted to think he was fair and he knew that his reputation as a warrior meant there weren't many who would challenge him. After almost fifty years of peaceful existence, he wondered if his reputation would be enough to dissuade the Alpha of Willow Creek from taking this matter further.

Grant paused outside the door and took a deep breath. The scent of his mate filled him with a desire that for now at least, he knew he couldn't fulfill. Closing his eyes he pulled his wolf back until he felt he had control. He opened the door quietly and walked inside. His eyes immediately fell to the slight swell of pale globes. Richard was lying on his stomach with the covers tossed to the side. He had a full view of his naked mate along with the damage that had been done.

Angry red lines still covered the man's back, ass and thighs. A closer look showed scarring from previous beatings marring the pale marble skin. Yet the

45

Alpha never saw anyone so beautiful. The scars would fade in time and being a wolf and a warrior he only saw them as a badge of courage to be worn with pride. He placed the food tray on the dresser before he moved closer and gently pulled the covers over the exposed flesh. He didn't want the man to be embarrassed when he woke. As he pulled the blanket higher, he couldn't resist running his hand through the shoulder length hair. The soft waves of reddish-gold rings shimmered against the dark skin of his hand. He smiled as the man moved into his touch even though he slept. At least his mate's body wanted him, now if he could just convince the man.

Grant stepped back as a soft groan floated up from the bed. He watched as his mate struggled to turn, his back obviously making the move difficult. Without thinking the Alpha reached forward and began to help. "Take it easy, Richard. If you break any of those stitches the Doc won't be happy with either one of us."

He felt the man stiffen for a moment, before, with a sigh, he allowed him to help him sit up. He quickly pushed some pillows behind the injured man. "I brought you some breakfast. Doc Houston said you need to start eating more to get your strength up." He noticed Richard swallow before looking down at his hands. "Do you need something?"

"Ah, well…" Richard glanced toward the doorway, which lead to the ensuite bathroom. From the way the man squirmed, it didn't take much to figure out the problem. Without saying a word, he helped his mate to the bathroom and stood outside the door while he did his business. A short time later, he had Richard back in bed with the tray of food sitting on his lap. Grant took a seat in the chair and continued to watch his mate. After a few bites the man put down the fork and looked at him with stormy hazel eyes.

"What do you want to know?" Richard asked, as he took a sip from the orange juice on his tray.

The Alpha leaned forward. "I need to know it all, Richard. But first, why don't we start out with the easy stuff. Are you or your brother related to or…" Grant paused and took a breath, "…involved with Alpha Clifton?"

Richard choked for a moment before he sat back and glared at Grant. "We are not related to that bastard other than through bad judgment on my part. He offered us a home and a place in his pack, which I accepted without reading the fine print. As to the rest," the man looked down and pushed the tray aside. "I didn't ask for any of it but I had no choice. As long as I did what the Alpha wanted, Sandy was safe." Grant watched as the fire that had blazed in the hazel eyes quickly faded just before Richard dropped his eyes.

"Our parents died when I was eighteen and I thought," the human chewed on his lower lip for a moment before he continued, "Maria seemed so sure that Alpha Clifton would help." Angry hazel eyes looked up. "I thank God she found my father because Alpha Clifton would have destroyed her."

"So Maria was your step-mother and she was a shifter. How much did she know about Alpha Clifton and his pack?" Grant prodded. He wondered why she hadn't just made Alpha Clifton Sandy's guardian. A soft sigh caused him to look at his mate. Richard's lower lip was slightly swollen. The tip of tongue peaked out briefly only to dart back inside. Grant bit back a groan as he crossed his legs to hide his cock straining against his zipper. The dream he had in the shower surged forward and made it difficult for him to focus on what the young man was saying.

Richard sighed softly and plucked at a piece of lint on the blanket in front of him. "I don't think Maria really knew Alpha Clifton that well. From what she told me about him, they had dated a few times. There had been talk between the Alpha of her old pack and Alpha Clifton about allowing her to join Willow Creek and become the Alpha's mate. She was on her way to meet with Alpha Clifton to eat when she bumped into my father at the diner." A soft smile formed on the man's face. "She told me she knew that my dad was her true mate, the light in her soul. But I always thought it was the opposite. When she entered the room, the sun seemed to shine. Sandy is a lot like that, too. I just wish." Grant watched as Richard swallowed before he shook his head. "Well, it doesn't really matter since she's gone."

"Did you ever see her wolf? Was she the same color as Sandy?" Grant leaned forward.

Richard tensed immediately. The man's lips formed a straight line as he remained silent. Even the fingers that had been busy a moment before curled inward until only fists remained on the human's lap. Grant waited and watched but it appeared that Richard wasn't gong to answer the question.

"Look, if you want my help you need to answer my questions and answer them honestly. It isn't just you and your brother that I have to consider here but over three hundred members of my pack. Do you realize what your presence

47

here means?" Grant growled as he stood and moved towards the bed. Before he could take a step, Richard rolled to the opposite side and scrambled out of the bed. The scent of fear was so thick; Grant thought he might choke on it. He watched as the man staggered for a moment before he fell to his knees, his arms curled over his head as he hunched in on himself.

The door opened and a snarl filled the air. A white wolf raced across the floor and stood between Grant and Richard. Realizing this was getting out of control, the Alpha turned on his heals and strode from the room. He walked down the hallway and knocked on the door where the doctor was staying. When it opened, he ordered Doc Houston to check on his mate and then continued down towards his office. The wolf in him was screaming at him to go back, to comfort his mate and yet the human part of him knew he was the last person Richard needed right now.

Grant had just managed to down his first glass of scotch when he heard someone approach the door. He turned his chair and reached for the bottle he kept on the sideboard behind him. The door opened and closed but the Alpha continued to refill his glass and fill a second.

"Was he injured?" Grant asked as he turned to greet the doctor and hand him his own glass. He watched as the pack doctor accepted the drink before he sat down in the chair and gazed down into the amber depths. "Well?" The Alpha prompted.

"If I hadn't known you since you were a pup and if I didn't know that your father raised you to be a fair and good Alpha, I would be taking that man and the boy and leaving here." Doc Houston looked up and shook his head. "I had to give him something to make him sleep. What in the hell happened, Alpha?"

Grant sucked in a breath as he thought back over the way he approached the conversation. He hadn't been threatening his mate but he had pressed him for answers that Richard obviously didn't want to provide.

"He wouldn't confide in me about Sandy being an Omega. I could tell he was holding back and I needed answers, damn it! How can I keep him—" The Alpha stood and held his arms wide, "—all of them safe if I don't know what I'm facing?" He dropped his arms and walked towards the window. "He's my mate but even not knowing that, he was part of a pack and should know when an Alpha gives his word, it is kept."

"Unless you are Alpha Clifton from the Willow Creek Pack," Doc Houston said softly. He took a sip from the glass, considering his words before he continued. "According to what Sandy told me and the little I've gleaned from your mate, the same promise was made before they joined the Willow Creek Pack. Not all Alphas uphold the old values in the way you do Alpha Grant." The doctor leaned forward, "You have never been challenged by anyone except maybe your family and even they bend to your will. You see Richard's fear to speak as a failure to submit to your position."

Grant huffed as he turned to look at the doctor. "You sound like David. I'm not a King and I don't rule as one. Everyone here has a choice to stay or leave as they see fit. But a strong Alpha has to set the rules and enforce them or the pack will flounder. My father never bowed to anyone and he expected his orders to be followed without question." Grant walked back to his desk and took his seat. "All I ask is that he tell me the truth so I can protect them all, is that being unfair or cruel?"

Doc Houston looked at Grant for a few moments before he sighed and sat back in the chair. He finished the rest of the Scotch and placed the empty glass on the corner of the Alpha's desk.

"What you ask isn't being unfair or cruel, Alpha Grant. However, what you fail to take into account is the manner in which your mate came to you. Put yourself in his place. He was abused and tortured by the same Alpha who promised safety. I'm not sure how much Sandy actually saw, but from the little he told me your mate suffered greatly at the hands of that pack. He is a human who was thrown into pack life without a life preserver. He didn't understand all the nuances of pack politics. Hell, he didn't even know that he could tell the Alpha no or that he could leave and take his brother with him by simply notifying Alpha Clifton of his intent," Doc Houston growled. "He was declared rogue without so much as a hearing or a chance to plead his case before his Alpha. To be honest, Alpha Grant, I'm surprised your mate is still able to challenge you at all but if he were my mate, I'd be proud that he still can."

Grant sighed and rubbed a hand down his face. "I need answers but you're right Doc, I should have been more patient. I'm just not used to—"

"—having your authority challenged. Even if it's by a badly abused human and his whelp," Doc Houston finished for him. He stood and winked at Grant, "Actually, given time I think you'll be able to get your mate to believe you and

49

accept your word but Sandy? Well, you may have to do a bit of groveling with him. When I left he was laying at the foot of his brother's bed, growling at anyone who approached."

The Alpha chuckled. "Well I do have to admit, the pup has the makings of a fierce warrior even before he becomes a full fledged Omega. I'll go up and begin groveling with a plate of those sugar cookies he's so fond of."

The doctor nodded and smiled as he rose and turned to leave the room.

"Richard, should sleep for a few hours. Maybe you should have Jason bring him lunch and try to talk to him?" The doctor suggested as he clapped Grant on the shoulder. "Remember, you really don't have to do it all."

CHAPTER SIX

ICKY WOKE SLOWLY AND GROANED AS HE TRIED TO MAKE his mind focus. The last thing he remembered was talking to Alpha Grant and then, he'd panicked. God, the Alpha wanted to know about Sandy. It was obvious he already suspected that his brother was an Omega but would he try to use him the same as Alpha Clifton? One thing had become clear, they couldn't stay here. He'd made that mistake once and refused to make it again. Maybe the best thing to do would be for them to just disappear.

He glanced down at the slight weight lying across his legs.

A smile curled his lips as he saw the white fur of his brother. "Hey, short stuff," he said softly as he gently nudged his brother. "How about you shift and get off big brother's legs? My toes are a little numb." He watched as light blue eyes glanced up at him before with a slight shimmer in the air his brother's human form emerged.

"Are you okay, Ricky?" Sandy asked softly as he moved to sit on the corner of the bed.

"I'm fine, but I'd be even better if you could find both of us some clothes," Ricky said softly, looking at the door. They were probably locked in. He glanced at the window and tried to figure out if they could escape that way instead. He jumped when his brother dropped a stack of clothes on the bed beside him.

"You want us to leave don't you?' Sandy asked as he began to pull on his own clothes. "Did Alpha Grant hurt you, Ricky?"

The older sibling moved slowly to the edge of the bed and began to get dressed. He winced as he pulled the T-shirt over his healing back. He wasn't as strong as he would like to be, but at least the room didn't spin when he stood to finish dressing. Ricky saw the duffle bag he'd brought with him laying against the wall. At least he hadn't lost everything.

"Ricky?" Sandy's insistent voice broke through his musings.

He sat back on the bed and sighed. How was he going to explain to his younger brother that the Alpha scared him more than just physically? He didn't understand his own feelings; much less the reason that he still felt drawn to the shifter more than his need to get away. But he'd made a mistake accepting Alpha Clifton's word that they would be safe and now that Alpha Grant was questioning Sandy being an Omega, he just couldn't take the chance. He absently rubbed the tattoo on his upper arm as he answered his brother.

"He didn't really hurt me, Sandy, but I'm not sure this place will be safe for you or me." Ricky watched as Sandy began to chew on his lower lip. "I know you like it here but we really don't know these people and until I can be sure, I have to do what I think is right to keep you safe."

Sandy looked up and shook his head. "But where will we go? You said the bad shifters would find us if we didn't come here. The Alpha came in while you were sleeping and he was really sorry he scared you. He even brought me cookies and let me stay with you. Alpha Clifton never let me stay with you..." Sandy paused for a moment. "...and this place is supposed to be safe. Jake said so too and he's your friend, right?"

Ricky stood and carefully knelt in front of his brother. He had to admit since being here his brother was looking much better and was coming out of the shell he'd crawled into while they lived with the Willow Creek Pack. What Sandy said was also true. Other than the Alpha asking questions, he hadn't been hurt and he'd been treated like one of the pack. He just wished he could be sure. Then there was his attraction to the imposing man.

"Going somewhere?" A man walked in carrying two trays filled with food. He was a smaller version of the Alpha except his dark black hair was worn short and was spiked on the top. His face also seemed softer somehow. The shifter continued into the room and placed the trays on the bed before he turned and held out his hand to Ricky. "My name is Jason Walker. I'm Grant's younger and smarter brother."

Ricky couldn't help the slight twitch of his lips as the man knelt down and ruffled Sandy's hair. "I understand you tried to take a bite out of my brother again shorty. Give me five!" He held up his hand and laughed when Sandy smacked it. He stood and motioned towards the bed. "Why don't you two eat before you make any decisions? I find it's always easier to think on a full stomach, don't you?" Jason paused and looked directly at Ricky. "And if you don't mind I'd like to talk to you about why Alpha Clifton declared you a rogue when you're definitely not a shifter."

Ricky sighed as he nodded at Sandy to go ahead and start eating. What little appetite he had was gone as he sat on the edge of the bed and faced Jason. "Like I told your brother, we joined the Willow Creek Pack after my parents died. It seemed like the best solution since Sandy was just over a year old. I mean he was born in his human form but once he started shifting, I really had no idea how to raise a baby much less one that could shift." He glanced at his brother and smiled softly.

Jason shook his head. "It must have been hard. You were only eighteen at the time right?"

The human nodded. "Yeah, and I didn't even have a job. We could have stayed with Robert I guess but Maria had been so sure about Alpha Clifton."

"So what changed?" Jason asked as he sat back in the chair and crossed his legs. Ricky looked at his brother for a moment before he continued.

"I thought everything was going fine. At first the Alpha treated us both like his own sons. But then he found out." Ricky swallowed and glanced over at his brother again.

Jason nodded his understanding.

"If you're up to a short walk, I'd like to show you what I've found on the Willow Creek Pack through my own research. Maybe you can help me fill in some of the blanks. My office isn't far and I won't keep you long." Jason looked at Sandy and smiled. "And if it's okay with your older brother, don't you have an appointment with Sparky to go into town and get some clothes? I seem to recall you now only have the pair of pants you're wearing."

Sandy jumped up and looked at Ricky. "Can I go with Sparky? Can I? I know you'll like it here, too. I mean they have a huge house and the lady who cooks makes the best cookies. She said if I was good, she'd make me one that looked like a wolf..." Ricky laughed and held up his hand.

Jason grinned and added, "Don't worry, Sparky will keep a close eye on him and Grant will send along a couple of Sentries just to make sure there aren't any unpleasant surprises. Not to mention the town Sheriff is a shifter and a good friend of ours. He was with us when we found you."

The elder Landon knew when he was being double-teamed. He glanced over towards his brother. "Fine, but you listen to what you're told, don't talk to strangers and for heaven sake…"

Ricky paused as he saw his brother roll his eyes and finish his sentence in a sign song voice, "Don't shift where others can see me. I know Ricky and I promise I'll behave. Can I go?"

Ricky nodded. "Fine, I'll see you when you get back short stuff and then maybe we can have dinner together okay?" He stepped back as his little brother launched himself at him to wrap his arms around his waist. He hugged his brother back before releasing him. Sandy waved at Jason and raced from the room calling out the name of the other shifter as he went. Ricky tried not to let his worry show but a strong hand on his shoulder showed he still wasn't good at hiding his feelings.

"He'll be fine, Richard. Now if you'll come with me maybe we can figure out a way to make sure you and your brother are both safe and feel comfortable here." Jason opened the door wider and motioned for the reticent human to walk ahead of him.

As they walked through, Ricky couldn't help but notice there wasn't a lock on the door. Maybe he was over-reacting after all.

"Ricky," the young human remarked absently as he walked beside Jason.

"What?" Jason asked

"I usually go by Ricky. Richard makes me sound ancient," he replied as he watched Jason smile. For the first time since he arrived he actually felt like things might be okay. Now, if he could just figure out Alpha Grant.

"Here we are, why don't you take a seat and make yourself comfortable. I'll just pop over to the kitchen and grab us a couple of sandwiches. I don't know about you, but I seem to always be hungry." Jason motioned to a comfortable leather chair.

Ricky glanced around in awe as he took in the multiple computer screens, a whiteboard with diagrams on it that made absolutely no sense to him and of course the desk that was cluttered with papers and folders. He'd never seen this much computer equipment in his life. Just as he started to get nervous, the door opened and Jason entered with sandwiches and a couple bottles of beer.

54

"Don't tell Doc Houston but you look like you could use something a little stronger than tea or coffee right now." Jason plopped down in the other chair and after settling in; he reached for a folder that was lying right on top. "So why don't I tell you what we do know and then you can fill in the missing information, okay?"

Ricky took a sip of the beer before he settled back in the chair. He was pretty sure this would take a while and he had to admit he was curious what was in the folder. He picked up the sandwich and took a small bite. He groaned as the taste of egg salad exploded across his tongue. The human couldn't remember the last time he'd had egg salad, much less one that tasted this good.

He glanced up as Jason chuckled. "I see you like Meg's egg salad as much as I do. Don't worry, she'll make you as many as you like. Nothing makes Meg happier than someone who enjoys her cooking. Unless it's playing mother hen, it drives my brother Grant crazy when she does it to him."

"I didn't think anyone could get under your brother's skin," Ricky replied before he could stop himself. He quickly looked down and placed his hands in his lap. How could he be so stupid? Jason would report what he said and then he'd be punished. How many times had he let his guard down with one of the members of his old pack, only to have it come back to bite him in the ass. He jumped as a finger was placed under his chin, pulling his gaze up to meet dark brown eyes. But instead of anger or censure, he only saw understanding.

"I realize you don't know us and I also know that my brother can sometimes be..." Jason paused as if trying to find the right word, "...intense. But no one here will ever hurt you or your little brother." The shifter backed up and sat back down. He placed his finger on his chin before he smiled. "Why don't we start with me telling you a little about Windy Creek Pack?"

Ricky nodded even though he was still not sure he believed that he wouldn't be punished. Jason pulled a picture from the side of his desk. It showed three men standing with an older couple. The mountains that showed outside the office window were in the background. They all smiled and looked happy. He recognized Alpha Grant and Jason so the rest had to be their other brother and parents.

"This is my family. As you know, shifters live for a long time but we'll start with more recent history. Over two hundred years ago my father and his pack were traveling through the mountains when they came upon a small Indian

Village that was under attack by a rival tribe. The smaller tribe was being overrun and it was likely all were going to be killed when my father interceded. Most of the men had lost their lives, so my father agreed to stay on and help defend the tribe. When the Shoshone moved on, they gave my father the land in gratitude for his help."

Jason smiled as he looked down at the picture. "It was my father who decided that his pack would become a sanctuary for anyone who needed help. Even during the Great War between humans and shifters, this area remained a place where those who needed protection would come." He paused and looked at Ricky. "Even humans were sheltered here during the War, which was unheard of. It caused some packs to resent my father, but luckily they quickly learned that challenging the Walker Family patriarch and his oldest son would result in a quick death. Neither my father or Grant have ever lost in battle."

Ricky could hear the pride in Jason's voice as he talked about his family. It sounded like their family had been close, unlike his own. For a moment, he wondered what it would have been like to have a family like the Walkers. But then it wouldn't do any good to look at the past, as it wouldn't change anything.

"So, Alpha Grant said you have over three hundred members in your pack right now?"

The shifter grinned. "At least and still growing. Luckily, we have more than enough land in these mountains to shelter everyone. But it does make it hard on Grant." Jason sighed. "And also is why he can be a jerk at times. But don't worry, my brother David is still trying to get him to loosen up and learn to delegate more. Grant is still old school in his thinking when it comes to an Alpha's responsibilities."

"What do you mean?" Ricky couldn't help but ask.

"Well for one thing, most packs aren't anywhere close to this large or spread out. Even my father's pack was much smaller. But since Grant has taken over, word spread and people have come seeking his help. He never turns anyone away and feels responsible for every member of his pack." Jason stopped and looked at Ricky. "He thinks he has to bear all the weight for keeping the pack healthy and safe which doesn't leave him much time for his own needs. Something David and our cook Meg love pointing out on a daily basis."

Ricky sighed as he sat back in the chair. "And now he has to worry about me and my little brother. Maybe it would be better if we moved on. Alpha Grant was right; he has enough people to worry about without taking on our problems, as well."

"And that would be where you are wrong." A deep voice came from the doorway as the Alpha entered the office.

Ricky jerked and would have dropped the plate with his sandwich if Grant hadn't been quicker. As their hands brushed he sucked in a breath at the electricity that seemed to flow through his skin directly to his cock. What the hell was wrong with him? He was acting like he was in heat or something.

"Sorry about startling you but I thought I'd join you and Jason, if you don't mind." Alpha Grant stood to the side and handed the plate back to Ricky.

"Sh—sh—sure," Ricky stammered not sure why it seemed like all the oxygen had left the room as well as his brain it seemed. Great, the shifter probably already thought he was damaged and now he would be convinced. The human glanced down at the sandwich in his lap and swallowed. Maybe if he closed his eyes, the Alpha would disappear and he would be able to breathe again.

A soft chuckle sounded from the desk. "You two really need to have a conversation or at the very least find a room." Jason continued to snicker as Ricky glanced up at the Alpha from under his lashes. He swore he could see the beginning of a blush under the tanned skin.

"Jason." A warning growl came from Alpha Grant that caused Ricky to shiver in apprehension. He jumped as a hand landed on his shoulder, squeezing it lightly as the Alpha continued to speak, "I thought you were discussing our problem with Alpha Clifton; not my social life."

Jason continued to chuckle as he held his hands up in surrender. "Okay, okay. You're right. Ricky and I were just getting acquainted before you barged into my office. Which by the way, this is my office, right?"

Ricky watched in amusement as the Alpha shook his head and stepped to the door and knocked loudly. "There, satisfied? Now can we get serious and discuss our problem? I haven't heard a word from Alpha Clifton and it's been four days since we found Ricky. Surely the Willow Creek Sentries have reported back to him by now."

The eldest Landon brother felt as if a cold bucket of water had been thrown over him. Alpha Clifton knew he was here? And worse, he'd let Sandy go into town. What if the shifters found his little brother? His chest hurt and the room seemed to be getting darker when he heard a deep voice next to his ear as his head was forced down. "That's right, deep breaths now, Richard. You are safe. Alpha Clifton won't come to our pack lands without announcing his presence. You have lived in a pack and know that is a transgression that can be punished with death, especially if he does something to harm anyone under my protection."

Ricky took a deep breath and tried to get his wits about him. He knew the signs and if he didn't get himself under control, he'd end up in a full panic attack. The last time that happened he'd passed out and woke to a world of pain. He opened his eyes and saw Jason kneeling beside him, a glass of water in his hand. He nodded his thanks and took a drink, his hand shaking but at least he could breathe and see again. "Thanks, and it's Ricky, not Richard."

"Okay, ah Ricky, take deep breaths and relax," Alpha Grant said softly as he massaged the tense muscles in the stressed human's neck.

Ricky sighed and leaned into the touch. For a moment he felt a connection he didn't understand. He looked up into the dark eyes of the Alpha and recognized the look of lust. He'd seen it too many times not to shiver. Yet, for the first time he felt his own body answer the call. He groaned softly as the Alpha lowered his head and gently placed his lips on his, seeking permission. Ricky opened his mouth and sighed, as he tasted the man that had suddenly become more than his shelter in a storm.

A soft cough caused both men to separate "I'm sorry, Grant, but you and your mate will have plenty of time to get acquainted later. Right now we need to talk about why Alpha Clifton wants Ricky and his brother so badly that he's willing to start a war between packs and even the humans."

Ricky felt himself blush as he sat back in the chair. His cock pressed uncomfortably against the zipper in his jeans as he tried to refocus on what Jason was saying.

"What do you mean?' Ricky finally managed, as he watched Alpha Grant take a step back, but still kept his hand on his shoulder. He decided it would be better to focus on Jason than what he was feeling at the moment. It wasn't the first time he'd been referred to as the Alpha's mate since he'd been here. But he thought he'd imagined it. It certainly explained the reason he wanted to climb the Alpha like a tree. The large imposing man standing beside him was his mate.

Maria had explained it to him. Shifters could really mate with anyone, just like humans. However, the goddess Gaia in her wisdom would sometime intervene and give them a nudge in the right direction. A shifter could scent their mate and humans would feel a slight pull towards the shifter but unlike many romance novels, that was all it was. The two people involved could decide to act on the pull or they could walk away. The only problem with walking away was it doomed the pair to never feel complete. To mate with your fated match meant both would be bound together in a way that no one could interfere with. It would be a life match and would bring both parties great happiness. He'd seen it between his father and Maria.

Yet, he couldn't give into his own needs, not when his brother's life depended on him making the right decision. He couldn't let anyone use him the way the previous Alpha had intended to do. Hell, Alpha Clifton had talked of taking him as a mate to ensure he would never be able to leave. So he couldn't give in, even if he suspected it might mean he would have to walk away from the shifter who was beginning to mean too much to him.

Ricky was jerked out of his thoughts as a low voice sounded next to his ear, "You are my Semme', Ricky, the one I was meant to love above all others, but I also understand that you may want to take this slow. I will not force you to do anything you do not want to do." Alpha Grant continued to massage Ricky's neck before he turned towards his brother. "Have you been able to find out exactly what is going on in the Willow Creek Pack?"

Jason shook his head. "No, which is why I was hoping your mate—er Ricky here could help us fill in the gaps." The other wolf blushed slightly as he glanced down at his folders.

It was clear they were all trying to give him a choice, which was more than his previous pack had done. He also knew now that he would be safe because the other thing Maria told him was, Semme' mates would never hurt the other. It was one of the reasons his father had changed so much after meeting her and was the reason he had killed himself when she was dying. Ricky placed his hand over the Alpha's as he took a deep breath and began to tell them what they needed to know.

59

CHAPTER SEVEN

ROGER SANDERS WALKED TOWARD THE MOUNTAINS, HIS backpack slung over his shoulder. It was finally the weekend and for the first time since Charlie had disappeared, he was able to go spend some time with his friends. They were all meeting up at their usual campsite in the mountains. His wolf was already close to the surface at the thought of a whole week of running and hunting in the mountains. Thanks to Alpha Grant, his father had all the help he needed and his father had encouraged him to join his friends. The young wolf couldn't wait, especially since Rebecca had said she'd be there too.

He took a deep breath as he entered the lower forested area but frowned as he realized he smelled more than one wolf in the area. The scent was strange to him, which immediately caused his hackles to rise. He dropped his backpack and quickly shifted, his ears lay back as he turned to face the strange wolves now coming through the trees. For a brief moment he felt the need to defend his territory but then common sense kicked in. He turned tail and ran back towards the Alpha's house, howling as he went. Unfortunately, before he could get too far a large form jumped on him and brought him to the ground. His last thought before darkness took him was that he was glad Rebecca wasn't here.

• • ❖ • •

Ricky sat back in the chair, his head falling forward as he listened to the voices of the Alpha and his brothers around him. About mid way through his story, David had joined the other two Walker brothers in the small office. They had asked him if he was okay with the middle brother joining them, which was nice. He'd agreed because it didn't matter at that point how many people heard his sad tale. Soon everyone would know what a loser he was anyway.

It had been a grueling couple of hours, but now they not only knew of his shame but also how weak and stupid he'd been while he'd been a member of the Willow Creek Pack.

"Would you like something to drink or eat, Ricky?" The human jumped as a hand was placed on his thigh. He'd been so absorbed in his memories that he hadn't noticed Jason kneeling in front of him. Ricky shook his head as he glanced at the other two shifters in the room. David was sitting in one of the other chairs in the office while Alpha Grant was standing with his hands clasped behind his back while he gazed out the window.

"You realize that this wasn't your fault, right?" Jason continued as he stood and patted Ricky's shoulder. "From what you've told us, your stepmother didn't really give you enough information to make the right decisions for you or your brother. Of course, she probably thought she would have time to help you understand more about us."

The eldest Larson shrugged as he glanced down at his clasped hands. He didn't want to think about that part of his life. Instead, he concentrated on the men that currently surrounded him. Now that all three brothers were in the room, he could see the family resemblance. Jason looked the most like Grant, but a slightly smaller version. He wore his black hair shorter and spiked. Of the three brothers, he seemed to be the one who balanced out the other two. Grant reflected his name in mannerisms while David seemed to be the joker of the group. But Jason had a way of making you feel immediately comfortable, sort of like an old friend.

In a way, he could see himself becoming friends with them. In fact, the longer he stayed here, the more he thought just maybe this could be a safe place for himself and his brother. He couldn't deny the strong attraction he felt for the Alpha either. Even now his cock throbbed and his hole twitched at the thought of having Grant in his bed. Thoughts that just a few weeks ago would have caused him to have a panic attack, now felt like something he was beginning to yearn for. Ricky was brought back from his musings when David spoke up.

"Jason is right. You are not to blame, but Alpha Clifton certainly knew better!" David shook his head as he glanced over at his silent older brother. "He knows an Omega can't be controlled by any shifter. It's why they were hunted during the Great War by both sides."

"What do you mean?" Ricky asked as he glanced up at the middle brother. The similarity between David and Grant was apparent but he didn't have long silky dark black hair. If Ricky was honest with himself, he couldn't wait to see Grant's hair loose so he could run his fingers through it. David on the other hand wore his light brown hair in a short military cut that belied the shifters lighthearted demeanor. The eyes though were the same color brown as his brothers', except they seemed to be filled with mischief most of the time.

David grimaced. "How much do you know about Omegas?"

Ricky thought back to the little Maria had told him and realized other than knowing his brother was a special kind of shifter and needed to be protected, he really didn't know much about his brother's abilities. "Actually, not much. In fact, as you all found out, I really didn't know much about shifters in general." Ricky blushed. "I remember the first time I objected to Alpha Clifton taking Sandy out on his first hunt. He was only two years old at the time. I mean at two years old humans can't take care of themselves so I just assumed it was the same for wolves."

Alpha Grant turned around and shook his head slightly. "Shifters have to mature more quickly in some ways than human children. As soon as our pups are able to hold their shifted form, they are taught to hunt. It was necessary for survival, especially in the time before humans knew of our existence and became even more important after. During the years where we warred with humans, many pups found themselves without anyone to protect them."

Ricky glanced at the Alpha for a moment before he looked down at his hands again. "Yeah, Alpha Clifton filled me in on what would be expected of Sandy to be a vital part of the pack. Before we left, my brother was able to hunt with the pack and showed that he was able to defend himself while in his wolf form. I try to remember it's different for shifters, but when I look at Sandy, I see a six year old boy who loves cookies and ice cream…"

"It's understandable, Ricky, and in some ways you're right, he is still a pup and needs to be allowed to mature emotionally. He must be prepared so that when he comes into his powers at age twenty-one, he'll be ready to accept them and use them," Jason replied.

Ricky jumped as he felt a strong hand on his shoulder.

"He still needs guidance, maybe even more so than a normal pup," Alpha Grant said gravely. "If he is raised in the wrong kind of environment, an Omega could cause great damage."

"Sandy wouldn't hurt a fly," Ricky said quickly. He glanced around the room and saw the grim looks on all the shifters' faces. For the first time since he came here, he felt afraid for his brother. "Alpha Clifton tried to convince Sandy that humans were inferior. It was one of the reasons he told my brother that I had to be trained…" Ricky swallowed and closed his eyes as his memories threatened to overwhelm him. The hand on his shoulder squeezed tighter for a moment and suddenly he felt like he could breathe again.

"No one here will hurt you or Sandy. Your brother has already shown he is not only smart and resourceful, but he is also loyal to you. However, even if that weren't the case, we would still protect him and you." Alpha Grant glanced at his brothers. "I believe Alpha Clifton never intended to kill Ricky, but instead he meant to use him…"

"…like a collar," Ricky said quietly, as he glanced up at the Alpha for a moment before he leaned forward in the chair. "The reason I left when I did wasn't just because of how I was being treated. As long as Sandy was being cared for, I thought…well, in a way Alpha Clifton was right in that I deserved what I got. If I hadn't been so careless with Robert, then Maria would be alive and Alpha Clifton could have eventually married her."

"I call bull!" David said loudly as he slammed his fist on the desk. "That bastard knew the chance of him getting Maria as a mate was gone when she found her true mate."

Ricky shrank back from the sudden violence from the middle Walker brother.

"But…" Ricky started to protest but stopped when he heard a low growl next to him. He sat back and quickly looked down at his hands. Years of training to never look at those deemed to be better than him kicked in as he waited for his punishment for disagreeing with the other wolf. He closed his eyes and tried to keep his breathing steady, once again the room felt as if there wasn't enough air.

"Ricky! Listen to me!" Alpha Grant's voice broke through the white noise until he couldn't help but look up into the intense dark eyes. "That's right, you need to calm down. I told you no one would hurt you here and you need to accept it."

Ricky heard David snort as Jason rose and once more knelt down in front of him. "What my older brother is trying to say is, eventually you'll learn to trust us. But for now, why don't we concentrate on trying to figure out what Alpha Clifton is up to huh?"

The frightened human took a deep breath and nodded. He watched the Alpha move back to the window, his back once more turned to them as he looked outside.

"I'm sorry…" Ricky tried as he glanced at the obviously upset wolf. He didn't mean to make the Alpha angry.

"There's nothing to be sorry for, Ricky," David said as he smirked. "I can guarantee that my big brother's bark is worse than his bite. In fact, somewhere inside beats the heart of a marshmallow, right ,Grant?"

The Alpha turned and glared at his brother before he looked back at Ricky. The Alpha took a deep breath and softened his voice as he continued, "When a shifter finds his or her Semme', it is a bond that lasts a life time. Your father's life would have been extended to equal Maria's longer life span. Alpha Clifton knows this and he also knows that once both parties accept the Semme' mating bond, nothing can break it. So you see, Ricky, no matter what happened, you could not be blamed for Alpha Clifton losing his right to mate Maria."

Before Ricky could respond Jason stood and walked back to his desk. "I imagine the Alpha thought he had struck gold when he found what possibly could be the only Omega currently living. It would give him a good reason to keep Sandy in his pack. But I would think he would have treated Ricky better. After all, Sandy could have chosen to leave at any time. If Ricky had been killed, there would be no reason for the Omega to stay with the Willow Creek Pack. In fact, it would have guaranteed that Sandy would leave the pack." Jason sat back at his desk and glanced at the computer screen before he sighed. "On the surface he looks squeaky clean."

"But we know that usually means he's just really good at staying under the radar," David replied, as he ran a hand through his short cropped hair. "Surely

64

he had to know if word got out about what he did to a human, the peace that has existed for over fifty years would be shattered."

Ricky sighed as he cleared his throat. "I overheard Beta Biff and Alpha Clifton talking before I left. I didn't understand at the time, but Alpha Clifton was angry at Biff for being too harsh with his latest round of 'training' with me. He told him they needed me to keep Sandy under control." He leaned forward and looked at the shifters. "Why is Sandy so important to him? Just exactly what will my brother be able to do?"

Alpha Grant sighed and faced them again. "Omegas have a special gift provided by the goddess Gaia. They can command any animal to do their bidding..." The Alpha paused before he continued, "...including our inner animals. Not even an Alpha is immune, although according to my father some Alpha's may be strong enough to resist. But that is only rumored."

"So Omegas are feared because they can control you?" Ricky swallowed. "And humans don't like them because they could turn all of the animals against mankind?"

The sound of the clock ticking on the wall could be heard through the silence that descended upon the room. Each person was lost in their own thoughts for what seemed like a long time, but in reality it was only a few moments. Ricky couldn't believe his brother would eventually harness such power. How was he supposed to keep his brother safe from not only the human hunters, but any paranormal who might want to either use his brother or kill him for what he could do?

He'd believed Alpha Clifton when he told him he owed him retribution for the death of his former fiancé. The choice had been between his servitude and obedience or giving over custody of Sandy to Alpha Clifton. Now he found out none of that was true. He'd suffered and his brother had been traumatized for no reason other than he was stupid.

He absently rubbed at the tattoo on his upper arm. Maria never should have trusted him with something so important. He knew she had felt his little brother's latent power just as he still felt it. Ricky didn't need to wait until Sandy turned twenty-one. He knew his brother already was special and had already exhibited some of his abilities. Even now if he opened his mind, he could tell his brother was having a good time with Sparky. For years they were both able to tap into what the other was feeling. The fact that his brother would not only

65

be sought after, but also hunted because of his ability only made him feel even more overwhelmed.

A chill caused him to shiver as he realized how close he'd come to turning his younger brother over to Alpha Clifton. When he'd heard the Beta and Alpha of Willow Creek discussing how they would use him to keep his brother under control once he came into his abilities, Ricky hadn't understood the significance. Now he finally understood why Alpha Clifton hadn't killed him. He was to be the leash that kept his brother loyal to Alpha Clifton and the Willow Creek Pack.

Suddenly, he felt strong arms lift him as he was pressed against a strong chest. Ricky struggled for a moment but then sighed as he let his body relax into the feeling of safety the arms offered him. "Don't worry, Ricky, everything will be fine. I will make sure no one hurts you or your brother. But for now I'm taking you back to bed so you can rest." Alpha Grant's deep voice rumbled in his ear.

Ricky looked up at the Alpha. "What about Sandy? Will he be safe in town?" The thought of Alpha Clifton getting his hands on his brother was enough to almost fully bring him back to full wakefulness. The Alpha continued to walk up the stairs. He opened the door to the master bedroom and gently deposited Ricky on the bed. For a moment the eldest Landon thought he was going to be ignored until the side of the bed sunk in. A gentle finger traced the tattoo that showed below the sleeve on the T-shirt he wore.

"Did Maria ever explain to you what this tattoo means?" Grant asked quietly. Ricky shook his head. "According to my father, humans who accept this binding symbol will always be at the side of the Omega Wolf. Both the human and wolf will share a bond closer than any on this land, including Semme' mates. Just as you would die to protect Sandy, your little brother will do the same to protect you." The Alpha smiled as he rubbed an area on his lower leg,. "In fact, he already has to the detriment of my favorite jeans."

Ricky couldn't help the chuckle that escaped. He knew his brother was just as protective of him and he'd shown it more than once. But now that he knew what the future held for his little brother, he couldn't help thinking someone made a colossal mistake in choosing him for the job of protector. He jumped when he felt a finger under his chin lifting his eyes up from the blanket he'd been examining.

"Maria made a mistake when she chose me," Ricky said softly as the hopelessness he felt filled his eyes.

"And that would be where you are wrong, Ricky. You think brute strength is all that is required to protect an Omega?" Alpha Grant continued to gently trace the tattoo. The feeling of his calloused finger on Ricky's skin was sending small electrical currents through his body and directly to his cock. The injured human couldn't help leaning into the man as he nodded his answer to the shifter. "Well, you'd be wrong. What you did, letting those bastards use you so that your brother would be spared shows more strength than many men or shifters I know."

"Right, like I really saved him. If it hadn't been for my friend Jake, we'd still be trapped there!" Ricky started to protest but was stopped by the Alpha's claiming of his lips. For a moment he relaxed into the kiss, even exploring the warm mouth on his, tasting and groaning as his cock filled. The Alpha tasted of the chicory flavored coffee Ricky enjoyed whenever he'd been able to drink it. He allowed the kiss to deepen as a soft moan fell from his lips. He'd never been kissed like this, as if he actually meant something to the shifter. Even his initial forays into kissing with Robert hadn't been this intense. If they kept this up, he was going to have to do something or explode from the tension building in his body.

The hand that had been stroking his arm moved slowly downward before stopping to tease at the hidden bulge beneath the fabric of his jeans. Ricky groaned as he leaned up into the touch, rubbing himself against the firm hand as he opened his mouth even wider. He allowed his tongue to explore the inner recesses of the Alpha's mouth with a fierceness he'd never used before. He should feel repulsed, but his body seemed to understand something his mind was just now starting to accept.

He now understood what this attraction meant. Even though Maria and Alpha Grant had both explained Semme' mates to him; he figured it was something close to what most humans called a 'soul' mate. It had felt surreal until this moment. The feelings of belonging and safety that being around the huge wolf gave him were now making more sense. The fact that his body also reacted this way was also a big clue. It had been years since he'd felt aroused.

Just as he thought he'd pass out from lack of oxygen, Alpha Grant sat back and gazed at him with lust filled eyes. "You should be resting, Ricky. I'm sorry,

I shouldn't have started this. We will have plenty of time to go further when you are feeling better."

Ricky looked down at the tanned hand still rubbing gently against his throbbing erection. Of course, Maria had also explained that unlike in the romance novels, true mates still had a choice. After what he had just told the Alpha and his brothers, it was a wonder that the wolf could even touch him.

"It's okay, I understand." The human tried to pull himself from the Alpha's arms but was stopped as the hand that had been cupping his head, traced a line down his cheek.

"No, you don't. If we keep this up, then I won't be able to stop myself from claiming you as mine. I refuse to be like the others who used you and hurt you." Alpha Grant smiled ruefully. "And I don't want to be the one to tell Doc Houston why your stitches broke open." Ricky jumped as he felt the zipper on his pants lower. "But I can help you out with this before you get some sleep."

Ricky watched as the dark head lowered and wet heat enveloped him. "You don't have to…oh, ah…" the young human groaned as the Alpha continued to suck his throbbing cock. He'd never felt anything like it before. He'd been forced for so many years to service others this way and yet the favor had never been returned. He felt a moment of guilt as his cock slid further down the Alpha's throat, the constriction of the muscles made him push further even as his mind argued this wasn't right. He knew he hated doing this for others and didn't want the Alpha to demean himself this way.

Ricky sucked in a breath as the man pulled off briefly only to suck on his sack. "You don't…oh…you don't have to…" he tried to protest as he felt first one ball and then another sucked into the Alpha's talented mouth. The silky tongue traveled up the vein on his cock, only to have soft lips nibble at the sensitive nerves just under the head. Just when he thought it couldn't get any better, the Alpha's tongue pushed gently into his slit, tasting the pre-come that dripped slowly from his engorged member.

"Relax, little warrior. Have you never experienced this before?" Alpha Grant asked in a husky voice as he gazed up from between Ricky's legs.

"No, ah, this is the first time," Ricky admitted and then moaned with a soft smile, the Alpha reclaimed his cock and began to suck harder while gently rolling his balls between his large fingers. There was no way he was going to be able to stop as the human felt the tingle in his spine build until with a shout of warning he felt himself erupt. For a brief moment, Ricky felt a sense of euphoria as his cock continued to empty his seed into the welcoming mouth of the Alpha. Then reality over what had happened kicked in.

Ricky shoved away from the Alpha and rolled to the other side of the large bed. The pain in his back a reminder of what happened when he came without permission. He landed on the floor and moved as quickly as he could towards the bathroom door. Before the Alpha could stop him, Ricky managed to duck inside and close the door. He locked it but knew it would only be a matter of time before the Alpha broke down the door. Ricky glanced around the room for any exit he could find. The only window was too small to be of use. He was trapped.

With a sob, Ricky entered the shower stall and closed the door. He lowered himself into the corner and pulled his legs up to his chest as he tried to make himself as small a target as he could. While he waited for his punishment, he found himself reliving the first time he'd been caught jacking off in the shower while a member of the Willow Creek Pack.

Even now, Ricky couldn't help the shudder that went through him as he thought about Biff, one of the Beta's and also one of the meanest wolf shifters he'd ever met. The large shifter was built like the hulk and he used every bit of his imposing presence to scare Ricky into submission. The vivid tattoos that covered the shifter's body were the things of nightmares. Alpha Clifton had given him to Biff for six months to help him learn his new position within the pack. After more than three months of being used to do any demeaning task Biff could think of during the day and then being taught to be totally sexually submissive to the huge shifter at night, his body had screamed for some kind of release.

Beta Biff had told him to get clean and be in position before he returned from a meeting with Alpha Clifton. The human knew he didn't have much time to make sure he was ready for the evening's session just like he knew there would be no pleasure for him when the Beta returned. He glanced nervously around Biff's bedroom before entering the attached bathroom to prepare. As the warm water cascaded down his body, his thoughts once more went back to his friend Robert. His cock filled as he pictured Robert kneeling before him, his full lips smiling up at him as he leaned forward and began to lick the vein that ran on the underside of Ricky's cock. With a soft sigh, the captive human

69

continued the fantasy, stroking himself until with a soft cry he came against the shower wall.

Before he could make sure the water washed away all trace of his activity, the shower door was yanked open as the panicked man was yanked from the stall. "How dare you!" Biff roared, as Ricky tried to pry his arm from the stranglehold the Beta had on it. "Obviously you have learned nothing about control or your place human."

"I'm sorry…it's just been so long and I…" Ricky stuttered as he was thrown down on the floor of the bedroom. A heavy foot kicked his side with enough force to send him rolling across the floor. Before he could get his knees under him, he was yanked up by his hair until he stood at the end of the large bed. His arms were shoved into the shackles that hung from the top of the heavy wooden posts while his ankles were restrained to the lower end. Helpless to prevent what would happen next, Ricky closed his eyes and tried to find the place he went to when the pain became too much.

Unfortunately, this time he was forced to open his eyes as his cock was pulled up until he stood on his toes. "This no longer belongs to you, human. Maybe I should just permanently relieve you of your needs." The Beta allowed his claws to form on his other hand. "Perhaps I should hang these around your neck as a reminder of your place." The clawed hand held Ricky's balls in a crushing grip that caused him to cry out. He could feel a trickle of blood as it flowed down the inside of his thigh.

"Please…" Ricky managed to groan as he tried to keep himself from throwing up.

Biff laughed as he stepped back, a thoughtful look on his face. "Perhaps you're right. I might be a little too hasty since some of the female wolves are sure to enjoy what your puny human cock can do for them. But I guarantee before we are done tonight, you'll learn to get hard when ordered and you'll learn to curb your desire for release until you are given permission or female wolves or not, I'll remove the temptation permanently. After all, I'm only interested in filling your holes, boy; I don't need the rest of the equipment to enjoy myself."

Ricky pulled his knees tighter to his body. He no longer heard the pounding at the door or the demand for entry from the Alpha of Windy River Pack. Instead he did the only thing that had allowed him to survive all the years of punishment, first by his father and later by the Willow Creek Pack members. He slowly rose to his knees and placed his hands behind his head in the perfect slave position. Ricky allowed himself to drift into the one place where no one could ever hurt him and for the first time he thought about not coming back.

· · ❖ · ·

Sandy looked on in awe as his newfound friend showed him around his garage, The Spark Plug.

"So you are the only one who knows how to fix all these cars?" The young wolf asked, as Sparky pointed to one of the tools on the tray beside Sandy. He was helping out by passing over tools, just like he had done in the past for his brother. They were going to finish their shopping trip with a new hairstyle until the mechanic's phone had rung with an emergency. It seemed the town's main fire truck had broken down and the only one who could fix it was Sparky.

"Hard to believe, huh?" Sparky grinned as he twirled the screwdriver in his hand. Sandy found his gaze following the glittered purple handle. The young wolf thought the brightly colored tools were cool even though he doubted many people would be caught dead using them. But he'd learned quickly that Sparky didn't care what people thought about him or his strange tastes.

"No, I believe you," Sandy quickly assured the wolf. "Maybe once my brother is feeling better he could help you."

"You're brother likes to work on cars?" Sparky asked as his head disappeared into the engine. Sandy grinned at the tight blue jeans with the glittering rainbow on each of the back pockets. His own new jeans didn't have any decorations, even though the older wolf had tried hard to get the young wolf to expand his wardrobe past blue jeans and plain t-shirts. The fact that Sandy now owned a bright yellow t-shirt that stated "Don't worry, Zombies only eat people with brains" was as far as he had gone from what he always wore.

"He used to work on the cars in our old pack. Of course, they never paid him." Sandy scowled for a moment before he looked up to see Sparky looking at him with sympathetic eyes.

"That must have really sucked. Don't worry, if Ricky wants a job here, he'll be paid just like everyone else." Sparky wiped his hands on the bright orange rag that hung out of his pocket. "But first, young Jedi, we must introduce you to the dark side. What do you think about blue highlights?"

"Ah, well…" Sandy tried to think of a nice way to say no when the other wolf chuckled.

"You know it's okay if you want to just get it trimmed up a bit. After all, not everyone can be as stylish as me—there'd be too much competition for best dressed in this town." Sparky winked as he slammed the hood down on the fire engine. He stepped back and cocked his head to the side as he looked at the young wolf. "Although, fire engine red might really look good on you kiddo…"

Just as Sandy was getting ready to decline the offer, he felt a familiar ache. It was one he'd become too familiar with while they had lived in the Willow Creek Pack but he knew what it meant. "Ricky's in trouble," Sandy said in a monotone voice.

"Wait, what?" Sparky said as he moved closer to the youngster. Sandy felt an arm go around his shoulders, but he was too busy trying to figure out why his 'spidey senses' were going off. He hadn't understood when it first started happening. The unsettled feelings and phantom pain that sometimes happened to him had scared him. When he told Ricky about it, his brother had looked at him strangely for a moment before he'd just told him it was normal. But as the feelings continued to get more intense, his big brother had finally admitted that they were bound together so that each of them could look out for the other.

Sandy shrugged off the wolf's arm and stepped back. "My brother's in trouble and I need to go to him!"

Before Sparky could comment, the young wolf shifted and took off toward the Alpha's house. He heard the shifter's yells behind him, but he didn't care. Ricky needed him and that was all that mattered.

CHAPTER EIGHT

GRANT PRESSED HIS EAR AGAINST THE DOOR THAT SEPARATED him from his mate. It took all of his will to keep his wolf from emerging and barging through the door to get to the man he'd come to admire in such a short time. As he thought back over what had happened, he still couldn't figure out what he'd done to cause this kind of reaction. The man had been enjoying what he did to him, he could tell. The scent of arousal was strong and Ricky's body had come alive under his touch.

"Ricky?" Grant said softly as he tried the knob once more. "Open the door and we can talk." The slight growl in his voice couldn't be helped. The longer the door remained closed, the closer to the surface his wolf surged.

Just as he was about to break the lock, he heard movement followed by the sound of the lock being disengaged. The Alpha took a deep breath and tried to get his own emotions under control as he slowly opened the door. Nothing could have prepared him for what he found on the other side. "What the…" Grant started but stopped as he took a step into the room.

Ricky knelt on the floor completely naked with his knees spread to reveal himself. His arms were locked behind his head and his back was ram rod straight. He recognized it as the position a sex slave would take, but he didn't understand why Ricky was greeting him this way now.

"What the hell did you do to him, Grant?"

The Alpha turned to face David and growled. "I believe this is my bedroom, what are you doing here?"

David crossed his arms and glared at his brother. "Oh, nothing much, just saving your jeans from another shredding from a certain Omega. He showed up

73

a few minutes ago looking like he was ready to kill anyone who got in his way. Jason is trying to calm the pup down but it won't be long before..."

A loud growl sounded from the bedroom doorway before a white blur raced into the small space and placed himself between Ricky and the other wolves. Grant had to give the pup credit, he had no fear. But this was getting ridiculous. He was the Alpha here.

"Stand down!" Grant ordered, pushing his power towards the young wolf. He watched in fascination as Sandy stepped back for a moment, cocked his head to the side before shaking himself and baring his teeth again. "I said stand down, pup." Grant allowed his wolf to surface briefly. He could feel his eyes shift and his teeth lengthen as his claws pushed through his hands. Like other true Alphas, he was able to control his shift and could even fight in this form. If Sandy was going to be part of this pack, he would have to learn who was in charge. Especially if what they suspected about the young pup was true. If the Omega would not accept him as his Alpha and obey his commands, they would be in trouble once he gained his powers.

"Well if everyone is done showing his dick, I think we should all back out and give the boy some space." Sparky's voice echoed in the small space. "Or we could braid each others hair. David, we might need to give you some extensions...but I can work with the others."

There was a shimmer as Sandy shifted back to his human form. The look on the pup's face was priceless as he stared at the outrageous wolf. David chuckled and even Grant managed a slight twist of the lip.

"Why would we braid our hair?" Sandy asked as he glanced to the other two wolves for help.

"Don't look at me, I need extensions remember?" David shrugged as he glanced back at the mechanic.

Grant sighed as he rubbed his hand down his face. "Silence!" He growled. The irate leader glared at the other two wolves before he motioned for everyone to leave the small room. During the whole exchange Ricky hadn't reacted at all. He sat calmly, his head lowered. If he hadn't seen the man's chest move, he would have thought he was looking at a statue. He saw Sandy once again ignore his order as he knelt next to his brother, his eyes filled with tears.

"Not again, please, Ricky—I need you!" He said softly as he stroked his brother's hair. Grant shook his head as he followed his brother and friend into

74

his bedroom. The two men glared at him, but for once kept silent. The Alpha paced for a few minutes, trying to regain control of his wolf. It was bad enough that his mate wasn't well and obviously in no shape to be claimed, but his wolf was also reacting to what it saw as the failure of the others to submit.

David and Sparky must have realized how close his wolf was to losing control. He glanced at his two pack members and saw them tilt their heads, their eyes now looked down at the floor. Grant sighed. Just once he wished he could let loose and say or do what he wanted like the others. The need to just shift and run through the forest was strong. But he couldn't. He had to keep a tight reign on his wolf.

"David, get the Doc in here and Sparky, you can explain how Sandy arrived here without his escort!" He saw a flash of guilt cross the mechanic's face as he continued to remain silent. His brother left without a word, but not before patting their friend on the shoulder. Grant glanced back into the bathroom and sighed. Sandy was whispering to his brother, but Ricky still hadn't changed position. He couldn't help his mate but he could find out how Sandy was able to escape. "I'm waiting for an explanation. How could a young pup manage to get away from one of my best Sentries?"

Sparky shuffled his feet before he sighed and glanced at the young pup that had shifted again and was lying beside his silent older brother. "It was the darnest thing I've ever seen—" The mechanic looked back at the Alpha. "Are you sure he hasn't, you know, come into his powers already?"

Grant glanced back at the young pup before he returned his attention to his Sentry. "According to the legends, an Omega doesn't show his or her true self until their twenty-first year. At the time of the Wolf Moon the goddess appears and bestows her gifts to her chosen."

"Well something strange is going on, Alpha. I swear the pup knew his brother was in trouble. It was almost like they were connected." Sparky continued as he shook his head, "Before I could figure out what was going on, Sandy had shifted and taken off."

"Did anyone see him?" The Alpha asked as he realized they might have another problem.

The Sentry shook his head. "Only Markus and Bret. I have them standing guard outside though just in case." Both wolves looked back at the bathroom. The silence from the room was deafening. The Alpha moved closer, his wolf

75

howled within at his inability to soothe his mate. Yet it was clear the man needed more than he could give him. Grant turned as a hand clasped his shoulder.

"He's waiting for your command," Sparky said softly.

"And how do you know what my mate needs?" Grant asked as he turned his attention back towards the other wolf. He watched as his friend squirmed for a moment before looking up to meet his gaze. "Well?"

Sparky shrugged. "I have been to a few clubs in my time, mostly before I came to stay here." He glanced over towards the silent human. "I never really got too heavy into the whole Dom/Sub BDSM scene, too much sweat and blood for my taste, but some of the members did." There was sympathy in the wolf's gaze as he glanced back towards the Alpha. "He's been trained to be a submissive Grant."

"He told us about the Beta at Willow Creek training him, but I've never given him any indication I expect the same from him," Grant growled as he glared at the wolf standing in front of him. He knew about Doms and Subs of course, but he'd never actually experimented with it. Being an Alpha, he knew he was a natural Dom but he'd been too busy learning to take over as leader of their pack to delve into the practice. Besides, he had hoped that he could show his mate the side of him that no one else could ever see.

There was a soft sigh as the other wolf shook his head sadly. "My guess is your mate isn't really a submissive by nature. There's too much fire in him from what Sandy has told me. But it is possible to force someone to submit." There was a haunted look in the Sentry's eyes that gave Grant pause. While he knew some of what had happened to his friend in the past, there was a part that the flamboyant wolf never spoke of to anyone.

Grant glanced back at the still form of his mate. The man continued to ignore his brother as he gazed at the floor. "So what do you suggest? I will not force anyone in my care to submit against their will."

Sparky snorted. "Alpha, I hate to break the news to you but your nature demands those around you to submit." The wolf stepped back as Grant turned and growled low in his throat. Not to be cowed, the shifter placed a hand on his hip and pointed his finger at the glowering Alpha. "You just proved my point. Look, no one here is challenging your authority and you know I don't back down to anyone but you…" he paused and tapped his chin with his finger, "…and maybe that cute new waiter at the diner…"

"Sparky!" Grant ground out.

"Okay, look this is really easy. Just use your Alpha voice and command him to do what you want. If he's been trained, it's the only way to reach him right now. From the way Sandy is acting, this isn't the first time he's seen his brother do this either." Sparky tapped his temple. "It's some kind of coping mechanism that he probably uses to get away from what he can't face."

Grant shook his head. "But all I did was show him pleasure. After hearing all he's suffered, I wanted to help him…"

The other wolf glanced at the bed for a moment before he looked back at the Alpha pacing the room. "If he's reverting back to his training, he probably feels he broke some rule."

"Rules?" Grant asked.

"Most Doms have rules for their subs. Things like never wearing clothes or even not coming without permission—" Sparky jumped back as Grant turned suddenly and moved towards the bed. The large shifter glanced down at the rumpled sheets for a moment before he glanced back at the bathroom.

"He came after I…" Grant blushed slightly before he continued, "…after I helped him release some of the tension. But he enjoyed it. I know he did."

"Did you tell him to come, Alpha?" Sparky asked quietly.

"Of course not! Why would I need to." Grant stopped and rubbed a hand down his face. "He's been trained not to come without permission?"

Sparky nodded. "That would be my guess and from his reaction, I'd say not obeying meant more than just a couple of slaps to the ass."

Suddenly the whip marks on his mate's body took on a more sinister meaning. A low growl rumbled in the Alpha's throat. He could feel his eyes change as he thought about what had been done to his mate. It took everything in him not to shift and go after the Beta who had caused so much pain to Ricky. A low rumble from the floor brought his attention back to the problem at hand. He had to try to at least get his mate back to the bed and off the cold floor. He couldn't imagine the pain the position was causing the man. He still hadn't healed from the damage done to his back much less regained enough strength to maintain the pose for much longer.

Grant took a step towards the doorway into the bathroom. He cleared his throat and looked directly at the kneeling human. "Ricky, you will rise and go to the bed." He watched in fascination and horror as the man slowly rose to his feet and began to walk stiffly towards the end of the bed. Without a word he stood and turned, his arms raised over his head and legs spread wide as if he expected to be restrained. Grant could see the slight tremors that ran through the man's body as he struggled to maintain the new position. Before the Alpha could order Ricky to drop his arms he heard a growl and was knocked to the ground. He rolled, instinctively shifting his hands into claws to defend himself. He shoved the white wolf away from him and heard a slight whimper as Sandy hit the wall.

The Alpha stood quickly to face the still growling wolf. "Stand down now!" He ordered as he tried to keep his wolf from attacking the perceived threat. He noticed Sparky had also shifted and had moved to stand in front of him. The Sentry growled softly at the young wolf but didn't advance. The Omega paced for a moment before he dropped his front end down in preparation to charge again. Before he could move, Sparky advanced and grabbed the young wolf by the scruff and shook him slightly.

Grant took a deep breath but before he could intercede he heard a softly spoken word from behind him. "NO!"

He glanced back and saw Ricky step from the bed towards the two fighting wolves. He raised his hand and waved it as if he was tossing something aside as he spoke again. "Leave him alone!" Grant whirled around as he saw Sparky fly across the room and crash into the opposite wall. The wolf whimpered softly as he lay on the floor shaking his head. His gaze was drawn back to his mate who now stood in front of the cowering Omega.

"You will not hurt him," Ricky said with a monotone voice.

"No one will hurt either one of you, Ricky," The Alpha stated as he retracted his claws and tried to appear non-threatening to the pair. "Sparky would never hurt Sandy and neither would I. However we will defend ourselves." There was a shimmer as the white wolf transformed into the youngest Landon. The boy placed a hand on Ricky's extended arm.

"I'm okay, Ricky," Sandy said softly. Grant noticed the slight look of awe in the young pup's eyes. From his reaction, this must be something new. He glanced back up at his mate and noticed the tattoo on the man's arm glowing.

Interesting, it seems like the protector had made his appearance. For a moment he wondered why Ricky hadn't used his ability to stop what had happened in the Willow Creek Pack, but he'd have to solve that puzzle another day as the young man began to sway and would have fallen if Grant hadn't rushed to catch him.

"Ricky!" Sandy cried as his brother's eyes rolled upwards and closed.

"I see I arrived just in time," Doc Houston grumbled as he walked into the room. "Place him on the bed so I can check him out. The rest of you leave." The Doc glanced at the limping mechanic. "I'll check on you when I'm finished."

"It's nothing, Doc, I'll shift once I get outside and it should take care of it," Sparky remarked slightly subdued as he gave the man in the bed a wide berth. "I'll just check on the other Sentries Alpha and make sure they understand about not talking about what they've seen. Let me know if you need me for anything else." The wolf glanced briefly at Sandy before he left the room.

Sandy glanced up at the Alpha with tears in his eyes. "I didn't mean to cause trouble. It's always my fault. Please don't punish my brother. I'll do whatever you want, just don't hurt him no more."

Grant sighed as he placed a hand on the boy's shoulder and followed him out of the bedroom. He kept his hand on the Omega's shoulder while they walked down the hallway towards the kitchen. "I'm not going to punish anyone, Sandy. We're part wolves and sometimes we act like them. However, you and I do have to talk about what happened in town today."

Sandy shuffled toward the kitchen table and sat down; his head was lowered as he placed his hands in his lap. For a moment, Grant just wanted to pick the young pup up and hold him, but he also had to make sure the Omega understood how dangerous it had been for him to shift in town. He walked over to the fridge and pulled out the carton of milk. He grabbed the plate of cookies that seemed to always be on the counter these days before he took a seat opposite the young wolf. He poured a glass for each of them and took a bite of one of the cookies before he nodded for Sandy to do the same. He watched as the young pup dunked his cookie in his milk before taking a bite. A soft moan could be heard as they both continued to eat in silence for a moment.

Grant began to think back over what had just happened. It was clear that the goddess Gaia had already bestowed some gifts on these two. He'd need to call his father and see if there was anyone who could give him some more guidance on what to expect. Until then, he'd have to tread carefully with the two new members of his pack. Whether they knew it or not, they both needed his protection, maybe more now than ever.

"Do you think Ricky will be okay?" Sandy's voice broke the silence of the room.

"The Doc will make sure he hasn't done any damage to his wounds," the Alpha answered before he asked a question of his own. "How did you know Ricky was in trouble, Sandy?"

The young pup shrugged. "Ricky calls it my 'spidey' senses. I'm not 'sposed to talk about it." The Omega traced a pattern on the table. "I know I shouldn't shift when others are around and I can't trust anyone 'cause I'm supposed to be special. But I don't feel special." Teary sky blue eyes looked up at Grant. "Alpha Clifton would always punish my brother, even if I did something wrong. If I wasn't quick enough or able to hunt and fight the way the Alpha taught me, he'd whip my brother." Sandy paused and looked back towards the bedroom. "I don't understand..."

Grant followed the boy's gaze. "What don't you understand, Sandy?"

"Ricky's never fought back before. I mean, he was like some super hero throwing Sparky like that. Do you think he might be like Superman?" Sandy looked back at the Alpha, his voice low as if they were sharing a secret. "Cause that would be so cool and it would mean no one could hurt my brother again, right?"

Grant couldn't help the slight grin that formed on his face. Sometimes he forgot how young the boy was in front of him. While in his wolf form, he'd shown his ability to handle himself better than most his age, but he still had a ways to go towards maturity. "Has your brother ever told you about the tattoo on his arm or how he got it?"

Sandy shook his head. "No, I know that once Alpha Clifton tried to burn it off but the flame couldn't touch it." The young wolf shuddered as he rubbed his own arm. "Why would our old Alpha do that?"

Grant took a deep breath and forced himself to remain calm. "Because he isn't a good Alpha, Sandy. There is good and bad in all things. It is the way of our world. What Alpha Clifton did to you and your brother was wrong. A good Alpha takes care of all the members in his pack. It is his responsibility to make sure they are protected from those who would hurt them and to make sure they are cared for. It is a hard job and not all Alpha's can handle the responsibility that comes with the power they are given."

Sandy nodded. "You're not like Alpha Clifton."

"No I'm not," Grant confirmed.

"Can we stay with you?" Sandy asked quietly.

"You and your brother became a member of my pack the moment I brought you to my house, Sandy. If you wish to stay, it will be up to you and your brother. But if you do stay, there will be rules," Grant replied, as he sat back in his chair. He watched as Sandy chewed on his lower lip for a moment before he straightened his shoulders.

"If I agree to follow your rules, will you promise to never hurt my brother, even if we do something wrong?" Sandy sighed. "I don't want my brother hurting no more Alpha. I'll do anything to keep that from happening to him."

Grant sighed. The boy had no idea what he was offering. He took a deep breath and hoped he could get the pup to understand. "Sandy, you can't make a pledge like that lightly and I don't demand it from you." He held up his hand before the boy spoke. "To be a part of this pack, you simply have to agree to obey me. That means all the time, not just when you want to. If you can't submit to me, then you place not only yourself at risk, but the whole pack. Do you understand what I'm trying to say?"

"So I can't protect my brother?"

The Alpha shook his head. "No, you can protect your brother. But you have to also trust that I will also protect him. If you had attacked me with any other wolves of my pack present, they would have tried to protect me and you or Ricky could be hurt. Some day you will understand more about pack loyalty, but for now just try to trust me when I say I won't intentionally hurt either you or your brother. I'm Alpha and I take care of my pack." Grant stood and let his wolf eyes flash for a moment before he glanced down at the young wolf.

"Okay, Alpha Grant." The pup stood and held out his hand.

Grant took the small hand into his much larger one and shook it. "We have a deal."

A soft chuckle sounded from the doorway. "New initiation ceremony, Grant?" David asked as he entered the room and glanced at the table. "A handshake over cookies and milk? Why couldn't you have done that with me?"

Sandy cocked his head to the side. "What do you mean, David?"

The Beta looked at Grant before he answered, "Didn't your former pack explain to you what is involved in pledging your loyalty to the Alpha and the pack?"

"No, other than showing respect by tipping my head and doing what I'm told, there wasn't anything else. Why?" Sandy asked as he reached for another cookie.

"Well, young Jedi, let me explain it to you." David took a seat and began to talk quietly to the young pup.

Grant stood and left them alone as he walked toward his bedroom. As he passed his office he stopped and stepped inside. He walked towards the desk and picked up his cell phone. For a moment he gazed back towards the kitchen and then he made his call.

"Hello, Dad? Can you and Mother make a trip home sometime soon?" He listened for a moment and smiled. "Next week is fine. I'll see you then." As he hung up the phone he relaxed. Hopefully his father would be able to provide him with some of the answers he sought. Besides, he might need more than advice.

CHAPTER NINE

RICKY GROANED AS HE OPENED HIS EYES. HE GLANCED OVER at the window and noticed that another day had passed. The moonlight spilled across the windowsill, bathing the floor in its pale light. For a moment he allowed the peacefulness of the room to envelope him in its embrace. But before long memories of what happened came forward and made him shiver. He didn't remember everything, but he did recall throwing the wolf that was attacking his brother across the room with nothing more than a thought.

He raised his hand and flexed it for a moment before he lowered it slowly. Had he actually done it or was it just a strange dream? In all his years, he'd never done anything like it and yet, he could still feel a slight tingle coming from the tattoo on his arm. He remembered Maria telling him that the goddess would provide him with the strength to defend Sandy when the time came. But he'd never believed it. Especially after what he'd endured at the hands of his former pack. Surely if he'd had these powers before, he would have been able to use them.

The thought of his brother had him sitting up in the bed and glancing around. Had Sandy been hurt by the other wolf? Were they now prisoners because of what he'd done? Too many questions swirled in his head as he slowly placed his feet on the cold floor. He had to find his brother and then he'd make plans for them to leave. There was no way the Alpha would let them stay now.

At least someone had put clothes on him. His last memory before coming to and seeing Sandy being attacked was taking them off and preparing himself for the punishment he knew would be coming. Ricky frowned as he realized that there hadn't been any punishment for his transgression. It confused him and worried him more than he realized. In the past, punishment had been swift and brutal, but so far in this new pack, nothing had happened. Of course, maybe the new Alpha was waiting until he was more aware so that he could accept his punishment. That had to be it. Once he was healed, the new punishment would be dealt.

As he reached the door leading to the hall, he paused. There hadn't been a lock on the door, but what if there was a guard on the other side? Ricky squared his shoulders and quickly opened the door. If there was a guard, then he'd at least have someone to ask about his brother. As the door opened, Ricky tensed, waiting for an attack that never came. Instead he was met with an empty hall. He quickly made his way to the room his brother had indicated would be his. As he quietly opened the door he stepped inside and sucked in a deep breath as he glanced around. The room was smaller than the master bedroom, but not by much. He saw what looked like a bed shaped like the Batmobile in the center of the room. Various action figures littered the floor while posters with his brother's other favorite superheroes hung on the walls. As he moved closer to the bed he smiled softly as he saw his little brother sleeping peacefully in the center of the bed, the figure of Spiderman clutched in his hand.

Ricky pulled the blanket up higher to cover his brother as he leaned forward to brush a lock of stray white hair from his sibling's cheek. Normally Sandy would have woken by now, but he continued to sleep. For the first time, Ricky realized that his brother might not only be safe, but he must also feel safe. If he was honest with himself, there was nothing these wolves had done to hint that they wanted his brother in the same way Alpha Clifton had. In fact, he'd noticed genuine affection for his brother from the Alpha and his brothers.

Assured that his brother was safe, Ricky quietly left the room and stood in the hallway. He rubbed his hand over the tattoo on his arm as he tried to figure out what exactly had happened. But nothing came to mind. Of course, it was just one more reason why the Alpha wouldn't want him as his true mate. For a moment he thought back to how his body had reacted to the Alpha's touch. Maria had told him enough for him to realize that his reactions to the Alpha and the way the wolf looked at him meant they were true mates. But he also knew the Alpha did not have to accept him. In fact, he might be better off if he didn't.

Yet as he thought about never being claimed by the big Alpha, Ricky felt the loneliness that always lingered grow until he thought it would swallow him whole. He touched his lips for a moment, remembering the taste of the Alpha as he plundered his mouth. The gentle touch on his skin, that caused him even now to get hard. If only he had met Alpha Grant first things could have been so different. Something in him needed to believe that it wasn't too late as he made his way down the hall towards the kitchen. Maybe he and Sandy had found a home after all.

Voices echoed down the empty hallway. Ricky recognized the Alpha's voice along with the voices of his brothers. He paused for a moment just outside the kitchen. He didn't want to intrude on the brothers. But before he could turn to leave he heard his name.

"You know Ricky is your *Semme'* mate, Grant." Jason's voice was low and soothing. "I've done some research and the only way to stop Alpha Clifton from taking him or having him killed as a rogue is for you to officially claim him as your mate. *Semme'* mates trump the mark he bears of the Willow Creek Pack and it's Alpha."

There was silence for a moment before Ricky heard Grant's strong voice. "I can't claim him Jason. The man is damaged beyond anything I am able to fix!" The sound of a fist hitting the table made Ricky jump, even as his eyes filled with tears. He listened as his last hope of having true love disintegrated. Of course the Alpha didn't want him, who would after what he'd allowed his former pack to do to him.

"Alpha Clifton has no claim on Sandy. As an Omega, he can join any pack he chooses. But by declaring Ricky a rogue, he has signed the man's death warrant and you know this," David responded.

"Sandy has asked for sanctuary for him and his brother and I have given it," Alpha Grant stated. "No one will harm any who has been placed under my protection."

A soft sigh filled the room. "It's not that easy and you know it, Grant. We also signed the treaty with the humans. If you don't kill Ricky or return him to Willow Creek Pack for retribution, then you could bring war to us. Are you sure you want that?" Jason asked softly.

Ricky didn't wait to hear any more of the conversation. He walked quickly towards the front door of the house, his steps determined. It was clear Sandy would be safe with this pack and had already settled in. The only way he could truly protect his brother was to make sure that war did not come to this pack.

He paused by the door to an office. From the looks of it, he guessed it belonged to Alpha Grant. As he searched the desk for a pen and paper, he glanced at the moonlight coming through the window as it splashed across the desk. As the light moved higher to the tattoo on his arm, he swore he felt a slight pulsing but shook his head as he continued to write.

Once he'd finished, he placed the note where he was sure the Alpha would find it. With one last glance back towards the room where his brother slept, Ricky did the hardest thing he'd ever done in his life. He shut down his emotions and walked out the door. Hopefully with distance the strange connection between him and his brother would fade, along with the memory of him.

• • ❖ • •

Grant glared at his brothers. How dare they question his ability to protect his pack? "They would not dare to challenge me. These lands have long been recognized as sanctuary for all regardless of their past. Besides, from what I've heard, Ricky was never given an opportunity to state his side of the story. You heard what he told us, Alpha Crazy thinks he is going to use Ricky to control his brother. Can you imagine what that would mean to not only the shifter world, but to all the other paranormals and humans?"

"I understand the risk, but will the rest of the pack be willing to make the sacrifice that might be necessary?" Jason continued as he stood from his chair. "What you are willing to risk is a lot for one you don't want to take as your mate." Jason jumped as a chair sailed through the room and landed not far from him.

"I never said I didn't want Ricky, but how can I claim him when he becomes catatonic when we have sex?"

"Wait, you had sex?" David sputtered. "With Ricky?"

Grant rubbed a hand down his face as he returned to sit at the table. "That's none of your business, brother," he ground out even as he felt himself blushing like a virgin bride.

"You did!" His middle brother chuckled. "Well, I'll be; I never thought I'd see the day when my big brother would admit he used anything other than his left hand."

Jason slapped David on the back of the head. "Do you have to be so crude? Seriously, dude, you need to stop worrying so much about our brother and get yourself laid."

David rubbed his sore head and still laughed. "Never a problem for me. I've got numbers upon numbers to call whenever I feel the itch. But big brother here? The last time he got lucky electricity hadn't yet been invented."

"Are you through?" Grant growled as he stood and glared at his brothers. He knew they were just trying to lighten the mood, but it wasn't helping. Especially when all he could think about was the smooth alabaster skin on the man sleeping in his bed upstairs. The need to claim his mate was riding him hard but he just couldn't put Ricky through any more trauma.

"I've asked Father and Mother to come home. Maybe they'll have some answers to the best way to proceed with our two new members. Until then, we'll just have to stay vigilant. I doubt Alpha Clifton will act in any great haste. If he was going to do that, he would be here already."

Jason sighed. "That's what has me worried."

"I've ordered some new hardware that should be here tomorrow. I'll be upping the security on the grounds as well as on the house. Nothing will get in here without my knowing about it," David said, as he stood and placed a hand on Grant's shoulder. "Don't worry big brother, Ricky is your *Semme'* mate and I'm sure Gaia wouldn't have given him to you if you didn't have what was needed to help him. Now I'm going to bed because that order will be here bright and early tomorrow."

Grant watched as his two brothers left the kitchen and headed for their rooms. He stood and followed them, pausing briefly outside his own room. He placed his hand on the doorknob, but stepped back without opening the door. He'd have to talk to Ricky soon about the future of their relationship. Even if they couldn't have sex, he still wanted the man in his life. Maybe he could find someone to help Ricky deal with what had happened to him. He'd have Jason check into a psychiatrist. He might not be able to claim his mate in the way of their kind, but he knew it didn't matter because his heart had already bonded with the man.

The Alpha collapsed onto the bed in the spare room. Tomorrow he'd talk to Ricky and make sure he understood that both he and his brother were now safe. Then he'd call a meeting of the Sentries to bring them up to speed on what was happening. Eventually he'd have to tell the rest of the pack. He'd give them the chance to stay or leave. Perhaps those who didn't want to fight could relocate to one of the other friendly packs he knew of. As thoughts of what he needed to do swirled through his mind, it was the vision of hazel eyes glazed in pleasure that finally allowed him to drift into a troubled sleep.

● ● ❖ ● ●

Ricky was surprised at how easy it had been to walk away. He'd expected there to be guards around the house, but there hadn't been any. As he continued the long walk towards the small town of Sugar Creek, he concentrated on keeping his emotions at bay. He'd learned long ago that his little brother somehow tapped into them. The truth was, he could also sense his brother. He knew when he was happy or when he was worried. It was one of the reasons he'd been able to leave. Sandy was happy for the first time in a long time.

He glanced nervously around. If another wolf spotted him and knew he was rogue, he knew what would happen. Even though he didn't understand how a human could be held to the ways of the shifters, he really didn't want to test the theory. At this point he figured all he had to do was get to town, 'borrow' another car and get as far away as possible. With luck he could find a mechanic job in some small town and just disappear. He was just thankful that he'd healed enough to make the journey. Even though he still felt a bit weak and his back twinged now and then, he felt better than he had in years. Of course, his limp slowed him down a little, but with luck he'd make it to town within the next hour.

As he walked around a curve, he stopped dead at the sight in front of him. For a moment he thought it was his imagination, but when the tall man in front of him smiled he knew it was his nightmare returned.

"Well, look at what we have here. And I thought I'd just be leaving this note for that stupid Alpha of yours." Biff chuckled as he held up a piece of paper before dropping it on the road.

Ricky followed the path of the paper as he tried to figure out a way to escape. "You shouldn't be here…"

Biff shook his head. "Wrong, you're the one who shouldn't be here. Of course, it would have been better if your little brother was tagging along—he wouldn't be running close by, would he?" The Beta of Willow Creek grabbed Ricky by the arm and yanked him forward. "Do you hear me, Sandy? If you're out there, you need to come now, or I'll make your big brother cry again."

"He's not here, you bastard!" Ricky ground out as he tugged his arm away from the larger man's grip. "Even if he was, there is no way he'd come to you. In fact, he's probably most of the way back to the Alpha's house getting help."

Biff stopped and stared at the woods for a moment before he turned to glare back at Ricky. "You're bluffing, human!"

"Stay and find out, Biff. Either way, you won't be getting out of here in one piece—argh!" Ricky cried out as a fist slammed into his face. He felt his nose give way as he fell to the ground. Before he could try to get back on his feet the Beta grabbed him and began to run into the woods.

"Let me go!" Ricky screamed as he beat against the muscular back.

"Quiet, or I'll do more than break your face. You forget yourself pet. Once I have you someplace safe, I guess I'll have to remind you of the proper way to act." Biff laughed as he continued to move further into the forest. Ricky remained quiet as he tried to figure out a way to slow the shifter down. Even with his added weight the Beta was able to move quickly through the brush. Ricky's only hope was that the wolf wouldn't be able to get out of the Windy River Pack territory before the Alpha could find him.

Part of him wanted to use his connection to Sandy to alert his brother of his predicament, but then he realized bringing Sandy to him was what the bastard would want. In fact, he was probably counting on it. That was why he was leaving him conscious. He was hoping his sibling would follow. Ricky concentrated on quelling his feelings. There was no way he was going to allow these bastards to get their hands on his brother ever again. He'd kill himself before he allowed them to use him that way.

Just when he thought his head was going to explode from being carried like a sack of potatoes, they came to an old logging road. Ricky's heart sank as he saw a faded blue van parked on the side of the roadway. Before he could struggle further, he was dropped onto the ground and a fist connected with the side of his face. He couldn't prevent his fall into darkness. Ricky could only hope that this time he wouldn't wake up.

CHAPTER TEN

THREE DAYS. IT HAD BEEN THREE DAYS SINCE GRANT HAD found the note left by his mate. As he sat at his desk, he glanced down at the paper in his hands for the hundredth time.

Alpha Grant:

I'm sorry for the trouble I've brought to you and your pack. All I ask is that you keep my little brother safe. He never asked for any of this. I believe you to be an honorable Alpha and that you meant what you said when you vowed to protect him. As long as I'm a rogue, I can't be with him so I entrust his care to you. With this letter I revoke my rights as guardian for Sandy and make you his new legal guardian.

I'm also sorry I couldn't be the Semme' you needed. But you're right, I'm too weak and damaged. I would never be the mate you needed and will only bring you pain. I can't and won't be the reason that war is brought to you and your people.

I thank you for making me feel safe for the first time in years. It is because of this that I release you from any claim and entrust you with my brother's care. My only hope is that some day you will find someone else to stand by your side that is everything you deserve.

Don't look for me. It's better this way.

It didn't take much to realize that somehow Ricky had overheard their conversation the other night. The doctor had told him his mate would be out for the rest of the night. But apparently the man had surprised them all again with his resiliency. He glanced at the other note on his desk and felt anger welling inside of him. It had been found when they had tried to track Ricky down. The scent of a strange wolf had been on the paper but the words clearly identified where the shifter had come from.

91

Alpha Clifton was holding one of his pack hostage. The young boy, Roger, had been taken. A quick check with the boy's father indicated he was supposed to be camping with some of the other young wolves of the pack. Dakota had gone up to the campsite only to find out the boy had never shown up. His girlfriend had been upset, but figured he'd had to stay home to help out. It had happened in the past so no one worried when he didn't show up as expected.

For the first time in his life, Grant felt out of control. His mate was missing, most likely taken by someone from the Willow Creek Pack and one of his own pack members had also been taken. Other shifters were sneaking into his territory, something he hadn't had to worry about for over fifty years. It was an outright declaration of war by the Alpha of Willow Creek but instead of bringing the war to the Windy River Pack territory, he was forcing Grant to come to him. Well so be it. He would get his mate and pack member back and when he was done, Alpha Clifton would no longer be breathing much less leading the Willow Creek Pack.

"Grant?" Jason said softly as he stuck his head into the office.

"How's he doing?" Grant asked as he rose and motioned for his brother to join him.

"About how you'd expect; he misses his brother, Grant," Jason replied as he took a seat. "But he has promised not to leave the house for any reason. I don't know what you said to him, but for now at least, he's going to follow your orders."

The Alpha smiled grimly. "I told him the truth. If he is captured by anyone from the Willow Creek Pack, his brother would be hurt worse than before. They would hurt him just to make Sandy obey them. Eventually they might even kill him."

Jason shook his head. "He's only six years old, Grant!"

"And he's an Omega who needs to understand why his brother was made to suffer all these years. Did you know he blamed himself?" Grant ground out. He remembered the hard conversation he'd had with Sandy when they found Ricky missing. The boy of course wanted to immediately go after his brother, but when he found out his brother left without him he'd thought it was because Ricky blamed him. "The boy and my mate both should have been told more so they could make the right decisions. But instead, neither was told what to expect and look what happened!" Grant's fist hit his desk.

92

"He's still not eating, Grant, and he won't leave his room," Jason continued as he rubbed a hand through his hair. "And have you noticed Sparky?"

"What about him?" Grant asked as he glanced up at his brother.

"He hasn't been back here since the day Ricky threw him across the room. David tried calling him and Dakota stopped by the garage, but there's no sign of him."

"Do you think he was taken, too?" Grant asked sharply.

"I don't know but it's a possibility. He was acting strangely after the incident. If I didn't know him better, I would have thought he was afraid of Ricky and his brother. I asked him to try to cheer up Sandy the day Ricky left, but he came up with a lame excuse of having work that needed to be done. Later that same day he disappeared." Jason shook his head. "I don't understand what could be wrong with him."

"I do," David said quietly as he entered the room and sat down.

Grant and Jason both looked at the Beta and waited. A moment later David swallowed and looked up. "I swore I'd never tell but now, well, I think you need to understand why Sparky might have an issue with Ricky and his brother."

"Go on," Grant prompted as he pulled out three glasses and filled them with two fingers of whiskey. He watched as David downed the glass in one throw before holding it out for more. Grant filled it further before setting the bottle back on the sideboard.

David sighed as he finished the second glass and placed it on the desk in front of him. He took a deep breath. "Sparky had a partner before he came to stay with us. He told me because the bastard actually showed up one day to demand Sparky return to him. What Sparky didn't mention was his former partner was Magi."

"What?" Jason sputtered.

David nodded. "Yeah, that's kind of what I thought, too. I mean, they pretty much keep to themselves, which I don't blame them. But I do know that the Magi do not like to mix with other races. His ex-partner explained it was to keep their lines 'pure'." David used air quotes. "It was the reason the jerk gave to Sparky for mating someone else. At first he insisted he left Sparky and wanted a second chance, but after I ran the guy off I got a different story."

David paused before continuing, "It seems the bastard used his magic to keep Sparky a literal slave. You see, he saw Sparky more as a pet than a mate."

"Were they *Semme*?" Grant asked.

"Thank the goddess no. But Sparky had thought the man loved him. Until he brought home another Magi and mated with her. The bastard tried to tell Sparky she meant nothing to him, but it didn't take long for the truth to come out; which is why Sparky left." David sighed as he glanced out the window. "Winston apparently tried to get Sparky back more than once before. Each time he used his magic to bind Sparky. Luckily, our friend was smarter and learned how to escape the spells."

"No wonder he was a little freaked out. But surely he doesn't think Ricky or Sandy would do that to him," Jason remarked.

"I'm sure once he has time to think about it, he'll come around. But right now, it wouldn't surprise me if he was just spending some time with his wolf trying to figure things out." David turned at a slight sound in the doorway. All eyes looked at the small figure that stood just outside the door.

"I'm sorry, I didn't mean to listen, but I wanted to know if you found my brother." Sandy sniffed before he turned and ran back down the hall. The sound of a door slamming confirmed the small wolf was back in his bedroom.

Grant rose from his chair and walked towards the door. "We really need to close the doors from now on around here. It seems too many people misunderstand what is being discussed." He turned towards his brothers. "David, have you heard from your ex-military friends yet?"

"They're on their way and should be here…" David glanced down at his watch. "Any time now. In fact, they'll probably get here about the same time as Father and Mother."

"Good, let me know when they arrive. We need to make some plans to get our missing pack members back and to make sure Alpha Clifton understands the error of his ways." Grant turned and headed down the hall towards the closed bedroom door. He might not be able to help his mate at the moment, but he could at least help his little brother deal with this latest blow.

94

Ricky groaned as he slowly opened his one good eye. There wasn't an inch on his body that didn't hurt after the beatings he'd taken over the past few days. He glanced wearily around his old room, or prison cell as that is what it was. The Alpha had made it clear that he was not allowed to leave this room for any reason. Of course, his former belongings had been removed and all that was left was the cot and a bucket in the corner for him to relieve himself.

The sound of a key in the door made the injured human flinch. An open door meant more pain and humiliation. Why couldn't they just leave him in here to die? But it seemed the Alpha had other plans for him. The beatings were meant to weaken him so that his brother would sense he was in trouble and come running. How the Alpha found out about their secret, he didn't know. However, so far he'd been able to keep himself calm and had shut down the link to his brother. He'd learned early on how to block his brother from what was happening to him. However, he hadn't been able to do it all the time. He only hoped this time he could continue to shut down his feelings and save his brother from feeling his pain, anguish and fear.

As the door opened slowly, he tried to push himself further away but his body refused to listen.

"I've brought you some food and water." A young voice echoed in the room before the pup entered fully. He had a tray that he placed on the floor beside the bed. The youngster looked to be no more than sixteen years old with short brown hair that was slightly shaggy looking. Soft brown eyes looked at him and showed nothing but sympathy as he reached forward to help Ricky sit up.

"Who are you?" Ricky managed to croak as the room spun alarmingly around him.

"My name is Roger," the young wolf answered as he glanced nervously at the door. Ricky could see the bruises from past beatings on the boy's face and arms.

"Are you new to the pack?" Ricky asked quietly as he tried to get his body to obey his commands. He felt like he was going to flop back over but just before it happened a strong hand steadied him. He glanced up and saw a deep burning anger in the brown eyes.

"No, I'm from the Windy River Pack. These bastards grabbed me on my way to a camp out with my friends." Roger sighed as he glanced towards the barred window. "I tried to sound the alarm while I fought them off, but there were too many. When I woke up, I was here but I don't really understand why."

Ricky sighed as he glanced towards the doorway. They probably only had a few more minutes before someone came to check on the boy. "I'm sorry, Roger, but you're probably here because of me. The short version of the story is, I asked for sanctuary from your Alpha and was granted it. Alpha Clifton didn't like the idea, so I think he meant to use you to get me and my brother back."

"But why would he want you?" Roger took a step back and looked Ricky up and down. "I mean, you're just a human right?"

Ricky rubbed the tattoo on his arm for a moment before his shrugged. "Yes, I'm human but my brother is a shifter. Look, you need to be careful and if you get the chance, you need to escape."

Roger snorted. "You don't think I haven't tried? They keep too close an eye on me."

"Hey kid!" a voice yelled from outside the door. "Give the rogue his food and get out. No talking, do you hear me? Or do I have to remind you of your place, slave boy!" Roger stiffened for a moment, fear replaced anger in his eyes as he glanced back towards the doorway. Ricky couldn't blame the youth. He'd been on the receiving end of punishment more than once with this pack. He just hoped the boy would be spared some of the worst of it.

"Go on, kid. Get out of here before you get in more trouble. I'll be fine," Ricky tried to assure the youth. He could see the kid was thinking about disobeying but shook his head in warning. "It's not worth it—I'm not worth it. Just keep your head down and if you see an opportunity, then you run and don't stop until you get home."

Roger nodded as he headed back towards the door. He glanced back briefly before he exited, closing the door firmly behind him. Ricky glanced down at the food and shook his head. He hadn't eaten since he was taken. Obviously the Alpha needed him alive for his plan to work. But Ricky wasn't about to allow that to happen. He tipped the tray and lay back down on the thin mattress. He might not be a great fighter, but he would do whatever he could to ensure his brother was not returned; even if that meant he had to die to prevent it.

Grant sat in the living room as he glanced around at all the occupants. His father and mother had arrived just before the six large shifters who now sat in various seats around the room. His father, Forest Walker currently sat next to him while his mother had gone to take care of Sandy. The Alpha smiled as he saw the look on Sandy's face when he'd seen his mother. Although smaller in stature than her mate and sons, Vicky Walker was a force to be reckoned with when she made something her mission. It appeared that young Sandy had become her latest cause when she heard about what the boy had gone through. Grant knew if anyone could help Sandy, it would be his mother.

As he looked at the ex-marines his brother had hired, he had to admit David was right; these shifters looked like they could take on an army and walk away without a scratch. He glanced at their leader, Blaze. The shifter was as tall as him and packed plenty of muscle. Luckily from some of the comments made, the shifter was not interested in running a pack so Grant wasn't worried about a challenge. Although, he wondered if Blaze understood that in his own way, he was the Alpha of his small pack of mercenaries.

Everyone glanced up as Jason entered with Dakota and a very subdued Sparky. Grant was glad Sparky had returned unscathed, it was one less member he had to worry about. But he had to admit, he was beginning to worry about their unusually quiet friend.

"I'm sorry to hold everyone up, but I wanted to get the latest surveillance shots from the drones we sent." Jason moved towards the large coffee table and laid out various photos of the Willow Creek Pack lands.

"Cool, they have drones, Blaze!" Radar moved closer to the pictures and smiled. "Nice, so how do I get one of these?" The blonde headed shifter stood shoulder to shoulder with Grant's younger brother Jason and apparently shared his love of computers. He'd heard the two chatting earlier and still had a headache from all the techno babble they spewed. David had told him in addition to being their resident geek; the wolf also had a talent for tracking that had been legendary while they served together.

Jason chuckled. "Well you need to talk to David. It's one of his newest toys."

"I'm surprised the wolf pack didn't see them and shoot them down." Blaze remarked as he also moved closer to look at the pictures.

"That's only if you know what to look for." David smiled as he walked over to the fireplace mantle and picked up what looked like a stuffed raven. He gently stroked the bird's feathers before reaching into his pocket and pulled out a small control box. "This was my prototype," he said before he pressed a button and the bird began to fly around the room. "Of course this one doesn't have a camera, which came later. But we now have a flock of different birds that can fly undetected into enemy territory."

"If we're done with show and tell, maybe we can get back to the matter at hand?" Grant stood and walked towards the crowd now gathered around the table. He glanced down hoping to see the one person that meant the world to him, but there was no sign. However there was clearly something going on near what appeared to be the Alpha's house. There were a large number of vehicles, some with out of state plates parked around the dwelling and there were more guards than usual posted outside.

"Something's going on." The shifter name Falcon mirrored Grant's thoughts as he pointed to one of the Sentries standing off to the side of the house. "That's an M32 Semi-Automatic Grenade Launcher." He glanced at Blaze before looking back down at the pictures. "That's some serious fire power boss; it can shoot off six 40 millimeter grenades in less than six seconds. The last time I saw one was overseas and believe me when I say, the enemy never saw what was coming."

"Why would a wolf pack in Idaho need that kind of fire power?" Tank asked in a deep voice. Grant glanced over at the shortest fighter he'd ever seen. The man barely stood 5'5 and was slim in build. His long black hair was gathered in a ponytail giving the man an exotic almost oriental look. Yet the light grey eyes that looked out from the slightly slanted eyes held a steely determination in them. Everything about the man was a contradiction to his name. Yet the Alpha had a feeling this shifter was more than capable of taking down any of them in the room.

"My guess is they are expecting trouble." Blaze glanced over at Grant, his expression grim. "So much for the element of surprise."

"Does that mean I get to blow something up boss?" Dove practically cooed as the dark skinned man rubbed his hands together. Grant still couldn't get over the man's name. Who named their demolitions expert Dove?

"We still need ground Intel before we go in and start blowing things up Dove," Shadow rebuked softly. The dark haired man stood six foot five and was so skinny, it was a wonder he didn't blow away with the mountain breeze. The man seemed to go unnoticed as befitting his name. Until he spoke up, Grant had forgotten the shifter was in the room.

"Why don't you tell them what's at stake, son. They have a right to know." Forest Walker stood and placed a hand on Grant's shoulder. "You won't be able to keep it a secret much longer, especially if they are familiar with the myths."

Grant sighed as he glanced around the room. Part of him wanted to keep Sandy's secret safe, but his father was right. Eventually everyone, including his own pack would have to know about the Omega in their midst. "Fine, but for now, what is said stays in this room until David and I can finish working out a way to secure the pack lands."

"It must be pretty important for the Alpha of Willow Creek to invite a war with not only a rival pack, but the humans as well," Blaze remarked as he crossed his muscular arms over his chest.

"You can trust these guys, Grant," David stated as he slapped Falcon on the back. "They pulled my ass out of the frying pan more than once while I served overseas. Besides, once we get your mate back, I was going to see if these guys would stick around and help."

"The human is your mate?" Dove asked as his eyes grew bigger, "Why would another Alpha steal your mate?"

Grant held up his hand as everyone began to talk at once. "Quiet!" he ordered using his Alpha voice. The others in the room immediately fell silent, but from some of the looks he was getting, they didn't appreciate being reminded of his position. At this point, Grant didn't care as long as they helped him get his *Semme'* back where he belonged. He motioned for everyone to take their seat as he moved to stand in front of the massive fireplace in the room. While he waited, he ran his hand over the smooth stones of the surround and gathered his thoughts. He turned and looked at the solemn faces in the room.

"What I'm about to tell you has to remain a secret for a little while longer. The lives of my mate and his brother are not all that are at risk. If what we suspect is true, there would be many who would kill Sandy just because of what he is while others like Alpha Clifton would do anything to get control of him." Grant paused as he glanced around the room. "Sandy appears to be an Omega and my mate is his bonded protector as well as his brother."

The room was silent as each of the shifters absorbed the news. Blaze rubbed a hand over his short blonde hair before he looked at Grant. "You weren't kidding when you said it could change everything. I've heard the legends. There was a reason the Omegas were hunted and killed."

"So you would kill a six year old pup for what he might do?" Forest stood his full height and glared down at the ex-military man. For a moment, Grant was brought back in time when his father had stood in a similar way against those who would kill for no reason other than fear. Even though he was no longer the Alpha of Windy River Pack, his father still carried the power that came with years of being a leader.

Blaze sighed. "Of course not! My men and I have fought against many who killed for the wrong reasons. But not everyone will feel the same way. Omegas were hunted by our kind because they could control our inner animals. The humans and other paranormals feared them because they could control all animals down to the smallest insects, if the legends are to be believed."

"I heard Omegas were the direct decedents of Gaia," Shadow interjected softly. "Surely, the goddess wouldn't create something meant to destroy our kind. Are we not all her children?"

Grant nodded. "I never believed the Omegas deserved what happened to them. In fact, until I met Sandy, I'd never met one. By the time the wars ended, I had heard they had all been killed."

Forest nodded sadly. "They were the first to be destroyed out of fear for what they would or could be made to do. I heard of some that had been captured by the humans. They tried to unlock the magic bestowed upon them by the goddess. But they never could recreate it. Just as with many paranormals in this world, what was feared and could not be controlled had to be destroyed." The former Alpha walked towards the window and gazed out at the mountains. "I sent word throughout the lands that our pack would offer any

Omega who survived a place of refuge. But none ever came. I assumed that none had survived the slaughter."

"Well obviously, the goddess found another way," Radar stated as he tapped a few keys on the small computer pad he carried before turning it around and showing the group. "It says here that all Omegas had a special gene in their blood. It is thought that the Omega genes were carried by one or both of the parents, but apparently an Omega cannot produce another Omega. Of course, since they died out before genetics were understood, it was never verified. For all we know, it could just be something random." The tech expert of the team scratched his head. "Are you sure he's an Omega and not just a wolf with a weird shade of fur?"

Grant glanced at the computer screen before he nodded. "I'm sure. The pup carries the mark of Gaia on his inner wrist while in his human form. Eventually the mark will appear on his fur once he has gained his full powers." The Alpha paused for a moment before he continued, "According to Ricky, his father, who was human met his *Semme'* who was a shifter. Since both of them are dead, there's no way to determine for sure why Sandy was born. But the point is, he is here and until he comes into his full powers at twenty-one years of age, he will need to be protected."

"So will your mate, Alpha," Radar stated as he put his pad away in his satchel.

"What do you mean?" Grant asked as he turned to look at the shifter.

"He means Ricky may carry the Omega gene in his blood. He just might be more valuable than Sandy," Blaze said calmly.

"Holy Crap! But he's human, how could he be a carrier?" David exclaimed as the room became quiet once more.

Radar shook his head. "Like I said, no one is really sure how an Omega is born but if the father had the gene, it is possible he passed it onto his son."

Grant growled. "Well none of this is going to matter because I intend to get my mate back where he belongs. The time for talking is over and it is time to let Alpha Clifton know what happens when he takes the mate of a true Alpha!"

CHAPTER ELEVEN

IT HAD BEEN DECIDED THAT SHADOW WOULD INFILTRATE THE Willow Creek Pack and try to determine where Ricky and Roger were being held. Meanwhile, Blaze and his crew were discussing the best way to neutralize the guards without harming possibly innocent members of the pack. According to Sandy, not all of the wolves agreed with Alpha Clifton's rules but they were too afraid of him to do anything about it; except of course Jake, the wolf who had helped Sandy and Ricky escape. Sandy had provided a description to Shadow who would try to make contact with their friend inside. Hopefully the wolf would help them one more time.

Grant turned to the men sitting in his office. Jason was helping his new friend Radar as they tried to find out more about Alpha Clifton and his pack. However, his father, David, Sparky and Dakota had joined him to discuss how to protect the pack from what was sure to come. "My deputies can handle some rotations if needed." Dakota was talking to David about increasing their patrols around pack land. While he had a number of Sentries in his pack, over the decades of relative peace, the number had been reduced.

Who will look after the town, then?" Grant asked. "We have to make sure they're protected as well. David, can't we use some of your new toys to help with the surveillance?"

David smiled. "Already in the works, big brother. I've got Mack working on making a few new critters that will be placed around our lands. It will take time to get them in place but combined with the additional security I've already placed around here, no one will be able to sneak onto our lands again without us knowing about it."

102

"I can help, Mack. They're just machines and we all know I speak their language," Sparky piped in. He glanced at Grant and smiled ruefully. "I know I've been acting a little strange…" At David's chuckle Sparky rolled his eyes. "Okay, a lot strange. But, I honestly don't want anything to happen to the pup or his brother." Grant stood and clasped his friend's shoulder. He didn't need to say anything as the mechanic relaxed under his grasp.

Forest sat quietly in one of the chairs. He looked lost in thought while the others continued to discuss ways to ensure that not only the pack lands would be safer, but the Alpha house had to also be protected.

Grant glanced over at his father and wondered what he was thinking about but before he could ask his father looked up. "I just don't understand Alpha Clifton's plan. The wolf isn't the brightest and I knew he had issues with humans, but he never impressed me as being this ambitious. If we assume his end game is to control Sandy, the question has to be, what does he ultimately want?"

Grant sat back down in his chair and shook his head. "Who knows, Father. From what Ricky told us though, he definitely has talked about using the protector to control his Omega brother. I can only guess he intends to expand his pack somehow."

"It's too bad we don't know more about Omegas," Dakota spoke up. "All we have are the legends and some of them seem pretty far fetched to me. Some humans still think we only shift during a full moon and that a human who is bitten by one of us, becomes a werewolf."

Sparky laughed. "As if there is any such thing outside of those old Hollywood movies. Werewolves don't exist any more than Unicorns. I mean what do they think bear shifters are? Werebears? Not to mention, have you seen how ugly they make werewolves in those films? This…" Sparky ran his hand down his body, "…is not ugly in any form!" The rest of the men in the room chuckled at the mechanic's antics. Grant was just glad to see some of his friend's spunk coming back.

"Still, Dakota does have a valid point," Forest interjected. "I only met an Omega once for a brief time. I remember he and his protector were passing through before the Great War began. At the time, I offered him a place to stay but the wolf declined. He said my pack didn't need him as it was already at peace."

103

"You never told me about him," Grant replied, as he glanced at his father. "Are you sure there aren't any other Omega's out there? I mean what if they simply went into hiding?"

Forest shook his head sadly. "I can't imagine that would be the case son. I mean look at the Magi. They use their protective spells to hide their tribes from the world and yet now and then we still hear about them."

"Unfortunately," Sparky said softly before he turned away. Grant saw David place an arm around the man and talk softly to him. It was clear his friend was still suffering from whatever had happened in his past. He saw the question in his father's eyes but shook his head to warn him off. When the mechanic wanted to tell them, he would.

"Well then all we have are the legends," Grant stated. "Which means Alpha Clifton won't know more about Omegas than we do right?"

The former Alpha shook his head. "Not necessarily. Remember, he lived with Ricky and Sandy for quite awhile. You told me the two could sense each other and that Ricky was able to throw Sparky across the room using some kind of magic right?" Grant nodded as his father continued, "So what other tricks have those two shown in the past while they were in the other pack? They've only been here for a few days and already you found out some of their abilities. Maybe you should have your younger brother do some more research."

"Or you could find the Shaman who put the binding spell on the protector," Sparky stated as he turned back to look at Grant. "There is serious voodoo going on with your mate. Did you see his arm? That tattoo of his actually glowed while he was using his magic. There are many factions within the Magi, some with special powers including the ability to see into the future or the past. Others like the Shaman are healers as well as protectors of the Tribes." Sparky shivered slightly as if someone had walked over his grave. "There are many forms of magic in our world and not all of it is good believe me, I learned the hard way."

"Ricky said Maria took him to a strange man who performed some ceremony while giving him his binding tattoo but he never said where they took him," Grant replied. "I don't see how we can find him without my mate's help. Besides, at this point I really don't care what Alpha Clifton is trying to achieve. When this is over, I intend to make sure he doesn't live long enough to get what he wants."

"And are you willing to take on his pack as well as your own son?" Forest asked quietly. "You know the rules. If you kill Alpha Clifton, his pack becomes your responsibility."

Grant stood and flexed his shoulders. "I'll do what I have to in order to ensure that my mate, his brother and the rest of my pack are kept safe from those who would seek to harm them. It is what you taught me, father, and I learned my lessons well."

Forest stood and smiled. "Yes, son, you have. But you should also understand that even an Alpha has limits." The old Alpha held up his hand when Grant began to object. "I don't doubt your abilities, but as your mother has pointed out in the past; you don't have to carry the whole load on your own. I didn't…"

"Well I'm glad to hear you finally admit I'm right dear," Vicky walked into the room with a tray containing sandwiches. She set the tray on the desk and turned towards Grant. "Your father had good Betas who helped him and when you were old enough, he had you. I know you feel like you have to do it all, son, but you also have to live."

Grant watched as his father rose and walked over to pull his mother into his arms. He rested his chin on her head as he spoke. "You too have a mate and if he is anything like mine, you will have to learn balance or you'll lose him. Use his strength and the strengths of those around you, my son. If what I fear comes to pass, you're going to need all of us to get through what is to come."

Shadow pulled his cloak tighter around him as he walked down the path that led to Jake Williams' home. So far no one seemed to pay much attention to him, which wasn't that unusual. Most of his life he'd been invisible, even to his parents and siblings. The fact that he now used that to help others helped to fill the void in his life.

From what he'd seen so far, this seemed like a normal pack and yet, he couldn't help but notice it seemed to be a very poor one. Every structure he passed showed years of neglect. The small pups who played in the field he passed, had clothes that had seen much better days. Of course, that didn't mean there was anything wrong. Many packs had found themselves in rough circumstances.

He'd followed the directions that Sandy had given him and so far they had been pretty accurate. Unfortunately, he'd seen no sign of the missing youngster or Alpha Grant's mate. In fact, other than the pups he didn't see much of the other pack members. It seemed they stayed inside or were working someplace else. As he got closer to the hovel that must be Jake's home, he noticed the partially burnt barn off to the side of the small farm. A few chickens ran through the yard and there appeared to be a lone cow munching on some grass in the small paddock.

The sound of a door opening caused him to focus on the bedraggled she-wolf who peered outside at him.

"Hello. I'm looking for Jake." Shadow kept the request simple. He found that he usually didn't have to give much information as people tended to fill in the gaps themselves. Right now he looked like a traveling merchant. He even had a backpack that contained a few baubles and other home goods he could sell if needed for his cover.

The door closed partially while the small wolf turned to talk to someone further inside the building. A moment later, a larger wolf appeared at the door. The dark skinned man was tall and nicely muscled. He wore his curly rust colored hair loosely around his shoulders. But it was the honey brown eyes that caught Shadow's attention. For a brief moment the military man wondered what those eyes would look like if the man was smiling. However as he continued to examine the wolf before him, those eyes contained nothing but suspicion and fear.

"Samantha said you were looking for me?" Jake asked as he stepped outside the door and closed it behind him. Shadow smiled at the protective gesture. The wolf may fear him, but he still stood his ground. If it had been another time or place, he could see himself asking the man out.

"You're not from around here, are you one of the new Sentries the Alpha called in?" The wary wolf asked.

Shadow didn't respond for a moment, as he continued to assess the wolf before him. He could tell Jake was getting agitated, but was trying to put forth a calm front. The wolf had leaned back against the door and crossed his arms, but his body was anything but relaxed. When Jake remained silent, Shadow smiled.

The more time he spent with the man, the more he liked what he saw. But this wasn't the time or place to pursue what he suspected. "Actually, a mutual friend of ours recommended that I stop in and say hi while I was passing through."

"And who would that be?" Jake's tone held a hint of fear.

Shadow lowered his voice and leaned in closer to Jake. "Sandy says to tell you thank you for your help in the past." Jake immediately stood and looked nervously towards the direction of the Alpha's compound before he opened the door and motioned for Shadow to follow him inside. Once the door was closed, Jake turned and glared at the military man.

"Do you know how much trouble I'd be in if the Alpha found you here? He already suspected that I had something to do with Ricky's escape." Jake ran a shaking hand through his hair as he walked towards the small fireplace in the central room. Shadow glanced around and noticed the place was pretty small for two people. There was a great room that had a small kitchen area off to one side. He saw three doors on the other side of the dwelling that he guessed would be bedrooms and a bathroom. The she-wolf was probably hiding in one of the bedrooms.

"Is Ricky here, Jake?" Shadow asked softly, as he brought his gaze back to the wolf who had taken a seat in one of the worn leather arm chairs. Shadow moved to take the other seat and waited for a response. Jake glanced at the flames and sighed before he answered softly.

"Yeah, he's here along with some other pup that Alpha Clifton's goon squad brought back while hunting for Ricky and his brother. The poor kid has been made into Biff's new slave boy." Jake shook his head. "I don't think he's done more than scare the kid. The Alpha at least told him to keep his hands off the boy unlike he did for Ricky." Jake growled as he glanced up at Shadow. "No one should be treated the way the human was. The public displays were the worst..." Jake glanced over at one of the doors before he continued. "Not everyone agreed with what was going on, but we were all too afraid to do anything about it."

Shadow smiled. "All except you, Jake. I'll understand if you don't want to help me again, but if you can just tell me where they are holding Roger and Ricky, then I'll get out of your hair."

Jake stood and crossed his arms. "There's no way you will be able to get near them. The Alpha isn't taking any chances this time. That's why he hired outside muscle. No one is allowed into the Alpha's compound—"

"Except me…" A soft voice sounded from the now open bedroom door. The young she-wolf walked into the room with a confident air. She was slightly smaller than her brother but had the same reddish brown hair and honey colored eyes. As she moved to stand beside her sibling, she placed a hand on his shoulder. "I know you're trying to protect me, big brother, but remember you're only three minutes older than me. I can take care of myself."

Jake shook his head. "I never thought you couldn't, Sammy girl, but you know he was going to use you to torture Ricky the same way he did with all the others."

Shadow cocked his head. "How would the Alpha do that?"

Samantha sighed and moved to sit in the chair her brother had vacated. When she looked up the anger in her eyes made them the color of molten gold. It was pretty clear to Shadow who the real protector in the family would be. He bet more than one wolf had misjudged the young she-wolf in front of him and regretted it later. "Our Alpha thought it would be fun to use the young human as a sex toy for the pack. As if I wanted any part of what was being done to that poor boy." She glanced over at her brother as her eyes softened. "But no one in this pack says no to Alpha Clifton."

"It's one of the reasons I helped Ricky and his brother escape when I did. Sammy was supposed to go to the Alpha compound for the next exhibition to be held before the pack run." Jake glanced toward his sister before looking back at Shadow. "And I'd do it again if I thought I could get away with it. But those who cross our Alpha end up disappearing. The rumors are he sells those who don't agree with him to one of his friends as slave labor or worse."

Shadow shook his head. "Just exactly what was involved in these exhibitions?" He'd never heard of anything like it before. He wondered if Alpha Grant knew what had happened to his mate. Somehow he didn't think so or the man would have probably taken action before now to gain retribution for his *Semme*.

Samantha huffed as she sat back and crossed her arms across her ample chest. "In order to show everyone that the human was no more than a pet, he would choose a couple of the females in the pack to use him before the pack run. Of course, we had to perform in public for all to see unlike some of the Sentries who would be given special privileges with Ricky. After all, being gay in this pack is almost worse than being human."

Shadow didn't miss the slight shifting of Jake's feet as he glanced down for a moment before resuming his stance. Sammy continued in a soft voice filled with sadness. "Poor Ricky was not only human, but was also discovered to be gay when his boyfriend showed up." The young she-wolf shivered as she rubbed her hands on her arms. "The Alpha whipped Ricky's boyfriend in the public area inside the compound before he forced the man to run for his life. He only made it a few feet before the Sentries fell on him and tore him apart right in front of Ricky."

"The Alpha claimed Ricky was responsible for his betrothed's death and as retribution made him into the pack slave and Biff's pet," Jake continued the story.

"But humans aren't subject to pack laws. Why didn't Ricky and his brother just leave?" Shadow asked.

Sammy shook her head. "The boy came here with a pup only a little over a year old. He himself was barely more than a child at eighteen. The Alpha promised to keep them safe if they joined his pack. Of course Sandy was too young, but Ricky was old enough to make the decision for both of them. He accepted the offer, pledged his loyalty to our Alpha and accepted the Alpha's mark. The poor boy didn't realize he was in fact making himself the property of our Alpha."

Shadow stood and walked towards the shuttered window. He glanced through one of the cracks to make sure they were still alone before he turned to continue the conversation. "The practice of making humans slaves was outlawed after the Great War."

"True, but Alpha Clifton doesn't accept the truce. He still believes that shifters were meant to rule, not coexist with a weaker species." Jake stood and huffed in disgust. "Living in this pack is worse than living in a cult. The pups aren't allowed to go to school but are home schooled. They are taught to read and write but anything else is deemed to be unnecessary. Alpha Clifton believes in starting our training as warriors to protect the pack as soon as possible which doesn't leave time for much else."

The spy shook his head and sighed. "Well, if you and some of the others of this pack want to leave, then maybe you should get the word out. When we come to rescue Alpha Grant's mate and the pup, I'm sure he'd be willing to take any of you into his pack."

"His mate?" Jake asked, as his eyes grew bigger. "Alpha Clifton didn't say anything about taking another Alpha's mate!"

"If Ricky belongs to Alpha Grant, then why did our Alpha announce the mating ceremony?" Sammy remarked. "I'm supposed to go to the compound later with some of the other females to help make the food for the celebration."

"When is this supposed to happen?" Shadow asked.

"Next week, on the night of the full moon; Alpha Clifton will be claiming Ricky as his mate," Jake responded as he growled. "The bloody hypocrite. He claims same sex matings are an abomination for everyone else, but in his case, it is his divine right because he says Ricky is his *Semme'*."

Shadow smiled softly as he moved towards the door. "My guess is there will be a few extra guests attending his mating ceremony." The ex-military man turned and smiled at Sammy. "And I have an idea on how we can make sure it goes off with a big bang; that is if you're willing to help us out just a little."

Sammy smiled as she crossed her arms over her chest. "Just tell me what you want me to do."

CHAPTER TWELVE

RICKY STRUGGLED AGAINST THE TWO SHIFTERS WHO WERE holding him in the shower and cleaning him. As they began to scrub his private areas he cursed and fought harder. After his discussion with the Windy River Pack, he now knew they could not force him to do anything he didn't want to, at least legally. The fact that his brother was also safe had begun to give him courage to push back against his former pack members.

Yet there was no way he could get free of their unwanted touch. Not only were they stronger than him, but even now he felt the drugs that had been forced on him making it harder for him to concentrate. While in one respect he had been glad when the pack doctor had begun to give them to him, he knew it wasn't out of sympathy for the pain he'd been in. They had made even his smallest rebellion against his captors almost impossible. Worse though was Ricky had no idea how much time had passed since he'd been kidnapped since the drugs caused him to lose large gaps of time.

What confused him the most was why they were doing this to him? When he'd refused to eat, he'd been tied down to his bed and hooked up to IV's to ensure he wouldn't die. He could understand that the Alpha wouldn't want him dead until he had control of Sandy. But the beatings had also stopped and now they had removed him from his room to clean him up. For a moment, the human wondered if Alpha Grant had found him and demanded that he be returned.

Just the thought of the handsome Alpha caused an ache in his heart. It had been dreams of the shifter that had comforted him when he slept. Of course, the fact that the comfort soon morphed into much more often left him hard and wanting afterwards. Even now he felt his cock throb to life as he remembered the way the Alpha had touched him the last time they had been together. If only he hadn't panicked, hadn't assumed the treatment would be the same as it had been with Biff, he wouldn't be in this mess now.

"Control yourself, human!" Ricky grunted as his cock was squeezed painfully by one of the wolves attending him. The shifter turned to the other in disgust. "I still don't understand why the Alpha would want this one when he could have his choice of any she-wolf."

"You know it's because he says the human is his *Semme'*, Henry," the other wolf replied as Ricky was pulled from the shower and wrapped in a course towel. As he listened to the shifters he began to feel a thread of hope. It could only mean that somehow Alpha Grant had found him and had come for him. As he had languished in his room, he'd had time to think about his decision to leave the Windy River Pack and his brother behind. He had missed his younger brother horribly and felt a guilt that some days threatened to consume him. He had done the one thing he swore he'd never do—he broke his promise to be there for Sandy.

He also felt as if there was a part of himself missing. Maria had explained to him that while she could have refused to mate with his father, had she done so she would never have found true happiness. His father had been the 'one', her Semme' and even though she was promised to another, she had chosen to be with the person who was meant to complete her. He never understood until now what she had meant. While he still felt that Alpha Grant could find someone better than him, if the wolf felt anything like he did then perhaps Ricky had been too rash in leaving.

"I still don't understand why the Alpha didn't hold the mating ceremony before now," Henry continued to talk as he finished drying Ricky off. Well Ricky could answer that question; he was too damaged and worse, too weak to stand beside someone with as much power as the Alpha of the Windy River Pack. He could understand Alpha Grant not wanting to tie himself publicly to him but maybe there was a way they could both be happy. The Alpha of Windy River Pack had promised him sanctuary and hadn't forced his affections on him. In fact, as he thought back to their last exchange, he could see now that the Alpha had been more interested in making sure Ricky enjoyed himself. Even though he'd never considered himself submissive, he could actually see Alpha

Grant as his new Master. Maybe this time it could even be consensual instead of being forced, like it had been with Biff and the other members of the Willow Creek Pack.

Ricky was thrust back into the moment when he felt the towel yanked from his body. Before the human could protest he found himself standing completely nude in front of the shifters. A shiver ran down his spine. After years of abuse at the hands of Alpha Clifton and his Beta, he knew this couldn't be good. Even though he'd been forced to be nude many times in the past in front of the whole pack, he still found it difficult. The shifters began to pull him from the bathroom into the hallway.

"He says he needed time to get past the loss of his betrothed and he couldn't believe that fate would match him with her murderer." The other wolf shrugged. "It's not our place to argue or understand, you know that Henry."

The other wolf shrugged. "True, but if I found my Semme' I don't think I'd be able to resist claiming her."

"That's why he's the Alpha of Willow Creek, Henry. Besides, you heard him; the human will be merely a pet to fulfill his needs and nothing more. So don't worry, we won't have to treat him like a traditional Alpha Mate."

Ricky stopped and turned to face the wolf that had been speaking. Surely he hadn't heard correctly.

"Keep moving, human. You're to remain in your new quarters until the ceremony is held. The whole pack will be there and then as is tradition the pack run will happen as soon as you're mated. Of course, you won't be able to join with the rest of us but that can't be helped. I'm sure our Alpha will wear you out when he returns from his run." Both shifters chuckled as they shoved him forward but Ricky managed to duck and move to the side. He heard a soft growl but ignored it as he tried to focus. This couldn't be right.

"Are you—are you talking about Alpha Clifton?" Ricky finally managed to ask as he leaned weakly against the wall.

Henry moved forward and grabbed him roughly by the arm. "Of course! Even you must be able to feel the pull of your Semme'. Your body betrays you..." The shifter pointed towards Ricky's erect cock, "...even if you do not accept it." Ricky could feel his erection bouncing against his abdomen. Of course he was hard, he'd been thinking about Alpha Grant. Even if the man wasn't his Semme' he'd have been attracted to him—who wouldn't be? But there

113

was no way he would be acting this way for Alpha Clifton. Not only was the shifter cruel, but he was one of the ugliest wolf shifters he'd ever encountered. He sometimes wondered what Maria had seen in the wolf.

The human was yanked from his thoughts as he was pulled forward once more. "Come on, we don't have all day to waste on the likes of you! I'm just glad fate didn't saddle me with a human, much less a male. It's not natural I'm telling you, Ralph."

"I agree, but again we are not Alpha and I for one have no intentions of challenging him," Ralph growled as he shoved Ricky into a room he was too familiar with. The metal cage was still where it had been the last time he'd been here. He couldn't restrain the whimper of distress as he remembered what had happened in this room. It was the Alpha's bedroom and one of the places that often inhabited his worst nightmares.

Ricky fought against the two shifters who now dragged him towards the cage. Unfortunately, he might as well have been not fighting at all as they forced him to his knees before shoving him into what was little more than a large dog crate. He tried to turn to tell them the Alpha was lying but the cage door slammed in his face before he could get a word out.

"Your master will be here shortly, I suggest you work on your attitude or the public whipping post will be painted with more of your blood human," Ralph sneered as he turned and left the bedroom followed by the other shifter. As the door to the room closed, Ricky sat and pulled his knees to his chest as the horror of what was about to happen hit him. He was going to be mated to Alpha Clifton and there was nothing he could do to stop it.

• • ❖ • •

Shadow pointed to the map on the table in front of him. "According to Sammy, they have moved Ricky to the Alpha's bed chambers."

A low growl filled the room. Everyone turned to look at Grant as he struggled to keep his wolf under control. After a couple of minutes Shadow simply nodded and continued with the information he'd learned over the past couple of days. It had been over two weeks since the human had been kidnapped. "The pup is being kept here." Shadow pointed to a smaller house within the Alpha compound.

"That's Biff's house," Sandy replied quietly. He had joined the group of wolves as they stood around the dining room table. Grant had been convinced by his mother as well as some of the others that the pup should be included in the planning at least. His mother had been the most vocal in arguing her views on the subject. His lips quirked slightly as he recalled her reaction when he'd hesitated—anyone who had seen his mother at full throttle could appreciate where the real power in his parents' relationship resided. He had to admit, the change in the young pup was amazing. Not only was he eating, but he was quick at pointing out things that would be extremely helpful once they mounted the rescue operation.

The dining room had quickly been converted to a war room with maps and other information spread out for all to see. Jason had brought some of their computers in and there were now TV screens mounted on the walls giving live feeds of what was happening at the Willow Creek pack lands. Eventually, Grant would have to convert another area of the large house into a permanent war room, but for now this had been the only place that was large enough to accommodate all those who would be involved in the rescue.

He glanced up at one of the screens and saw the young pup they'd been discussing walk quickly from the Alpha's house to Biff's home. Roger's shoulders were hunched, but Grant smiled as he noticed the young wolf was still sneaking a look at his surroundings. A large shifter opened the door to the Beta's home and motioned for the pup to hurry inside. Grant remembered what Ricky had told them about the Beta. His hackles rose as he thought about what Roger might be going through at the hands of the wannabe Dom.

"If he touched Roger," Grant growled.

"According to both Jake and Sammy, the Alpha has told Biff to simply keep the boy as a slave but not to hurt him," Shadow quickly supplied. "I saw him once while I was there, and other than a few bruises he seems to be fine. Unfortunately it was too dangerous for me to get close to him, but Sammy will try to get word to the pup that we will be coming and to be ready. She has the best chance as one of the she-wolves who cook for the Alpha and his Betas."

"Alpha Clifton isn't a complete moron," David interjected. "He knows Roger's father could seek a more serious restitution from him if the pup was seriously injured."

"You assume he planned to return the pup to begin with." Blaze shook his head. "My guess from what you told me is he doesn't want his Beta compromised in the eyes of the pack. No one would condone having sex with a sixteen year old whelp. Although the fact members of the pack condoned forced sex of any kind has me wondering why you want to save any of them."

"Not all of them are bad," Sandy spoke up. "Most of them are just scared of the Alpha and his Betas." The young pup glanced down at his hands. "Some of the Sentries aren't too bad but they know better than to question the Alpha—it meant they would lose their position or worse. Besides, who wouldn't rather be guarding the pack than working on a farm or some other boring job? Alpha Clifton told me if I did what he said, one day I could be a Sentry and help!" Sandy paused and sighed. "I thought that would be awesome, but now I'm not so sure no more."

"What do you mean?" Tank asked quietly. The shifter placed his hand on the pup's shoulder to encourage him to continue speaking.

Grant was glad to see the enforcer take an interest in the young shifter. While Sparky still spoke to Sandy and had made it clear he would do whatever he could to protect the pup and his brother, there was a wall between them that hadn't been there before. Grant could understand it, but he also knew Sandy felt the loss of his first friend in the pack. After this current crisis was over, the Alpha would make sure the pup was introduced to other members of his pack that were closer to his age.

Sandy shook his head sadly before he continued. "No one should be scared of their Alpha right, Alpha Grant?"

Grant nodded and smiled. "That's right, Sandy. A good Alpha looks out for his pack and takes care of them."

"Then Alpha Clifton is a very bad Alpha. I've seen where some of your pack lives when I went to town with Sparky." Sandy glanced sideways at the wolf before he sighed and continued, "My old pack don't live like yours. They work hard but only Alpha Clifton and those he likes get richer. I asked Jake once why he gave them all his money when one of the Betas came by to collect it. He told me it was for the good of the pack. Yet I heard many of the others complain about how little was given back." The young pup shuddered. "They had to be careful though 'cause if Alpha Clifton heard, they would either be

116

punished or just disappear." The last part was whispered as the young wolf glanced around the room fearfully.

Tank patted Sandy on the shoulder. "Don't worry, pup. You don't have to worry about Alpha Clifton anymore. We won't let him hurt you."

Blaze nodded in agreement along with the other shifters in the room. "We'll be staying here after we rescue your brother and the other whelp."

"Don't let Roger hear you refer to him that way." Sparky chuckled. "He's likely to try to beat the crap out of you."

"He can try…" Blaze grinned.

Shadow cleared his throat as he tried to get everyone's attention back to the table. "As I was saying, according to Sammy, Roger and Ricky are rarely together in the same place. However there will be one time we can be sure they'll both be together." He glanced at Alpha Grant and swallowed before he continued. "According to Jake, everyone in the pack is required to be at the next pack run—no exceptions."

"Why?" Falcon asked.

"Because Alpha Clifton will be holding a claiming ceremony." The shifter paused when he heard the low growl coming from the Alpha. He hoped that Grant would be able to keep his wolf in check when he learned the full truth. So far he'd been impressed to watch how well Grant was able to keep his wolf under control. If his mate had been taken, he knew he and his wolf would have tracked down the bastard and killed him immediately without any thought to the consequences. "He says he has found his *Semme'* and wants to have the pack recognize his mate publicly," Shadow continued.

"Do you think he'll claim his mate in front of the pack?" Dove asked. When Shadow nodded, the explosive expert snorted. "Seriously, who still follows that old ritual? I can't imagine wanting to have my mate claim me in front of the pack."

"No, but you don't have a problem letting the rest of us hear you whenever you bring home your latest conquest," Tank remarked dryly.

Before they could get off track Grant raised his hand and looked at Shadow. "Who is he claiming?" The room was suddenly quiet as Shadow looked down for a minute.

He took a deep breath and glanced directly at the Alpha. "He claims Ricky is his *Semme'*, Alpha."

This time the roar that filled the room caused the windows to shudder. Alpha Grant stood up straight, his eyes had turned to red and his hands had changed to claws. The sound of clothes tearing filled the room, but rather than changing to his full wolf form, the Alpha remained upright. This was the monster that many humans envisioned when they talked about werewolves. However, only the strongest Alpha's were able to maintain this third form for any length of time.

Jason and David rushed towards Grant but it was his father's voice that reverberated above the howl coming from the Alpha's dripping maw. "Grant, you will stop this moment and return to your human form!" Forest commanded. He didn't back down or tilt his head as the others had done in the room, but instead walked forward calmly. "I said stand down!"

A soft whimper sounded before Grant's body began to shimmer. Dakota had disappeared from the room for a moment, but returned carrying a large bathrobe. As the transformation was completed, he handed it to Grant. At his Alpha's look, Dakota shrugged. "It will be easier for you to get out of this in case your wolf decides to come out again."

Grant nodded his thanks as he pulled the robe around his naked form. He glanced at his father who walked forward to place his hand on his son's shoulder. "I know this will be difficult, but you have been trained to be better, son. You have to maintain control if you want to get your mate back as well as the pup."

The Alpha took a deep breath and nodded at the slight rebuke before he turned to the others. "When will this ceremony take place?"

Shadow looked grim as he replied, "In four days, on the night of the full moon."

Blaze sucked in his breath. "That's not much time to prepare for what could be a full out war. Did you get a sense of how many of the pack members would fight for their Alpha?"

"I'm not entirely sure. From the way the pack has been run, there are those who have favor with the Alpha and those who don't. As Sandy said, the majority of the pack falls in the latter category. However, Alpha Clifton is not entirely stupid. He has brought in outside enforcers to help bolster his Sentries. Also, those who do back Alpha Clifton are extremely loyal and from the looks of things, capable fighters. This won't be a walk in the park, Blaze."

Falcon stepped forward. "From the surveillance pictures we've been able to also determine they are well armed with not only traditional weapons, but a few that could give us a problem if they get a chance to use them. They apparently don't plan to obey all of the old traditions—even if you challenge Alpha Clifton. I wouldn't put it past him to have a sniper or two hiding in the woods or surrounding buildings." The weapons expert rubbed his chin. "I assume this large clearing north of the compound is where they meet for pack runs, correct?"

"Yes, that's where we would gather and then we would head into the woods at the base of the mountain. I remember the woods are pretty dense until you get higher up into the mountains." Sandy offered as he moved closer to the map, "There's an old ranger spotting station located just inside the forest—here. I used to play there with some of my friends. But we had to stop 'cause the Alpha found out—I never saw my friends again after that..."

The weapons expert smiled as he tousled the young pup's hair. "Good job! Can you remember any other buildings or high areas of land that you or your friends may have used to hide and watch the clearing?"

Sandy bit his lower lip as he concentrated on the map for a few more minutes. "Well there is a ridge on this side of the clearing, it's not that high, but I know I hid there one time when Ricky was looking for me." The young shifter sniffed and rubbed angrily at the tear that threatened to fall.

No one in the room said anything as Falcon looked closer at the areas Sandy had indicated. "Well, I'd bet my last dollar that we'll find a few of the hired enforcers in both of these places. We'll need to get in and take them out quietly if we want to take their place."

Radar spoke up, "We can have some of the drones check the whole area to identify where they are hiding. I still can't believe that Alpha Clifton doesn't have more high tech surveillance on his pack lands. He's just asking for someone to invade."

Blaze nodded. "True, but that's a lucky break for us." He glanced at Falcon. "It's a good plan, but I'm betting there will be more than a couple of enforcers stationed around the clearing, we'll need some kind of distraction."

"How about a challenge to the Alpha?" Grant growled. "He will be expecting me to show and to honor the traditions of a challenge. By taking one of my pack he has broken our laws and by right I can seek retribution from him in the form of a challenge."

"You can't go in there alone," David objected.

Grant smiled. "I'm sure he will also expect me to come with protection." He turned to look at Blaze's small group of enforcers. "Since he doesn't know about you and your men, it makes sense that we walk in to the clearing and issue the challenge in the traditional way."

Tank shook his head. "That would draw attention. But all it would take would be one shout from one of his hired enforcers and the game would be up. Some of those who are close to Alpha Clifton are sure to also be armed. Besides, you say this shifter has no honor, so why wouldn't he just pull out a gun and shoot you?"

"He could claim he was defending his *Semme'* mate and refuse your challenge outright. No one can interfere—it is a death sentence," Shadow added.

Forest looked at Grant with a thoughtful look before he spoke up. "There may be a way to force the challenge and still avoid any fallout from a *Semme'* claiming—but it could be risky."

"What do you mean?" Jason asked.

The former Alpha glanced at Grant and took a deep breath before he continued, "Just how sure are you that Ricky is your *Semme'*, son?"

CHAPTER THIRTEEN

RICKY SAT BACK AS FAR AS HE COULD IN THE CAGE HE'D BEEN kept in since he'd been delivered to Alpha Clifton. As he fingered the thick metal collar that encircled his neck, he understood exactly what was in store for him in the future. The glorified dog cage was only the beginning. Alpha Clifton had made it clear that he would be expected to remain unclothed and on his knees, ready to do whatever was requested of him. He would not have the stature normally provided to an Alpha Mate because he was not deserving of the honor.

The captive human had been floored when Alpha Clifton declared he was his *Semme'* and as such it left him no choice but to mate with him. He didn't understand how Alpha Clifton and Alpha Grant could both declare he was their destined mate. Was it possible he could belong to both? It didn't make sense with everything he'd learned from both Maria and the members of the Windy River Pack. Not to mention his own feelings. While the thought of Alpha Grant filled him with a sense of belonging and safety, all he felt for Alpha Clifton was fear and disgust. Just the idea of being mated to the Alpha of Willow Creek made his skin crawl. The only conclusion Ricky could come to was Alpha Clifton was lying.

At least the Alpha's declaration had lead to a cease in the beatings. Even Alpha Clifton couldn't condone hurting his 'true' mate in the way he had in the past. He'd also made it clear no one would be tapping his ass after the ceremony. Again, the mating bond would not allow the Alpha to accept another shifter touching him in a sexual manner. However, Ricky knew this was more for show than actual fact. While the public beatings and sexual displays might cease, what happened in private would not be seen by those who might object. The human had no illusions that he would be used however the Alpha wanted and that there would be no one to stand up for him.

Which lead to his final problem, what could he do to stop the Alpha from mating with him? It was clear Alpha Clifton saw this as a means to get control over his little brother. He just hoped that Alpha Grant was as honorable as he thought and would keep his little brother away from the Willow Creek Pack. However, just in case, he had to find a way to thwart the Alpha of Willow Creek's plans. The question was could he do it?

Ricky had tried putting a permanent end to the crazy Alpha's plans by refusing food and water. Unfortunately, that had ended with a daily visit to the infirmary where he would be drugged and then hooked up to life saving fluids. Even now he could still feel the effect of the drugs that were being used to dull his senses. They made any resistance almost impossible—until Ricky felt the collar around his neck, which was a constant reminder of why he needed to be strong for once in his life.

As he traced the strange designs on the collar with his fingers, Ricky remembered Alpha Grant and his brothers telling him he didn't have to accept the mating. Unlike with Alpha Clifton, when the Alpha of the Windy River Pack had talked to him, he'd stressed the final decision was up to him to accept the mating. If he didn't, then no shifter could force him to mate. The question was, could he stand up to the Alpha in front of all the members of the pack and say no?

A loud creak suddenly filled the room and caused Ricky to flinch. He kept his eyes cast down towards the floor but refused to move towards the door of his cage. He knew what would happen, but part of him no longer cared.

"Why are you not presenting yourself?" Alpha Clifton's voice echoed in the room.

Ricky simply refused to answer as he remained still in the cage. In a way it was a nice side effect of the drugs, things that normally would have scared him didn't faze him.

Ricky did jump slightly when the front of the cage was banged with enough force to cause the whole structure to rattle. "You will present yourself or you'll be sorry!" Alpha Clifton growled.

Ricky didn't care; in fact a small kernel of hope bloomed. Maybe if the Alpha got mad enough, he'd do what the captive human had been unable to do and end his life. Before he could follow the thought further, he felt a surge of pain radiating from the collar around his neck.

Ricky cried out as his eyes glanced up towards the Alpha. "You think you can disobey me human? You will learn to do what I say without question or you'll suffer the agony of the slave collar!" The pain continued to increase as the Alpha continued to talk. "I really have to thank Biff for finding this little treasure for me. I thought all of them had been destroyed after the Great War, but he managed to find one that I modified slightly to ensure you never escape from me again."

"What—what have you done?" Ricky managed to gasp as he tried to pull the collar from his neck. His flesh felt like it was on fire as the pain continued to grow. He fell to his side no longer able to remain erect as the torture continued. After weakly tugging at the metal one more time, he gave up as his body twitched on the bottom of the cage. It felt like he was being cooked from the inside out.

Alpha Clifton laughed cruelly as he leaned against the cage and showed Ricky a small black box that had been hidden in his hand. "I was able to convince a down on his luck Magi to give me a spell that would ensure my gift to you can never be removed except by my hand. He was able to help me create the ultimate slave collar. One that not only punishes without leaving a mark, but can only be removed by me..." Alpha Clifton leaned in closer, "...or when the wearer of the collar dies." Ricky gasped in horror. "That's right, my pet, you're not only my property, but you live only at my will. If you ever leave, well let's just say you won't live a long and happy life!"

As the pain continued to race through his body, Ricky could feel his heart pounding while breathing became more difficult. He couldn't help the whimpers of pain that continued to escape past his lips as he endured the extreme torture. Just when he thought the Alpha would take it too far he heard the door burst open and another voice filled the room.

"Stop! Are you trying to kill him?" Ricky recognized the voice. It belonged to the new pack doctor. However, the pain continued to increase as the Alpha growled at the intruder.

"How dare you question me, Artemus?"

The captive watched as the doctor fell to his knees and tilted his head in submission before he continued to speak. Under other circumstances, Ricky had to admit the man was handsome. His thick waist length hair fell forward slightly to surround his form in a shower of reddish brown hair. Even in the dim light of the room, the man's hair looked as if it was interspersed with a glowing flame.

"I'm only trying to warn you that if you continue, the human will die. If that is what you desire, then by all means continue." As Alpha Clifton paused the doctor continued in a bored voice, "If you don't believe me, then use your senses—his heart slows even now."

Ricky wished the doctor had remained silent. He had begun to feel himself falling away. He didn't even have the energy to whimper or to tell the doctor to mind his own business. His death would solve so many problems. However, the doctor continued to speak, "Alpha, if you seek to mate with the human tonight, then you need to stop!"

The argument seemed to get through to the Alpha as the pain suddenly ceased. Ricky tried to move, to curl into a fetal position, but his body refused to obey him. As his limbs continued to twitch uncontrollably he wished he could black out, but even that seemed lost to him. Instead he listened as the two discussed his future.

"Fine! I thought Biff had trained this one, but as you can see he is still fighting my commands. I need him to obey me..." The Alpha leaned down and looked directly into Ricky's eyes as he smirked. "I know he thinks he can say no to the mating." The Alpha glanced back at the doctor. "You will make sure that he is amenable to the proceeding tonight, right Artemus?"

Ricky felt his last hope dashed as the doctor rose to his feet and nodded. "Yes, Alpha. I will take him to the infirmary and ensure he shows his excitement. He will agree to anything you demand of him without protest. But I must warn you that I'm not sure if the mating will take since he will not truly be able to make an informed choice."

"That is unimportant. All I need is for the pack to recognize him as my *Semme'* and no one will challenge my claim in the future," Alpha Clifton stated as he stood to face the doctor.

"There is a risk to what I will have to do to him. From what I've observed, some beings lose their sanity when their free will is taken from them. He may not be the same person; in fact the human may end up not being able to make any decisions for himself going forward. He could become no more than a shell of what he was." Ricky could hear the sadness in the doctor's voice.

As he listened he finally began to feel the fear that had eluded him the past few days. Unfortunately, the only response he was able to give were the tears that fell from his eyes as he listened to the Alpha's decision.

"Do it. What do I care if he only becomes a hole I have to fill occasionally? It may be better in fact because I certainly intend to bring in a female to warm my bed and provide my heirs. If he weren't my *Semme'*, then I would have killed him long ago." The Alpha laughed as he turned to leave the room. "Make sure he's ready for the ceremony tonight or your abomination of a half-brother will be delivered to me. I'm sure you don't want to see him visiting the whipping post again do you?" Ricky watched as Artemus swallowed before shaking his head. "Good! Oh, and I'll be sending Biff in shortly to help with the final preparations. I'm sure he can remind my future mate of his place." With a grin, the Alpha left the room.

Artemus stood and stared at the door for a moment, his fists clenched by his side as he took in several deep breaths. When he turned to look at Ricky, there was pity in his eyes. "Come on, human. I will see what I can do to ease your pain a little."

The cage door opened and Ricky felt himself pulled from it. The doctor sighed and picked him up, careful of his neck as he carried him from the room. Ricky licked his dry, cracked lips and said the only thing he hoped would help. "Please—let me die."

His hopes were soon dashed as Artemus continued to walk towards the infirmary. "I'm sorry. I really am. But if I don't do as the Alpha wants, I'll never be able to find and save my brother Charlie. That bastard is the only one who knows where he is and who can help me get him back. Believe me if there was any other way, I would gladly help you." Another sigh escaped the doctor's lips. "If it's any consolation, I will try to make sure you are strong enough to get through tonight. With luck, you'll come out of this without any complications."

Ricky couldn't help the sob that escaped as tears fell once again from his eyes. This was it; there was no hope for him. As he was laid down on the hospital bed, he let his emotions free for the first time since he'd been taken, he didn't try to block anything from his brother. He just hoped his brother could feel how sorry he was that he'd broken his promise.

• • ❖ • •

As the members of the Windy River Pack arrived at the airport, Grant took a deep breath and glanced at the shifters who had joined him. Blaze's Rogues as they liked to call themselves were talking quietly in the back of the private jet. Only this group of shifters would take the name that meant certain death in their society. Yet after being around them for the past few days, he had to admit, the name did fit.

He glanced around the large jet, which was divided into a seating area along with a section that contained a table for planning and even had a small separate sleeping area. While he didn't use it often, Grant was more than happy that he had purchased it a couple of years ago. At the time, it seemed like an expense that wasn't needed, but David had insisted it would come in handy should they need to travel long distances. Of course at the time, he suspected his brother just wanted a new toy but now he appreciated the logic of having a means that allowed them to stay below the humans' radar. There was no way they would have been able to get the weapons they carried on a commercial aircraft much less have the room to spread out and continue to go over the final preparations for the rescue mission.

David and Jason were fiddling with some of the weapons they had brought with them to make sure any last minute adjustments had been made. They were taking special care of their 'surprise', Grant was pretty sure the enforcers and Sentries of Willow Creek would not see what David and Dove had coming. He grinned as he watched Dove and Falcon wander over toward his brothers. They obviously wanted to make sure everything was ready on the weapons front as well. He glanced up front and couldn't help smiling at the antics of Sparky who was currently doing his best to impress the pilot with his 'skills' and then there was Dakota who decided to take the time to catch up on some sleep. In all the years he'd known the wolf, he'd never seen him other than calm. It was one of the reasons he was such a good Sheriff for the town. All in all, he knew the best wolves he could have on a mission surrounded him. And yet—he still worried.

"Everything will be fine, son," Forest said softly from the seat next to Grant.

Having his father beside him in battle again felt like old times. He turned and saw a gleam in his father's eyes that he thought had gone out long ago. They had faced many battles together and had never lost. Yet, this time the stakes seemed so much higher, that Grant couldn't help wondering if his luck may have finally run out.

"I'm not worried about the battle father. It's just..." He paused and looked directly at the man who had come up with the riskiest part of the plan in Grant's opinion. "Are you sure you are right?"

Forest gazed out the window of the plane for a moment before he looked back at his son and smiled. "I can only go by what the legends say, but in my mind it makes sense that there would be a fail safe. Don't worry Grant, we'll get your *Semme'* back where he belongs and hopefully get rid of an Alpha who never should have been given the title." The last part was growled as his father's eyes darkened. "Whatever happens, son, you must keep your wits about you. Alpha Clifton is not stupid. I believe he will try to use Richard as a distraction. You mustn't let it happen. I can't help but feel that there is more at stake here than just regaining our lost pack members."

"I know, father. Don't worry. This is one challenge I have no intentions of losing." He felt his father pat him on the back.

The truth was he felt guilty about how complacent he'd become over the past five years. With the Great War far behind them and no real threats to contend with, he'd made the mistake of assuming the peace would last. Oh he'd made sure his Sentries were well trained and had also made sure they had an adequate police force to keep local disagreements or fights to a minimum. But he'd thought the pack lands were safe using routine patrols. He now knew how wrong he'd been. Two members of his pack had been taken, on pack lands, which was unacceptable.

"David was right, father. I should have let him put in more security to protect the pack. Maybe he should have been named Alpha." Grant jumped when his father turned to glare at him. For a moment he felt like a young pup as his father's displeasure rolled over him.

"Are you saying you want to step down, son?" Forest growled.

Grant shook his head. "No, this is my mess and I am responsible for cleaning it up. I know I can't change things in the past and I have no intention of leaving us open to future attacks. I just should have been a better Alpha for our pack."

Forest shook his head as he glanced out the window of the plane. "Do you think I never made mistakes? There isn't a being on this planet that wouldn't change a few things in their past or wished they could have a crystal ball to see into the future." The old alpha sighed. "Besides, why do you think I retired when I did?"

"Because Mom wanted to have you to herself?" Grant couldn't help teasing his father.

Forest chuckled. "Well there is that. But honestly not only did I think you were more than ready to lead our pack, but I also saw no threats in our future. Now, it feels as though this current trouble is only the ripple on the surface. I'm not sure what is going on, but Alpha Clifton never impressed me as being particularly smart or ambitious. In fact, I always thought he was content with his small pack in Idaho."

"We will soon find out why he has decided to challenge our pack Father and then I'll make sure no one else gets the idea that they can challenge the Windy River Pack," Grant replied.

"I never doubted that, my son," Forest said simply as he settled back in the seat and closed his eyes.

• • ❖ • •

Ricky turned his head and watched as the doctor began to gather his supplies. He wasn't sure what was in the various jars and bottles, but from the frown on the doctor's face it probably wasn't something he'd enjoy. His eyes traveled up slightly to watch the slow drip of life saving fluids as they traveled into his arm. He could tell there was also something in the IV to lessen the pain left from his experience with the collar. At least this time he wasn't restrained.

He glanced at the leather bands that had surrounded his upper arms, wrists, thighs and ankles since he'd been returned to Willow Creek. He was more than familiar with the attire as it had been used by Biff during his training. With little effort, he could be restrained into a number of different positions, many of them painful with just a few metal links. Of course, in his weakened condition they were no longer necessary. But he guessed, like the collar the leather restraints were meant to remind him of his new station in the pack.

He jumped as he felt a hand on his shoulder. He glanced up into the darkest green eyes he'd ever seen. They almost reminded him of a Jade stone his stepmother had kept in her jewelry box. "What—what are you going to do?" Ricky managed to rasp.

Artemus squeezed his shoulder gently before with a sigh he stood. He emptied a syringe into the IV line before he turned to pick up a cup that contained a dark liquid. "Don't worry, human. I've only given you something to ensure that you show the proper 'excitement' during the ceremony. While it may feel uncomfortable, it will wear off shortly after the mating ritual has been completed."

Ricky shuddered as he felt his cock begin to harden. His glanced up and shook his head. "Why do this? If Alpha Clifton were my *Semme'* then why wouldn't my body react naturally?"

The doctor shrugged. "In your condition, I'm surprised you're even still aware enough to ask. The human body does have its limits. This is just to make sure, because if you are not erect when you agree to the mating, then some in the pack might question your resolve on the matter."

Ricky sighed. "I will not agree to the mating."

The doctor shook his head. "I realize that as a human, you may not feel the mating pull as strongly as the Alpha. But after you have been claimed and the bond has been completed, you will understand and accept what fate had destined for you." The doctor added another ingredient to the glass and began to reach forward to place it at Ricky's lips.

"NO!" Ricky cried as he turned his head. "I am not his *Semme'!*"

"Hush, human! Do you need me to get Biff in here early to help me get this into you?" The doctor paused and glanced at the door before he lowered his voice. "Look, I have made the potion weaker than normal so that there is a good chance you eventually will gain your free will back."

Ricky took a deep breath and turned to look at Artemus. "Can I ask you a question first?"

With a sigh, the doctor placed the glass back on the table. "Fine, but make it quick because Biff still has to finish with your preparations before the ceremony."

"Can someone have two mates—can I have two *Semmes*?" Ricky held his breath as the doctor gazed closer at him.

"What do you mean, human? I don't see any marks of claiming—"

Ricky interrupted. "That's because he hasn't claimed me yet. He told me it was my choice to accept the mating or not, that he would abide by my decision."

Artemus glanced at the door for a moment before he glanced back down at the captive human. "How do I know you speak the truth?"

Ricky shrugged. "How do you know Alpha Clifton tells the truth? From what I've been told by my stepmother and by members of the Windy River Pack, even if I deny Alpha Clifton, the fact that I was his *Semme'* would mean he would not be able to harm me. I know you haven't been here for long, but you're a doctor. Even you should be able to see the scars I bear from my time with this pack."

The doctor shook his head. "No, Alpha Clifton told me that was done by your father. He took you and your younger sibling in. Any punishments you received, he was bound to allow because you refused to follow pack rules—after you accepted his mark."

"Again, how do you know he tells the truth?" Ricky said softly. For a moment he thought he gotten through to the doctor, but the man shook his head.

"It matters not who I believe, young human. To be honest, even if I were to believe you there would be nothing I could do. Alpha Clifton has hired a small army to ensure that the ceremony goes as planned. If I help you and he finds out, my half-brother would be lost. You have a brother, would you not do anything to keep him safe?"

Ricky could feel the tears well in his eyes as he thought about Sandy. He could understand the need to keep family safe. He was surprised when the doctor stared at him for a moment before he placed his finger on the center of the captive human's forehead, his eyes were closed as he mumbled words that Ricky could not understand. Before he could ask what the man was doing,

130

Artemus stumbled back with a puzzled look on his face. "This cannot be right…"

"What?" Ricky asked.

"Your aura flared and I sense a power surrounding you, protecting you in a way that I have only ever felt from long ago." Artemus' eyes had a far away look to them as he continued, "Only the Protectors were given such power, but they were all killed during the Great War. I should know because my father was killed trying to save the last one along with his charge."

"I still don't understand," Ricky said softly as he watched the doctor begin to pace. He ran his long fingers through his hair in an agitated fashion. Before he turned and walked towards the bed. He quickly removed one of the leather armbands and then hissed as he ran a finger over the tattoo that had been hidden beneath. "You *are* a Protector!" A look of pain filled the man's eyes as he put the armband back in place. He glanced at the door once more before he leaned down and began to talk softly.

"This changes things. I'm not sure how the potion I have prepared will affect you but my guess is it will not be able to restrain your will for long." He held up his hand as Ricky began to speak. "Listen carefully, young human. The potion I will be giving to you will take your will from you. The loss of will, even for a short time for some beings is enough to destroy their minds because you are aware of what is going on around you, but are forced to obey any command given."

"NO!" Ricky cried as he tried to struggle to sit up. Strong hands kept him pinned to the bed until the small surge of energy left his body. It was clear the doctor would still force him to drink the potion. It made sense; Alpha Clifton would not suffer any chance of him standing against him. The small kernel of hope he'd felt died as he watched the doctor move to get the glass from the table.

"I know you think this is the end for you. However, I have a feeling that our Alpha will be in for a big surprise. Even he cannot force one protected by the goddess to mate. Have faith that she will provide you with the power you need to fulfill your role. I only wish I could help you more." Artemus placed the glass to Ricky's lips and this time the human allowed the liquid to flow into his mouth. He didn't know if he believed anything the doctor said, but he also felt as if he owed the man a chance to save his sibling. It was the least he could do since he had failed so miserably in protecting his own brother.

As a strange calm stole through his body he watched as the doctor leaned in close to whisper into his ear. "Remember this, should you break free of Alpha Clifton, you must allow your *Semme'* to claim you within ten days."

Ricky tried to understand what the man was saying as he struggled against the strange feelings invading his mind. He felt as if he were inside a locked room with a window that allowed him to see out, but the window was slightly foggy. No matter how hard he tried to pound on the glass, he couldn't break through. Suddenly he heard the sound of the door open.

"Is it done?" Biff's voice echoed in the room.

"Of course, he is all yours, Beta," Artemus replied in a cool voice.

Ricky tried to shout, to make any kind of sound to beg the doctor not to let Biff near him. But his body refused to respond. He wanted to flinch away as his former tormentor's face came into view and yet even that small movement was denied him.

"Alpha Clifton was not happy with your level of training, slave. So after the ceremony, he has asked me to help him work with you until you remember what you had been taught." Biff stood up and spoke in a stern voice, "Get on your hands and knees, slave. Make sure you reach back and spread your ass cheeks wide too. I have to prepare you for the ceremony. Although why the Alpha gives you this small mercy I don't understand. But then I'm sure even with the stretching, you'll still feel his displeasure."

Ricky fought to resist, but it was if he was a puppet and Biff was controlling his strings. As he turned over and got into position, he caught sight of the large butt plug the Beta was holding in his hand. His hole clenched in anticipation of the pain he knew was about to happen.

A light cough behind him was followed by a quiet question from the doctor who apparently was still in the room. "I see you forgot the lube, Beta, don't worry I have some right here that you can use to ease the way. After all, I'm sure the Alpha would not be pleased if you injured his *Semme'* before the ceremony could even begin."

Biff growled low in his throat, but apparently had second thoughts as Ricky heard the soft snick of the bottle and could feel a cool liquid dripping down his crack. Had he been able, he would have thanked the doctor but it

132

seemed even his voice had been taken from him. He couldn't help the wince though when two large fingers dove deeply into his channel, pushing the lube inside. There was no foreplay as the Beta removed his fingers and placed the large plug at his entrance. The human knew he should relax, but before he could he felt his opening stretch to accommodate the large object. A soft whimper managed to escape as the Beta shoved the plug inside, forcing stiff muscles to accept the object.

"Quiet, slave!" Biff ordered with a slap to his ass that almost sent him off the edge of the bed. "Now stand with your hands behind you while I finish your preparation."

Once again Ricky's body obeyed without question even though he was screaming inside to stop, to run, to do anything to prevent what was happening to him. He watched as the Beta quickly attached a leather cock ring. The human groaned softly as his now engorged member was place on display. He also knew it meant he would not be allowed any relief as it now appeared even the ability for release would be denied him. Memories of his past abuse threated to drown him but he fought them, trying to remain in the present. A small kernel of hope had begun to bloom after his discussion with the doctor. If there was any chance for him to escape, he wanted to be aware enough to take advantage of it.

An evil grin appeared on Biff's face as he stood and glared at the human. "You will follow me, two steps behind. I expect you to obey without question and when the time comes, you will answer our Alpha by nodding your head indicating your acceptance of his claim. You will not speak, you will not make any noise or show any sign of distress. If you understand these instructions, then nod your head."

Ricky felt his head nod even though he was screaming inside. How was it possible? He glanced over at the doctor and saw pity in the man's eyes. The only thing keeping him sane at the moment was the hope that whatever was affecting him would eventually wear off.

As he followed his captor from the room, he couldn't help the feeling of despair that threatened to drown him. Once again he realized how foolish he'd been in running from Alpha Grant. Unfortunately, his mistake would not only affect him, but also put his brother and maybe even Alpha Grant at risk. He felt the sob trying to break free; but his eyes remained dry and no sound escaped his lips. All he could do was hang onto the hope that someone really was looking out for him.

CHAPTER FOURTEEN

GRANT SIGHED WITH RELIEF AS THE PLANE FINALLY ARRIVED at the small private airstrip. He didn't know who it belonged to, but Blaze had assured him that not only could they use the airfield, there would also be transportation waiting when they arrived. They still had over an hour's drive to reach the Willow Creek pack lands.

As the plane coasted to a stop, Grant glanced at his father who was frowning at something on his cell phone.

"What's wrong?" Grant asked softly.

Forest's face was grim as he quickly typed in a response before shutting his phone down. "That was your mother. I told her I would text her when we arrived." The former alpha sighed. "She says young Sandy is trying to shift and leave the house."

"He won't get far; I've left extra Sentries around the house. They have instructions not to let anyone in or out of the house until I return," Grant replied while he began to remove his seatbelt. "I understand how he must feel—"

"Do you, Grant?" Forest interrupted. "According to your mother the boy has been spacing out more frequently. When he comes around, he's extremely upset and insists that he has to get to his brother before it's too late."

Grant paused. "You think the link he has with his brother is working again?"

"That would be my guess, son. This means we may be running out of time. Your mate has been protecting Sandy but something must have happened for him to drop his shields." Forest stood and glanced at the other wolves who

135

were listening in. "It could just be that he's tired but from what my mate says, Sandy is suffering so—"

"I will kill that son of a bitch!" Grant roared as he felt his wolf fighting to break free. He took deep breaths before he moved to exit the plane. As he reached the door he growled, "Get a move on! The longer it takes us to get to the pack lands, the longer my mate suffers."

Blaze clapped a hand on the Alpha's shoulder and squeezed tightly. "Well, then I guess it's a good thing our transportation has arrived." He glanced back at the rest of the team. "Let's lock and load boys!"

As they exited the plane Grant paused and sucked in a deep breath. Before he could respond, he heard Sparky squeal, "Sweet!" The exuberant wolf rushed down the stairs and went to examine the vehicles neatly lined up on the tarmac. Grant couldn't help the small grin that tugged at the corner of his mouth as he watched the mechanic reverently run his hand over one of the motorcycles that stood behind two large black SUV's.

The large bikes were all black, but each had details that made it clear these belonged to Blaze's group. Grant watched as Sparky traced the flame decal on the tank of the first bike. It was pretty clear that one must belong to Blaze. The size of the vehicles spoke of power. Even the modifications to the frame that probably allowed for the men to carry their various weapons and other things didn't detract from the pure beauty of the machines. Grant had to give it to Blaze; the wolf had come through for them. The Alpha smiled as he watched his mechanic almost have an orgasm over the bikes.

"Tell me these babies come in purple!" Sparky said in an awestruck voice. "And where I can get one!"

Falcon shook his head as he moved towards one of the bikes. The tank on the bike had the head of the regal bird painted on it with tan feathered wings trailing behind. He opened the storage compartment and began to load in the tools of his trade. As he placed a high-powered rifle in a specially made sheath; he finally glanced back at Sparky. "If you get any drool marks on my baby, I'll use your face to clean it off!"

The excited wolf took a step back but simply crossed his arms. "First of all, that doesn't even make sense and second, didn't your mommy teach you to share?"

"I don't remember my mother," Falcon stated calmly. "And even if I did, the only one who will ever ride this bike will be my mate—which you definitely, thank the fates, are not. Now move back while I finish loading."

Sparky placed his hand on his hip and pointed the finger of his other hand at the wolf. "As if I would ever want you as a mate!" The mechanic turned and walked towards Radar who was showing Jason something in one of the SUV's. He glanced between the two wolves and whistled. "I take it back, I want one of these!"

Radar laughed as he patted the wolf on the shoulder. "I see you are a fickle lover. Now pay attention and I'll explain some of the special features to you since you'll be driving the other one." The computer expert pointed out the GPS that already had their destination loaded. In addition there was a hand's free communication panel that would allow those in the SUV to hear and communicate with those in the other vehicles. Another screen would show them what the Rogues were seeing as they each had a small camera affixed to the special halters they would wear in their wolf forms. "And the best part is these vehicles are bullet proof and will even withstand attacks from IED's. These are the next best thing to an actual tank." Radar grinned as he slapped the side of the SUV.

"IED?" Sparky asked as he watched Dove walking across the tarmac with a cage of birds that he carefully secured on the back of his motorcycle. He glanced back as Radar shook his head.

"Improvised Explosive Device, basically a nasty piece of work that is normally used to mine roads that your enemy is expected to use. Hopefully this Alpha Clifton won't be stupid enough to use them, but after seeing some of the other artillery his hired guns are toting, we didn't want to take any chances." Radar handed a set of keys to Jason and Sparky before he turned to leave. "Good luck. We'll see you on the other side!"

David watched as the Rogues finished loading their bikes with the various weapons they had brought with. He could feel the tension radiating off his older brother as he stood beside him watching the preparations. "Don't worry, Grant; they know what they are doing."

"I'm sure they do, but will it be in time?" Grant glanced towards the location of the Willow Creek Pack. "Father said Richard is suffering. He was barely healed when he left, what if—"

David interrupted, "If Ricky is a Protector then he is stronger than a normal human. At least that's what I've heard from the tales. Don't worry, we'll get your mate back, big brother. Besides, I'm hoping he'll be able to finally remove that huge stick you always carry up your—"

Grant slapped his brother on the back of the head. "Some day you will meet your mate and I can't wait to see the show." He turned as Blaze walked towards him.

The Rogue's leader tilted his head in submission before he spoke, "Everything is loaded and ready. Don't worry, Alpha, we'll be able to get to the pack lands in no time at all." Blaze smiled as he nodded towards his men. "We'll take out the perimeter guards around the clearing and get our surprise ready in case things go south."

"We are still over an hour away," Grant growled.

Blaze grinned. "Obviously you didn't notice our transportation—" The wolf was interrupted by Sparky who had walked up behind them.

"Yeah, Alpha Grant, those bikes are wicked fast. I've been told they can go from zero to piss in your pants in less than two seconds." Sparky was almost drooling as he asked, "Have you guys even found the top speed yet?"

The leader of the Rogues chuckled. "On a paved road we can get over a hundred miles per hour. Luckily our shifter reflexes make that speed something we can control. Once we get to the creek bed, we'll have to go a bit slower. But we should be able to shift and have our positions well before you get there. Just like we talked about, once we get to the outskirts of the pack lands, we'll leave the bikes and shift for the rest of the journey. Jason will let us know of any unfriendlies who might get in our way since he'll be monitoring the surveillance drones we have in place throughout the area. Don't worry; we'll make sure the party doesn't start without you."

Less then thirty minutes later Grant watched the monitor in the back of the SUV with his brother Jason. The split screen showed various views of the Willow Creek Pack lands along with the views of Blaze's Rogues as they got into attack position. The Alpha leaned forward as Jason zoomed in on Shadow's camera. Even though it was dark out, they were still able to see thanks to the night vision lens. They both watched in awe as the warrior slowly approached one of the hired enforcers who appeared to be hiding in a group of bushes just outside of the clearing. The wolf was still in human form as he lay with a sniper rifle supported on a tripod. There was a slight blurring of the image as Shadow shifted back to his own human form. The camera angle changed as it was now filming from the man's chest. The special made harnesses were made to stay on no matter what form the wolf was in and allowed them to not only keep in contact with the team, but also carried the weapons they might need for the mission.

"We need to get some of those for our Sentries, Grant," Jason whispered as they both continued to watch Shadow approach his prey.

It was amazing to watch how close the enforcer was able to get without the other wolf noticing him. Before Alpha Clifton's enforcer was able to react, Shadow had him in a headlock with an arm around his throat. Shadow applied pressure until the wolf went limp in his arms. They continued to watch as Blaze's teammate quickly secured the downed wolf with silver cuffs on his arms and legs. He then rolled the wolf over and covered his mouth with a piece of duct tape. Finally he pulled out a syringe and quickly injected the unconscious wolf with an inhibitor that would not only prevent him from shifting, but would also keep him weakened until they could transport him to a secured facility.

Jason switched to Dove's camera and smiled as he saw the shifter place one of their new toys at the base of the fire tower. "I sure hope this works," Jason said as he continued to watch the screen.

"Don't worry, little brother, they'll never see it coming and even if they do it won't matter," David answered from the front seat.

They watched as the remote controlled squirrel climbed up the outside of the tower before it slipped inside. Jason switched to the camera installed inside the squirrel. Inside the fire tower there were three wolves. Two of them had long-range sniper rifles trained on the clearing while the third scanned the surrounding woods. A grenade launcher was leaning up in the corner of the tower, ready to be used if needed.

"We'll soon know if your new toy works. I just hope it doesn't raise any alarms." Jason worried his lower lip.

David looked over at his father who was driving their SUV. Sparky and Dakota followed in the second vehicle. "You'd think they would trust my genius by now, "David replied. "After all, if it weren't for my bird drones, we would have been going in blind."

139

Forest shook his head as he reached over and cuffed David behind the ear. "Overconfidence has lost many wars, my son. No matter how prepared you think you are, something always happens when you least expect it."

David rubbed the back of his head. "Geez, Pop—" He ducked as another hand headed in his direction. "...I mean, *Father*. Loosen up already. This isn't like the days during the Great War—we have better toys than the stone arrows and sling shots from your time."

Grant shook his head as his brother and father continued to banter back and forth. He knew David was only trying to lighten the mood, but there was no way he would be able to relax until he had his mate and Roger back on his own pack lands. Of course, if all worked out he'd also be ridding the world of Alpha Clifton's evil.

"Here we go!" Jason called out as Grant looked back at the view from the robotic squirrel.

In the other view provided by one of their drones, he could see Dove smiling as he issued a command through the special headset he wore. Suddenly one of the wolves shouted in pain. The squirrel had run up the shifter's body and bit him in the neck before jumping towards the second wolf. Before the other wolf could swat the pesky animal away, the squirrel managed to also bite the wolf in the neck.

"For crying out loud, someone kill the damn vermin!" the first wolf yelled as he held a hand to his bleeding neck.

The remaining wolf reached for a knife that was hanging from his belt. They all watched as the squirrel jumped back down to the ground and quickly ran towards the enforcer. "He wouldn't—" Jason gasped as the drone quickly scurried up the pant leg of the remaining shifter. A second later the knife fell to the ground as the wolf let out a scream. Grant watched as Jason unconsciously crossed his legs before he continued to speak, "I can't believe Dove had the squirrel bite him there!"

David leaned over to look at the screen and then began to laugh. "You can't blame the squirrel, Jason. After all, most squirrels are attracted to nuts."

"I'm just glad it worked. When you told me the squirrel was going to knock the enemy out I thought you were the one who was nuts, brother," Jason replied as he smiled at his older sibling. "I mean who thinks of putting a tranquilizer solution in the teeth of a squirrel?"

"Even after working together all these years, you still have no faith, little brother. My toys always get the job done," David said smugly. "Just watch and learn. Those wolves will never know what hit them!"

"You mean Mack's toys. He may be strange but he certainly knows his robotics. If it weren't for him, your toys would still be stuffed animals on a shelf!" Jason shook his head as his brother crossed his arms over his chest and looked forward once more.

Grant shook his head at his brothers' antics as he continued to watch the screen. The other wolves were trying to help their friend remove the squirrel. However, before they could move closer, first one then the other fell to the ground unconscious.

"What the—" the remaining wolf growled as he tried to grab the walkie-talkie sitting near the window.

Luckily before he could reach it to call for help, he fell to his knees and joined his two pack mates. The squirrel quickly climbed on top of the unconscious shifter and began to dance holding its arms above its head in a victory signal.

"Now who's showing off?" Jason replied dryly as they glanced at Dove, who did a fist pump before he began working his way up the ladder. A short time later Alpha Clifton's hired enforcers were secured and Dove began to set up his equipment. Grant watched as the explosive expert began to work the controls. A short time later, the sound of wings could be heard as their surprise arrived and perched on the edge of the open windows. He glanced at Jason who shook his head and replied, "I'm sorry but there is definitely something wrong with that wolf."

Grant nodded solemnly. He had to admit Dove enjoyed his work, maybe a little too much. "How long before we arrive?"

"We should be at the outer gate in about fifteen minutes, then maybe another five until we get to the clearing. Assuming we don't have any interference," Forest answered calmly.

"I doubt we'll have any trouble getting in, Father—it's getting out that I'm worried about," Grant replied as he glanced back at the SUV following them. He knew that Blaze and Tank would be clearing out any obstacles to their leaving but still, they were going up against a larger force. Sooner or later their

141

luck would run out. He just hoped that Richard and Roger managed to escape before it did.

CHAPTER FIFTEEN

INSIDE RICKY WAS SCREAMING AT HIS BODY TO STOP BUT NO matter how hard he tried, he meekly followed behind Beta Biff. The large butt plug was rubbing his prostate as he walked which made the ache in his balls intensify. Of course, with the cock ring on he wouldn't be able to get release, even if he could get his body to obey. Artemus walked stiffly in front of Biff. It was clear he wasn't happy with the turn of events and yet Ricky couldn't feel resentment towards the doctor. He understood the need to protect a brother.

As they walked from the Alpha's compound, Ricky once again realized the vast difference between how Alpha Clifton and his chosen lived verses the rest of the pack. He had never understood why the other wolves didn't revolt. But then, he remembered the stories of those shifters who had threatened to challenge the Alpha only to disappear. He knew there would be no help this time. Besides, he didn't want Jake or any of the other wolves risk the fate that had befallen the others.

From the emptiness of the village, it was clear everyone was already at the clearing. Ricky frowned as he realized that the moon wouldn't reach its peak for at least another hour. Apparently Artemus also noticed as he paused and looked back at Biff. "Beta, I thought the ceremony would take place at the moon's zenith?"

Biff shrugged. "It will take place when Alpha Clifton decrees it should take place. Besides, I think he plans to take his time with the human before the final claim is completed. Why do you care anyway?"

143

It was Artemus' turn to shrug. "I don't, just making an observation." The Magi turned and continued the trek towards the clearing where the ceremony would take place. Ricky couldn't help the shiver that ran through him as they passed the whipping post in the center of the village. He had contributed many of the dark stains that currently marred the wood and ground beneath. His back had mostly healed while he'd been held captive, yet he swore he could still feel the pain of each lash as it had hit his back. Once again he tried to break free of the spell holding him. Unfortunately, while his mind was yelling run, his body calmly followed the Beta as if he didn't have a care in the world.

The ceremonial circle was located in a clearing in the woods that ran along Willow Creek. As they continued along the well traveled path Ricky thought about Alpha Grant. The handsome face of the Alpha still made him feel safe, even if his mind knew he wasn't. It was this picture that the enslaved human clung to as he finally arrived at the circle. He no longer cared what happened as he traveled further into his mind.

Here the clearing was empty except for a blanket settled near a picnic basket. Alpha Grant sat on the blanket, totally nude. Ricky devoured the site of the sculptured muscles that rippled across the shifter's stomach as he slowly stroked his cock. All the human wanted to do at this moment was kneel and taste, something he'd never wanted to do voluntarily before. The Alpha crooked a finger at him, motioning for him to come closer.

As if he were a moth to a flame, Ricky moved until he was kneeling on the blanket. The fact that he was also naked didn't bother him. All he wanted to do was to begin tasting the man in front of him. He glanced up at the molten brown eyes of the Alpha. They reflected the same lust that had taken over the young human. Even though he didn't have much experience in initiating contact, Ricky leaned forward and tentatively placed his lips against Grant's. The Alpha opened and allowed the human a taste.

Before he could stop, the Alpha had gently placed a hand behind Ricky's head and encouraged him to explore further. Tongues dueled for dominance as the two continued to kiss until it finally became necessary for them to come up for air.

"Wow." Ricky gasped as he tried to catch his breath.

Alpha Grant smiled. "And that was just the beginning of what I want to do with you, my mate." Ricky's ass clenched at the thought of the large cock that sprouted from the dark curls on the Alpha entering his body. A yearning he'd never felt before had him almost begging to be filled and dominated by the shifter. As if he understood Grant gently positioned Ricky on his hands and knees. The soft snick of what Ricky assumed was a bottle of lube was the only warning he had before a thick finger began to stroke his entrance.

Ricky moaned and pushed his ass further back towards the feeling. Grant chuckled. "I see you're impatient. Don't worry, we'll get you want you need, my mate." Just as Ricky was about to tell the shifter to hurry, he felt the finger that had been teasing him enter his channel. He relaxed his guardian muscle to allow the intrusion and was rewarded when Grant immediately found his pleasure spot. He arched his back and mewled as Grant continued to stretch him. If the Alpha kept this up, Ricky would shoot his load before they even started.

A third finger was finally worked into his ass, stretching him until he felt he couldn't take any more.

"Easy, little one. We're almost there," Alpha Grant said softly as he stroked his other hand down Ricky's spine, calming him. "If you don't want this, tell me now and we can stop," Grant whispered as he removed his fingers and blanketed Ricky's back with his own body. The human could feel the hard cock against the cleft of his ass as Grant began to nibble at the tendon along his neck.

"Please…" Ricky whispered.

"You are mine, Richard, my mate and my partner for the time I have left in this world. No one else will ever take you from me," Grant said forcefully as he began to thrust his cock into Ricky's willing opening. For a moment there was a burning sensation; but that soon was replaced by pleasure as the Alpha began to ease inside until his balls were touching Ricky's ass.

Grant waited for a couple more seconds before he began to slowly move in an out. Each time he hit Ricky's prostate a shiver ran throughout his body. Even his toes were tingling. As the strokes grew faster, the Alpha reached around and began to stroke Ricky's steel hard cock. He needed to come so bad and yet his body fought against the release. He fisted the blanket beneath him as his balls drew up impossibly tight. Just when he thought he would explode from the need for release, Grant shoved his cock deep within his chute. "Come for me, my mate!"

Ricky howled as he spewed his seed on the blanket beneath him. His cock continued to erupt as Grant's hips stuttered and then filled the human with his own release. Ricky dropped his head onto his arms as he felt himself being pulled sideways. Harsh breathing was the only sound in the clearing as the two men tried to catch their breath.

As Ricky snuggled closer to the large shifter he felt Grant kiss his shoulder before he spoke, "Remember, Richard, you are my mate and belong to no one else. I will always protect you…"

A cuff to the back of his head caused Ricky to blink. "Disgusting human! Even with the cock ring on he managed to come!" Beta Biff's irate voice yanked the captive back to reality. Gone was Alpha Grant to be replaced by the nightmare of Alpha Clifton. The heavyset shifter grinned as he pulled Ricky closer to him. The shifter had always reminded him of a heavy weight boxer who had let himself go.

"Now, Biff, he's just overcome with the need to mate. I've heard that even humans can feel the pull although they call it 'love at first sight', I believe." Alpha Clifton glanced out at the other members of the pack who currently watched from outside the ceremonial circle. Ricky recognized Jake and his sister Sammy. Both looked around for a moment as if they were expecting something before their sympathetic gaze locked on him. He was glad to see Jake hadn't suffered for helping them escape.

Ricky wanted to flinch away from the hand that lowered from his shoulder towards his still hard cock. "See how hard he still is for his *Semme*? While I fought all these years against the pull, I can no longer deny that which fate has given me." Alpha Clifton looked out at the crowd. "As with traditions of old, I will take my mate in front of the pack and claim him. Then none can contest the union of our souls."

Ricky watched as a silent communication seemed to happen between Jake and his sister before Sammy stepped forward. She held her head high as she moved into the ceremonial circle. She stopped a few feet in front of Alpha Clifton and tilted her head in submission before she began to speak. "Alpha Clifton, I understand you feel you must do this but others have walked away. No one here would think less of you if you didn't want to complete the mating."

Alpha Clifton growled softly but Sammy continued, "He can't give you heirs and you clearly are not gay like that abomination to nature." She pointed to Ricky, her lip curled in disgust. She didn't meet his eyes as she moved a few steps closer and placed her hand on the Alpha's arm. "I could give you strong pups to carry on your line. I know we are not *Semme'* but surely fate would not require you to give up an heir to run the pack when you are gone."

The Alpha tilted his head and looked at Sammy as if he'd just seen her for the first time. He licked his lips as he let his eyes travel over the female shifter's body. Ricky knew she was good looking with her long reddish brown hair tied back simply in a ponytail. Her dark skin glowed in the light of the bon fire that had been lit in the clearing. But it was the honey colored eyes that she shared with her twin brother Jake that drew most people in. Although he never felt drawn to Sammy when he'd been in the pack, even Ricky could admit she was beautiful.

The Alpha actually patted the she-wolf's hand before he gently pushed her back. "Your loyalty is appreciated, Samantha. Yet as you know fate only grants us one *Semme'*. Who am I to question that which the goddess has seen fit to provide?"

Sammy glanced back at Ricky for a moment before she spoke, "Has the human agreed to this? Maybe he has another—"

Alpha Clifton growled and pulled Ricky closer. "Of course he has agreed!" The irate Alpha turned them both towards the crowd. "Ricky, do you accept my claim—do you acknowledge you will bind yourself to me for the rest of our days as my *Semme'*?"

Ricky screamed his denial in his mind but his body refused to obey. He felt his head nod sealing his fate.

"You see, Sammy? Even the human knows this was meant to be. I'm sorry, but the claiming will continue unless there are any further objections."

"I object and I issue a challenge since Richard is my *Semme'*," Alpha Grant's voice echoed through the silent clearing. Even the birds had silenced their song at the sound of the Alpha's voice. Ricky felt himself drawn tighter to Alpha Clifton as the man growled.

"How dare you enter my pack lands without my permission?" Alpha Clifton's hands had turned into claws that began to draw blood where they touched Ricky's skin. But the captive didn't feel the pain as his eyes locked with

147

Alpha Grant's. He couldn't believe the Alpha had come and that he was publicly claiming Ricky as his own. Hope fluttered where despair had been only moments before.

"I have come to take back the two members of my pack that you took without permission." Ricky watched as Sparky stepped forward with his arm protectively around Roger. Beta Biff growled behind him as he took a step towards the pair. But Alpha Clifton shook his head.

"I've never seen the pup before. If he is here, it is against my wishes. You may take him and leave. However, Ricky is a member of my pack and has only recently returned." Alpha Clifton looked down at Ricky. "You don't want to leave with Alpha Grant do you, my mate?"

Again, Ricky tried to fight the hold over his body but his body betrayed him when he shook his head. For a moment he saw Alpha Grant's face fall until Sparky leaned closer and whispered something in his ear. The rage he saw on the man's face made the human want to run in the opposite direction.

"You bastard! You've used magic to bind the human to your control. Since when do shifters resort to magic to force a mating?"

Alpha Clifton laughed. "You have no proof of anything."

Before anyone could say anything else, Ricky felt pain in his shoulder as Alpha Clifton bit down and tasted his blood. The human wanted to scream but he couldn't utter a sound. What was worse was his body's betrayal as his seed spewed across the ground. Yet there was no pleasure, only a hopelessness that threatened to engulf him.

Gasps could be heard from the other shifters as Alpha Clifton stood up straight. "He has been claimed and even you can't undo what the goddess has decreed." He reached down and using his finger, he gathered some of the cum still leaking from Ricky's cock. He slowly licked it with an evil smile on his face. "Delicious! Now that's he's mine I can taste him often." The Alpha looked directly at Grant. "And I plan to do so."

Another shifter that Ricky had never seen moved forward and held up his hand for silence. He must have been someone important because even Alpha Clifton took a step back. "Many of you know who I am and know that I have fought for all shifters during the Great War. As the former Alpha of the Windy River Pack, I can confirm that Richard and his brother Sandy both came to my son and asked for sanctuary. This was granted even though Alpha Clifton had declared the human Richard rogue. The fact that he basically placed a kill order out on his *Semme'* is reason enough to question the validity of his claims. However, Doc Houston has also confirmed that prior to coming to us, Richard had been both physically and sexually abused." Forest glared around at the pack for a moment before he returned his heated gaze to Alpha Clifton and his Beta.

"Even if this were true, I have claimed Ricky as my mate. According to our laws, no one can interfere upon pain of death." Alpha Clifton smirked as he stepped forward and ran his finger down Ricky's face. "This human is mine and no one can take him from me."

Forest smiled but it did not reach his eyes. "True. However, you are the one who has stolen my son's *Semme'* by entering our pack lands and taking him against his will…" Forest held up his hand before Alpha Clifton could respond, "…but there is a test that the goddess has given us to ensure a true mating has taken place."

There were murmurs among the other shifters but they became silent again as Forest continued, "According to the old ways, if a mate is forced or if someone claims that a mate is Semme' when he or she is not, the bite of the false Semme' mate will not hold." Forest pointed to Ricky's shoulder. "Look and see for yourself."

A loud gasp once again sounded in the clearing as everyone looked at the completely healed skin on Ricky's shoulder. It should have still been bleeding since the Alpha had not sealed the wound after biting him. Ricky looked but couldn't believe his eyes. How had it happened? He'd felt the bite. Before he could process what this could mean he felt himself jerked back into Alpha Clifton's arms.

"NOW!" Alpha Clifton yelled as he glanced towards the tree line. For a moment there was silence before Alpha Grant began to chuckle.

"Further proof that not only are you not honorable by accepting my challenge; but you don't deserve the title of Alpha!" Grant paused with a smile on his face as he motioned to the trees that surrounded the clearing. "If you are waiting for your hired assassins to attack, you will have a long wait. I on the other hand will still face you in the traditional challenge," Alpha Grant growled as he stepped forward. "Now release my mate and I'll make your death a quick one."

Ricky felt a clawed hand at his throat. He swallowed as the pressure increased causing blood to flow. "I will kill him if you do not leave my lands!" Alpha Clifton took a step back, bringing Ricky with him. Before the Alpha of Willow Creek could take another step, the air was suddenly filled with a flock of doves. The birds circled the clearing for a moment before they flew closer. "What the Hell!" Alpha Clifton growled as one of the birds hovered a couple of feet in front of him. The next moment the air was filled with loud explosions as the birds began to explode. Ricky fell as Alpha Clifton and Biff quickly stepped back and covered their faces.

Chaos erupted as some of the shifters changed into their wolf forms and began to attack Alpha Grant's small group. Ricky felt someone kneel beside him. "Get up and run!" Sammy urged him as she pulled him to his feet. A growl sounded to his right as Sammy gave him a shove and turned to face the irate Alpha.

"What are you doing?" Alpha Clifton growled.

Sammy shrugged. "I told you he wasn't right for you—" She didn't get to finish as a clawed hand swiped at her, knocking her unconscious.

"Grab the bitch while I get the human!" Alpha Clifton ordered Beta Biff. Before the Alpha could get to Ricky, the befuddled human felt another hand pull him further into the crowd of fighting shifters. "I'm Radar and I'm with Alpha Grant. Come with me and I'll get you to safety!"

Ricky took another step but stopped as Alpha Clifton's voice ordered him to stop. Radar glanced at the human for a moment before he grabbed him and placed him over his shoulder. "Sorry, Ricky, but we don't have time to play Simon Says." The shifter took off at a run but stumbled and fell after grabbing at his shoulder. Ricky fell hard but managed to roll as a large wolf ran towards him. There was a shimmer as the wolf transformed, his gray eyes filled with concern as he glanced between Radar and Ricky.

Radar groaned but got to his knees. "Take him and get out of here, Tank. I can take care of myself!"

The man called Tank nodded and soon Ricky was once more being carried like a sack of potatoes from the fight. He glanced back and felt his blood run cold. Alpha Grant was in the middle of the battle, surrounded by at least fifteen wolves. Even though the Alpha stood tall in his half-shifted form, Ricky knew the odds were stacked against the wolf. Just as Tank put on more speed, the last view the human had was of the wolves surging to attack the brave Alpha.

Grant roared as he fought against the horde of wolves attacking him. He'd seen Tank running towards where they had the SUV's hidden. He hoped that Sparky had gotten there with Roger and would be able to get the pup and his mate to safety. A bite to his hindquarter brought his attention back to the battle at hand. He smiled as his brothers stood back to back taking down the wolves that attacked them. His father was also holding his own. The only thought Grant had left was to get rid of the ones who stood between him and Alpha Clifton.

With a loud roar, Grant began to toss the wolves away from him as if they were no more than pesky flies. He had chosen to shift into his third form which allowed him to remain upright. It was one of the advantages of being an Alpha. One of the wolves managed to grab his arm, biting down almost to the bone. Grant pulled the wolf from his arm and slammed him against the ground with a satisfying crunch. The wolf didn't move. He grabbed two more wolves and smashed their heads together before throwing them away. Slowly he was making his way towards where Alpha Clifton stood with two other shifters and a human. As he drew closer he could see the human mumbling something under his breath; so Magi then, not human.

"Hurry it up, Artemus!" Alpha Clifton growled as he stood behind the man. Grant could see a she-wolf fighting to free herself from another large wolf. Grant roared as he fought to get to the ones who had caused his mate so much pain. As he drew closer he could hear the Magi arguing with Alpha Clifton.

"I told you before; I'm a healer and not a Magi Warrior like my father," Aretmus ground out. "My father only taught me protective magic which won't last—ARGH!" The Magi screamed as he grabbed at his neck and pulled away what looked like a squirrel. "What the—" he never got to finish the sentence as he fell to the ground unconscious. Grant almost laughed as he glanced over and saw Dove grin before he ducked and with a move that would have made Bruce Lee proud, he took out one of the larger wolves.

There were still three large wolves between him and his goal. While he knew he could finish them off, it would cost him precious time. Suddenly a large reddish brown wolf leapt on one of the three wolves, ripping out the hapless wolf's throat before it even hit the ground. The remaining two wolves looked at each other before they sank to their bellies and bared their necks in submission. Grant glanced around and saw that the battle was over as those who weren't dead, were either unconscious or knelt in submission. Blaze had shifted back to his human form and was quickly pulling out zip ties laced with silver that he used to quickly secure the two wolves in front of him. He allowed his shift to flow over him as he glared at the Alpha he intended to kill.

During the fight Alpha Clifton had moved to the edge of the clearing. "I will give you the choice of what form you wish to die in," Grant growled as he began to walk towards Alpha Clifton.

"I think I'll take option three instead," Clifton sneered as he pulled a small bag from his shirt pocket. Grant surged toward the shifter at the same time he saw movement from the trees directly behind Alpha Clifton and his Beta. A small blonde wolf was surging towards the still struggling she-wolf. Alpha Clifton began to mumble in a strange language before he threw the contents of the small bag into the air. Still, Grant continued to run towards the evil Alpha. There was no way he was going to let the crazy shifter escape. A shout from Blaze caused him to pause.

"Alpha Grant—Radar NO!" Blaze screamed as the air around Alpha Clifton, the Beta and the she-wolf began to shimmer. Grant stopped but Radar ignored the command as he leapt the final two feet and landed between the she-wolf and the Beta. Before anyone else could move the figures in front of them began to fade.

"I'll see you again and when I do, I'll not only take what is mine but I'll make you watch as I fuck Ricky until he's raw!" Alpha Clifton sneered as he disappeared into thin air.

"Sammy!" A desperate cry sounded through the silence that had been left behind when Alpha Clifton disappeared. Grant glanced back to see the male version of the she-wolf fall to his knees on the ground. The despair in his eyes was reflected by each of Blaze's rogues. Grant couldn't help the howl that escaped his lips as he promised that no matter what it took, he would make Alpha Clifton pay for his treachery.

CHAPTER SIXTEEN

THE RIDE BACK TO THE AIRPLANE WAS SILENT. GRANT SAT WITH a too quiet Richard in his arms. If it weren't for the fact that he could see the rise and fall of the human's chest, he would have worried that his *Semme'* had left him alone. He glanced up to see even Sparky was subdued as they drove back towards the hanger. Roger luckily had escaped any major damage, but he still kept his head bowed as he sat in the front seat next to Sparky. His father and brothers had stayed behind with Blaze, Shadow and Dove. Tank, Falcon and Jake were following them in the other SUV that currently held their prisoner, the Magi who had helped Alpha Clifton. They also towed Radar's motorcycle behind their vehicle. They all agreed that it would be kept for when Radar returned.

His father and the others would stay in Willow Creek until the pack could be disbanded and relocated. After Alpha Clifton had disappeared, the original wolves of the pack were given an option to either pledge allegiance to Grant and the Windy River Pack or to relocate to another pack of their choice. The mercenary shifters that had been hired by Alpha Clifton were not given the same choice. They either chose to pledge their loyalty to Alpha Grant or they would be killed instantly.

Blaze had talked to some of them and discovered that many of them only fought because they had no other pack to call their own. As was the case with many lone wolves, they hired themselves out to various packs as enforcers. They never pledged their loyalty but rather fought for the money to allow them to continue their solitary existence. Blaze had convinced Grant that these wolves, most of which had military training would be useful in protecting the

153

pack. After discussing it, Grant agreed that Blaze would be responsible for training the wolves who would be on a probationary period. If any of them stepped out of line or were proven to be disloyal, they would be declared rogue and killed. It was risky, but it was clear they would need more fighters if they hoped to keep the growing pack safe from the threat of attack from Alpha Clifton and his followers.

Alpha Grant pulled the blanket his *Semme'* was wrapped in tighter as he felt Ricky shiver. He gently traced his finger along the side of the young man's face but there was no reaction. The hazel eyes that had blazed with life, now stared blankly from a too pale face. Sparky had explained that the spell that was keeping his mate mute would most likely wear off in time. But the collar that encircled Ricky's throat was another matter. Grant had tried unsuccessfully to remove it. Just the idea that his mate had it on made his inner wolf howl. His only hope was that the Magi they had captured would be able to shed some light on what the strange symbols on the collar meant and what was hurting his mate. If not, then the Magi would forfeit his life and Grant couldn't bring himself to care.

"We're almost to the hanger, Alpha," Sparky's subdued voice filled the silent cabin of the SUV.

"Good, the sooner we get back to our pack lands the better I'll feel," Grant growled as he gently shifted the human in his arms. He had to believe that whatever ailed his mate could be reversed and that he'd have the opportunity to explain how he really felt about the man in his arms; the man he suspected he was already beginning to fall in love with.

• • ❖ • •

Ricky slowly opened his eyes and sighed as he saw a familiar scene. His brother slept in his wolf form at the end of the bed while the large frame of Alpha Grant slept in the chair that had been brought into his room. Neither of them had left since he'd been returned, which made him feel safe and yet it also increased his guilt.

It was hard to believe that it had been over a week since his rescue. He blushed as he remembered the pack doctor removing the large butt plug and cock ring during his initial examination. While there hadn't been any severe damage done to him during his captivity, Ricky could feel that he was still dying. He slowly reached up to touch the collar around his throat. No one had been able to figure out a way to remove it and as luck would have it, Alpha Clifton hadn't been lying about the effects.

Even now Ricky could feel his energy being drained, slowly and painfully. Every joint and muscle in his body ached as if he had aged a hundred years in the span of a week. The only bright spot had been his freedom from the spell that had controlled his body. Artemus had been right. It had only lasted for a day and yet the effects still lingered. The total loss of control only reinforced his belief about himself. He was the weak link; so much so that he actually was a danger to his younger brother. If Alpha Clifton had succeeded, he had no doubt his brother would have ended up under the evil bastard's control.

Then there was Alpha Grant. Ricky had to admit that the shifter had more than come through. The Alpha had spent the past few days trying to explain that he didn't see Ricky as being damaged and would be more than honored to have him as a mate. While he wanted to desperately believe things could work out, he'd been shown more than once his shortcomings. Alpha Grant deserved someone who could stand proudly at his side, to fight beside him and to be able to receive his affection without flinching or having a panic attack. As much as his heart wanted a closer relationship with the handsome shifter, his head argued it could never be.

He'd had plenty of time to think during his captivity and since his rescue. No matter how he looked at it, his death would be better for not only Alpha Grant and Sandy, but also for the pack that had offered him a home. If he was gone there would be no one who could be used to control his little brother. Alpha Grant would be able to find a mate worthy of him and if Ricky was being honest, he'd finally find some peace from the hell he'd experienced since his parents' deaths. In short he was tired.

Ricky sighed softly as he turned to look outside the window to his room. It wouldn't be long now. He refused to tell Alpha Grant about the possible way to remove the collar and save his life. How could he? He knew the shifter would claim him out of a sense of duty, the need to protect a member of his pack. He refused to allow that to happen. And so he waited for the inevitable.

A soft knock on the door caused Ricky to pull the covers closer. "Come in," Alpha Grant's sleep roughed voice answered. Sparky glanced at Ricky before he quietly entered and stood in front of his Alpha. Grant had explained why Sparky was a little leery around him and after experiencing mind control magic, Ricky didn't blame the wolf's hesitance. Of course he still had no clue how he'd managed to throw the shifter across the room. Sandy shook out his fur but remained guarding the end of the bed as he listened in on the conversation.

"Were you able to get any information from the Magi?" Alpha Grant asked as he sat up straighter in the chair.

Sparky ran a hand through his hair before he responded. "I just don't understand. The Artemus I knew would have never been involved with Alpha Clifton much less use magic to control another." He glanced over at Ricky for a moment before he continued, "If it wasn't for him, I don't think I would have recovered."

Alpha Grant growled. "And yet he refuses to help us now. I'm afraid he doesn't leave us much choice. Tell him if Ricky dies, his death will follow."

"NO!" Ricky said softly, surprised at the lack of strength in his voice. He watched as both men and his brother's wolf looked at him. He glanced down at his hands for a moment before he looked back up at the Alpha. "Please, you don't understand—"

Alpha Grant stood and moved to sit next to Ricky. The Alpha placed his hands over his nervously twitching ones. For a moment Ricky allowed the feeling of calm and safety to flow over him before he took a breath and looked up into the concerned eyes of the person who was quickly becoming his everything. If only—but there was no time to go back, no do-over's that could make what happened disappear. But there was something he could put right.

"Make me understand, Richard. Tell me why I shouldn't kill the man who caused you so much pain." For a moment, Ricky could see the wolf shining through Grant's eyes. He had no doubt the Alpha would carry through with his threat. Ricky sighed before he took a breath and began to tell Grant how Artemus had tried to help him even at the possible cost of losing the only link to his missing half-brother Charles.

"Artie has a half brother?" Sparky asked as he cocked his head to the side. "How did I not know this? I stayed with him for months after…" the shifter swallowed before he continued. "…well after Winston's last attack."

156

Alpha Grant stood up and gazed outside the window for a moment before he looked back at Ricky. "Did he give you a last name?"

Ricky shook his head. "No, he just called him Charles. But don't you see—he had no choice but to obey." He looked down at his brother. "How can I hold him accountable for doing whatever he could to save his brother? After all, I did things—allowed myself to be used..." He stopped unable to voice any more with his brother in the room. He knew Sandy was aware of the beatings and probably some of the more public displays, but he never wanted him to know how far he had gone behind closed doors to keep his brother safe.

Alpha Grant seemed to understand as he nodded before he stood and pulled out his cell phone. "Bring Artemus to me immediately," he paused as he listened to the other person speak before he growled, "I understand the risk Dakota but we need more information and I believe I've found a way to get it."

"What are you going to do?" Ricky whispered. He watched as the Alpha smiled softly down at him before he answered.

"I'm going to offer him a deal he won't be able to refuse—I'm going to help him find his half-brother. Besides, if what I believe is true, we've already been helping him without knowing it."

Ricky wanted to ask more, but was interrupted by a short knock at the door before it opened to show a chained Artemus being led into the room by the Sheriff. Ricky was alarmed at the appearance of the man. Gone was the self-assured Magi who had helped him. Dull jade colored eyes glanced up at Ricky for a moment before they dropped back to the ground. The man had obviously lost weight and walked as if the chains that held him would pull him over.

"What have you done to him?" Ricky gasped.

Dakota pulled the prisoner further into the room and indicated he should sit in the chair vacated by Alpha Grant. He then stood behind the captive man and shrugged. "He refuses anything other than water. Since he is more than likely to forfeit his life, I saw no reason to force him to eat."

Before Ricky could object, Alpha Grant stepped forward. "Enough!" The room fell silent as the Alpha glared down at the magi for a moment before he sighed and placed a hand on the man's shoulder. He squeezed it gently, waiting for the man to look up. Artemus took a deep breath before he finally spoke.

"I told Sparky, there is nothing more I can do to help you." He glanced over at Ricky and frowned. "You haven't claimed him? How many days have I been here?" Artemus glared up at the Alpha. "I guess the rumors about you and your pack were just that—rumors."

"What the hell are you talking about?" Alpha Grant growled as he stepped back and glared at the man. Ricky wanted to say something, but suddenly he was afraid. No matter what he said, he knew Grant would never forgive him for keeping this from him. He wanted to close his eyes and pretend he was unconscious as the Alpha moved to stand directly in front of the captive, his arms crossed as he ordered, "Explain to me this rumor."

Artemus glared right back at the Alpha, his eyes now as hard and cold as the gem they resembled. "You obviously aren't capable of protecting members of your pack; you've grown complacent over the years. You're hiding away in this stone castle while those who needed your protection are left to fend for themselves."

"I will ask you one more time, what are you talking about?" Alpha Grant demanded in a voice that had the other shifters in the room baring their throats. Even Ricky felt like he should bow his head at the power he could feel flowing through the room. Artemus simply smiled as he shook his head.

"Your Alpha powers will not work on me," Artemus sneered. Grant leaned over and placed a clawed hand on the magi's shoulder. He gripped it hard enough to make the man wince. Ricky hadn't even noticed the partial shift. It was pretty clear that Alpha Grant was quickly losing patience with the healer.

"STOP! Just—just stop, okay?" Ricky cried out as he tried to sit up in the bed. Unfortunately he didn't even have the strength to do that simple task. He threw his hands up in frustration before he continued, "It's not his fault, Alpha Grant. He told me how to remove the collar." He stopped as all the eyes in the room stared at him. But rather than look at the disappointment he was sure to see, Ricky glanced down at his clenched hands.

"Artemus told me there were three ways to remove this cursed collar. Alpha Clifton could release it, the person wearing it dies or..." Ricky couldn't go further as he shook his head.

"...your *Semme'* had to claim you within ten days after you left the influence of the owner of the collar," Artemus continued softly. The magi shook his head and looked up once more at the Alpha. "It seems I may owe you an apology. I just assumed you had denied the mating."

Alpha Grant took a deep breath before he moved to sit beside Ricky on the bed. For a few minutes nothing was said. Ricky jumped as he felt a hand gently squeeze his shoulder. He expected to feel the pain from the Alpha's claws but instead the hand moved to his neck and began to message it.

"Did nothing I said to you over the past week mean anything to you, Richard?"

He glanced up at the hurt he heard in the Alpha's voice. The pain he saw reflected in the chocolate brown eyes took his breath away. He couldn't let the shifter think it was anything he had done. "No—I mean, yes I believe what you said but that doesn't change the fact that you are all better off without me."

There was a shimmer followed by the human form of his brother who now knelt at the end of the bed, his eyes swimming with tears. "You promised, Ricky!"

Ricky sighed as he swallowed back his own tears. "I know, Sandy, but you have to understand, sometimes keeping a promise may not be the right thing to do." Before Ricky could say anything further his little brother glared at him.

"You promised you wouldn't leave me like mom and dad did. You promised to always be there for me. I don't care what you say, a promise is a promise." Sandy quickly jumped down from the bed and ran towards the door. Just before he escaped through it he turned angry blue eyes at his brother. "You suck!" The young shifter yelled before he ran out and slammed the door behind him.

Ricky couldn't help the tears that slowly fell down his cheeks. He jerked as a finger wiped one of the tears away followed by a sigh from the Alpha. It was just too much for him to handle any more. He turned his head and closed his eyes hoping that everyone would get the message and just leave him alone.

"Your brother is right, Richard. A promise made should be kept whenever possible. If it was easy to do, then making one would mean nothing." Alpha Grant stood and looked at the remaining men in the room. "Please leave us."

Sparky stood and walked over to help Artemus to his feet. "Come on, Artie, I'm going to take you down to the kitchen and you're gonna eat something or I'll sick the Alpha's mother on you and believe me—you don't want to be on that woman's bad side." The shifter shuddered as he started moving towards the door with the magi.

Alpha Grant moved to stand by the door. He glanced back at Dakota who simply nodded his understanding. He would watch the magi. "It seems you and I have more to discuss, Artemus." He held his hand out for the key to the chains holding the man captive. After quickly releasing the magi he held the man's gaze as he spoke. "It seems we have more in common than either of us first thought. Sparky, make sure he eats and then show him to one of the guest rooms. I will meet with you once I have finished here."

Artemus squared his shoulders as his eyes softened slightly. "Agreed. Perhaps there is more I can do to help." He glanced over at Ricky before he continued. "Apparently the human protector does not fully understand his importance to the Omega."

The Alpha looked over Artemus' shoulder as he replied, "He obviously doesn't understand how important he is as my *Semme'* either but I intend to begin his education shortly."

Sparky snorted. "I bet he gets an 'A' in that subject, I know I did!" The shifter winked at Ricky before he led Artemus and Dakota from the room. Ricky watched as Alpha Grant closed the door before turning to look at him. "I think our first lesson will be on keeping secrets—"

CHAPTER SEVENTEEN

GRANT MOVED CLOSER TO THE BED AND THE FRAIL MAN lying on it. He could smell the fear but he could also smell arousal. He didn't need to look beneath the blanket to know his mate's body called out to him. However, he knew physical attraction wasn't the problem. He needed to not only win his *Semme's* mind, but also his heart.

Richard looked down at his clasped hands, refusing to meet Grant's eyes. His strawberry blonde hair hung limply around the man's shoulders. The pale skin the Alpha admired when the human had first arrived was now almost translucent. Over the past few days he'd watched the cursed collar drain the very life from his mate. To find out that he could have prevented his mate's suffering made his wolf agitated. He should be furious with Richard for not telling him.

Yet he had to remember the human had come from a pack where the Alpha didn't protect his members in the manner that he should have. Richard had no idea how a true pack operated, nor did he have reason to blindly trust when apparently his life had shown him nothing but reasons not to do so. How could he get through to his mate that he wanted him?

Grant sighed as he sat on the bed and once again covered Richard's hands with his own to still the trembling digits. He reached gently under the man's chin and forced him to look up. The devastation he saw in the swirling depths of his mate's eyes almost took his breath away. Richard believed what he'd said. The man didn't see his worth not only to Grant, but to his brother as well as the rest of the pack.

"I wanted to give you, to give us, time to learn about each other," Grant said softly as he pushed a stray lock of hair off his mate's forehead. "But it seems as though we don't have a lot of options if we want to stop the curse." The Alpha traced the outlines of the collar with his finger. "But maybe it will help if I start by telling you a little about me and then we can talk about what we'll do next." He watched as Richard's eyes blinked rapidly as if he was trying to keep the tears that formed in them from falling. Grant leaned forward and gently kissed each eye, tasting the salty tears before he moved lower and sipped at his mate's lips.

Richard moaned softly as he opened his mouth, allowing Grant to press further inside to taste and encourage his mate to return the exploration. He was pleasantly surprised when Richard's tongue began to push back, dueling with his own as they continued to explore together. After a few minutes, Grant pulled back and smiled as he saw the lust blown eyes of his mate looking up at him. His wolf was pushing at him, whining in his mind with the need to complete the bond. It was the hardest thing he'd ever done to sit back.

"There are a few things you should know about me before we go any further with this," Grant said as he ran his thumb under the slightly swollen lower lip of his soon to be lover. He noticed Richard's eyes returned to his lap, but Grant wasn't going to let the human get away from him again. "Hey, none of that, Richard," Grant chastised gently as he once again used his finger to force his mate to look up at him.

"What we have here is a failure to communicate—" Grant paused as he saw his mate's lips quirk slightly.

"Did you just quote Cool Hand Luke? 'Cause I gotta say, you don't look or sound anything like Paul Newman." Richard chuckled softly.

Grant winked. "Don't tell my brother David, but I actually do get out and watch a movie now and then."

"You're telling me the last movie you saw was in the late 60's?" Richard's eyes grew wide.

The Alpha shrugged. "I didn't really have anyone to watch one with, but I'm open to you bringing me up to date, if you're willing that is." Grant watched as Richard's smile left his face. For a brief moment he'd seen a glimpse of what they could have if only his mate would believe in their future together.

162

"Look, I know that sometimes I can be a bit…demanding. But I never learned how to act any other way. Since I was a young pup, I was groomed to become the Alpha of this pack. Then there was the Great War and I had to focus on not only protecting my own pack, but to also fight against those who would hurt others simply because they weren't the same. My father was still Alpha at that time, but as his Beta we worked together with other like minded packs to bring about the peace we now enjoy." Grant paused as he stroked a finger down Richard's face. "There never seemed to be time to do more than fight and then once my father stepped down and left me in charge, time has been eaten up by caring for our pack."

"I'm sorry; it must be hard to be responsible for so many people. David told me you're pack has almost three hundred members right?" Richard asked quietly.

Grant nodded. "Yes, and it will be growing with the addition of those who wish to seek sanctuary here from the Willow Creek Pack. But I'm not telling you this for sympathy, Richard. It's just—"

"You don't know how to be anything else. I get it, Alpha Grant—"

"Call me Grant, Richard. When we are alone, even when we're not, you don't need to call me Alpha except during official functions. I don't want that distance between us, I need you to understand how much you mean to me and not just as my *Semme*." Grant leaned forward and brushed his lips across Richard's.

"Ricky…" His mate mumbled against his lips. Grant sat up and smiled. "Ricky it is, but if I forget, you have permission to remind me."

Ricky sat back and sighed. "I know you feel a pull to me because of this whole fate thing, but tell me this." His mate leaned forward and placed a hand on his forearm. "If we met in a bar, would you have even noticed me?"

Grant smiled as he ran his hand through Ricky's hair. "Even without fate, I would have seen you. I might not have acted as quickly because to be honest, I haven't dated often. Something my brothers remind me of often." Grant shrugged as he smiled.

"But if you met me in a bar and learned about my past, you can't tell me you'd want to continue a relationship. I mean, I don't even know if I can." Ricky blushed. "I mean I have panic attacks, I'm not even sure I can have sex without," his mate swallowed before he continued. "…without zoning out. Not to mention I come with a brother who has his own problems—"

Grant silenced Ricky by placing his finger on his mate's lips.

"I can state truthfully that what happened in your past means nothing to me, except I wish I could have prevented it from happening to you. I wish you could see yourself through my eyes." Grant sighed. "I'm really not good at talking about feelings like this, but I can tell you that from the moment I realized what you'd endured at the hands of first your father and then Alpha Clifton, I saw a man who I would be proud to call my mate."

Ricky snorted and shook his head. "But how could you?"

"How many men would have taken the punishment you did to save your brother? Roger told me how you tried to protect him while you both were being held prisoner. Sparky told me how hard it was to endure the mind control magic and still come out of it without being 'Cray Cray'." Grant used quote fingers as he shook his head. "Even Artemus admitted he'd never seen anyone as strong as you when faced with what Alpha Clifton had done to you."

Ricky shrugged. "It's not like I had a choice."

"Actually, you did. You could have walked away from the pack and left your little brother behind. But instead you ran with him, injured and scared of what would happen to you if you were caught. You could have let me kill Artemus, yet you chose to speak up even though from what you have experienced in your former pack, you believed there would be punishment. These are not the actions of a weak man, but of a warrior." Grant took Ricky's hand in his own. "I can teach a man to fight, but I can't teach a man to be honorable or to have the will to do what is right regardless of the cost to himself. That is something you contain and that is why I am honored to have you as my mate." Grant kissed his mate's fingers.

"So what do we do now?" Ricky whispered.

"That is up to you, Ricky. Even with the threat of death, I will not force you to choose me. But I will ask—" Grant stood and got down on one knee as he held Ricky's hand. "Please choose to live, not just to keep your promise to your little brother, but so we can discover what fate has wisely seen in our future. Let me learn to love you and to show you the strong warrior that I see." Grant held his breath as he watched Ricky swallow. For a moment he thought he'd lost when the human sighed and looked at the door. He wasn't sure how much time they had left, but he would give his *Semme'* as much time as he could to make his decision.

"I'll give you some time to think about it." Grant began to stand but was stopped when Ricky clasped his hand tighter.

"I choose you, Grant," Ricky said softly, his eyes glowed with something other than despair for the first time since Grant had met him.

"Do you agree to be my *Semme'*, my mate, my partner for as long as this life will allow?" Grant had to ask. He had to be sure Ricky didn't feel like he was being forced to mate with him.

"Yes Grant, I want—no I *need*, have needed you for longer than I can remember. I knew when I left that I was already falling for you. I just hope you don't regret it." Ricky shook his head but still smiled as a soft blush began to creep up his neck. "So ah, how do we do this?"

"Do you trust me?" Grant asked as he stood.

"Yes, I've always trusted you even before I understood why. You make me feel safe," Ricky admitted as the blush now reached his cheeks.

Grant smiled. "Good, then the first thing you need to know is if anything I do makes you feel afraid or uncomfortable, you just need to tell me and I'll stop."

"Okay," Ricky sounded unsure.

The Alpha was glad he'd talked a little more with Sparky about how to handle his mate. He'd try to play the role until Ricky understood that he didn't have to be submissive with him; at least not in the way he'd been taught by the bastards of Willow Creek. While Grant knew he was a definite top and could be controlling, he'd be more than willing to give up some control if it made his mate happy. But for now, he'd have to try to make sure he didn't hit any of Ricky's triggers.

He opened a drawer on the nightstand and removed a bottle of lube. He saw Ricky begin to pick at the blanket again. "Look at me, Ricky," Grant ordered softly. He smiled as his mate did as he was told. "Good, now we'll set the rules. First, if you want me to stop, then you will use the word 'red' and if you want me to slow down you will use the word 'yellow'." He could see the confusion in Ricky's eyes. "I realize that you have not had any choices when you were with the Willow Creek pack, but now you will have control."

"I have control?" Ricky asked, his eyebrow raised.

"You will always have control with me, Ricky," Grant assured the nervous man. "I also want you to make as much noise as you want because I love hearing how much I'm pleasuring you. Finally, you have permission to come; in fact I plan to have you come many times before we are through. Do you understand Ricky?"

It was clear the human was still nervous but he looked up and nodded. "Yes, I understand. Can I ask one thing?"

"Anything," Grant answered.

"Can you take me face to face?" Ricky twisted his hands in his lap. "I mean, you can take me from behind if you want, but—well, they all took me that way and I'm not sure..."

Grant cupped Ricky's face. "They were fools, my mate. Of course I want to see your pleasure as I take you. Are you ready?"

Ricky pulled the blanket aside and blushed as the tent in his pajama bottoms answered the question for him. "Hmmm, it seems that someone wants to come out to play. Why don't we get you a bit more comfortable?"

Ricky couldn't believe he was about to be mated to the Alpha. Even as he felt his pajama bottoms being removed, it felt more like one of the dreams he'd had than reality. He glanced up and watched as Grant slowly removed his shirt. Ricky couldn't wait to trace the toned abs with his tongue. The Alpha kicked off his boots and quickly removed his jeans. The shifter went commando, yum!

He couldn't resist looking at the large uncut cock that stood out proudly from the dark curls. For a moment his ass clenched at the thought that it would soon be filling him. He'd been taken by men with cocks as large as Grant's. He just hoped this time it wouldn't be as painful. He continued to look at the shifter and all Ricky could see was miles and miles of golden skin that begged for his touch. He could feel his own cock swelling as he continued to drink in the sight of the naked man before him.

"Like what you see?" Grant asked as he knelt on the bed.

Ricky nodded, unable to speak as he watched Grant open the bottle of lube and begin to put some on his fingers. His hole clenched in anticipation. He'd never felt this way before, not even with his former boyfriend Robert. It was as if his body recognized what it wanted even though his mind still swirled with doubts. Could it be as simple as letting go?

166

"You're thinking too much which means I must not be doing something right." Grant's whisky smooth voice made him focus on what the shifter was doing. Grant had moved onto the bed and was kneeling between Ricky's legs. Before he could respond, he felt a warm, wet tongue lick at his slit. "Mmmm, you taste so good." Grant paused and looked up at Ricky. "Remember, if you want me to stop—"

"I say red." Ricky panted.

Grant smiled softly as he leaned forward and gently kissed the top of Ricky's cock. Before he could respond, the Alpha swallowed him down to the root and began sucking. Ricky reached down to the dark head bobbing between his legs. The dark hair beneath his fingers felt soft as silk. He couldn't help the groan that escaped from his lips as the shifter's finger gently traced his puckered hole before pushing past the guardian muscle. He'd always had to prepare himself while at Willow Creek. The young human marveled at the strange, yet wonderful sensation of having the Alpha's finger inside him.

"Oh—oh!" Ricky's body arched up as Grant found the special spot within. He glanced down and saw the smile on the Alpha's lips as he continued to suck Ricky's cock. The dueling sensations were too much. "I'm going to—please— can I—Oh God! Yellow! Yellow!" The human could barely get the words past his lips, but Grant understood as he briefly pulled his lips from around Ricky's cock. A sexy smile graced the shifter's face as he responded to the unasked request.

"Do you want me to stop, my mate?" The Alpha asked as the finger that pistoned in and out of Ricky's chute slowed.

Ricky didn't know what to do, he didn't want it to stop but he also couldn't help the small fear that niggled at the back of his mind. Coming was bad in his experience and never something he'd desired, until now. But this was his mate not Beta Biff. As Ricky squirmed on the bed he heard his mate chuckle.

"Come for me, my *Semme'*—my mate," Grant ordered before he once again placed his lips around Ricky's throbbing member.

Dark eyes captured Ricky's and held him captive as a second finger was added to the first and both were now hitting Ricky's prostate with each pass. There was no time for him to think but only to react as his body finally couldn't take any more.

167

"Gah! Grant!" Ricky shouted as his cock began to spurt into the Alpha's mouth. He could feel his muscles clench around the fingers in his ass as his orgasm stole the breath from his lungs. Grant continued to suck until there was nothing left. As Ricky's spit soaked cock fell from the Alpha's lips, he could see the need in his partner's eyes.

Before he could catch his breath, Grant chuckled. "That was just the beginning my mate, are you ready for more?"

Ricky sighed as he rested back on the bed, his heart hammered in his chest but his body felt more relaxed than it had in a long time. His toes still tingled from the force of his orgasm. He glanced up at the man who was slowly breaking through his defenses. Without thinking he provided the only answer he could give. "Yes, Master."

Grant sucked in a quick breath but quickly covered his concern at his mate's response. He leaned forward and kissed the man beneath him, sharing his taste while he devoured the human. His body burned and his wolf howled as he deepened the kiss until he was finally forced to stop to allow them to breathe. If he wasn't careful, he'd be rougher than he wanted to be with his mate when the time came. He sat back and noticed the kiss swollen lips in front of him as they quirked up into a soft smile.

The Alpha noticed that his mate seemed to be exhausted as his eyes slowly blinked up at him. He wanted to take more time to show Ricky how sex should be between two people who cared about each other, but from the way the man beneath him was fading it didn't appear that he'd have the time.

Grant sighed. "I know you're tired, my mate, but you need to stay with me for just a little longer."

"Mm—kay," Ricky said softly but his eyes still remained at half-mast.

"I'm going to take you now, Ricky. I'll try to take it slow, but my wolf is riding me—just—just make sure you tell me if it becomes too much. I don't want to hurt you," Grant spoke softly as he inserted a third finger to prepare his mate for his cock. His mate groaned softly but didn't seem to be in any pain.

"Please—I need—please…" Ricky whispered as his hips bucked up from the bed. The human's cock was already hard and leaking again.

"Shh—I know what you need, my mate. I'm going to claim you now," Grant whispered as he pushed Ricky's legs up towards the human's chest. He slowly pressed his cock against his mate's entrance and could feel the slight resistance but it soon gave way. He couldn't believe how good it felt around his throbbing member. Ricky's muscles stroked him like a velvet glove.

Grant looked up to make sure his mate wasn't suffering. "God, Grant— stop playing around and fuck me already!" Ricky called out as he tried to push himself further onto Grant's cock.

The Alpha smiled as he saw a glimpse of how demanding his lover could be before he pushed fully into his mate. He waited again for just a brief moment to let his mate get used to him before he began to thrust slowly in and out of his mate's chute. He could feel the sweat cooling on his body as he continued to increase the speed of his thrusts. He was too close to the edge to last long.

Ricky's body was bent in half as Grant continued to pound into him. His mate's cock was weeping while his lover met each of his thrusts with the soft sounds of pleasure and need. The Alpha's balls had pulled up tight as his wolf roared with its own demands. It was time for him to claim his mate.

"Come for me my mate!" Grant growled as he slammed deep within his mate's channel.

He smiled as Ricky's body shuddered and a loud howl filled the room as come spurted between their bodies. Before the last spurt had left his mate's cock, Grant let his canines elongate. He leaned forward and nipped Ricky's shoulder softly. He glanced into his *Semme's* eyes; this was the last chance for him to stop the bonding process. Once he bit and tasted his mate's blood, the bond would be complete.

"Do it," Ricky said softly.

If it weren't for Grant's enhanced hearing, he probably wouldn't have heard it. He could feel his cock throb as he pushed deep within his mate's body, holding himself there until his cock exploded. As he began to fill his mate with his sperm, he bit down and tasted his *Semme's* sweet nectar. The blood flowed over his teeth and into him while he continued to empty his balls into his lover. As he pulled his teeth from his mate's shoulder, he quickly licked the wound to stop the bleeding.

Grant let his head fall onto Ricky's shoulder while he kept the rest of his weight off of his ailing lover. He breathed in the scent that was his mate's. He could feel the bond snap into place. For the first time in his life, Grant knew peace. Nothing else mattered to him except for the slight human who lay quietly

169

beneath him. The Alpha lifted his head to look at his mate and quickly rolled to the side. Ricky wasn't moving, in fact, he appeared to be not breathing.

"NO!" Grant howled.

CHAPTER EIGHTEEN

HE DOOR TO THE BEDROOM BURST OPEN AS DOC HOUSTON, Artemus and Sparky rushed into the room. Grant jumped from the bed and glared at them, his claws extended as he faced them in his partially shifted form. He let his head fall back and let out another mournful howl as tears leaked from his eyes. His mate was dead, the bastard Clifton had killed him and nothing short of the former Alpha's death would appease the wolf inside him. He could feel himself losing control as the doctor rushed towards the bed, followed closely by Artemus.

"Get away from him!" Grant growled, his voice barely human.

A hand on his arm caused him to look down at the tear filled eyes of Sandy. He glanced up and saw Dakota run into the room.

"I'm sorry, I tried to stop him—" The sheriff stopped as he saw the still form on the bed. For the first time the shifter appeared to be at a loss as to what to do. Sparky made a grab for Sandy, but the young pup ducked and ran towards the bed. They all watched as he threw himself on top of his brother and began to sob as if his world had ended. Before Grant could move towards the distraught Omega, Artemus walked towards the bed and placed his hand over Ricky's still form. The Magi closed his eyes and softly mumbled words in an unknown tongue. For a moment there was complete silence except for the quiet sobbing of the young wolf. Then chaos erupted.

"Sparky, get Sandy away from the bed." The Magi glanced up at Grant. "You need to transform back to your human form now if you want to save your mate!"

"What are you talking about, Artie?" Sparky asked as he gently pulled the young wolf away from his brother's too quiet body. "You're not going to practice dark magic are you?"

"Of course not! You know I only learned about it to help my father protect the last Custos. Once you go down that path, you can't come back," Artemus sighed as he ran a hand through his hair. "We don't have time for this right now. If you want to save your mate, Alpha Grant, then I need you in your human form."

Grant glared at the man for a moment before he closed his eyes and controlled his breathing. It was hard, but he managed to push his wolf back, but just barely. The beast was just beneath the surface waiting for a chance to punish all who had hurt his mate. "If he dies—"

Artemus actually grinned. "I know, I know, you'll kill me slowly." The Magi looked at the doctor who had moved closer. "Do you have either atropine or epinephrine?"

Doc Houston nodded. "I have both, but I fail to see how that will revive the young man. I can't hear a heartbeat, do you, Alpha?"

Grant shook his head, "No, but—"

"But you don't feel a break in the bond," Artemus finished as he glanced over at Sandy. "Nor do you, young Omega. If Richard was truly gone, you both would feel it." The Magi glanced back at the doctor who stood with a syringe in his hand. "Now this is what we need to do. I can feel the magic of the collar that prevented its removal has been lifted, but the key is obviously with Alpha Clifton. We need to break the lock and then destroy the collar or it will continue to drain Richard's life force."

"What the he—er—heck is going on?" Sparky asked as he held the struggling young pup tightly.

They all looked at the human lying on the bed. His form was surrounded by a strange golden aura and the tattoo on his arm pulsed with the same strange glow that had happened when Sparky was thrown across the room. "If that means what I think it does, I'm outa here. I don't intend to fly Air-Ricky again anytime soon."

Artemus shook his head. "I haven't felt anything this powerful since the last Bellatorum and Omega were killed."

"We don't have time for a history lesson. Tell us how to save my mate, Magi!" Alpha Grant placed his hand on Ricky's hair. He leaned down to whisper into his mate's ear. "You hold on, *Semme'*, remember your promise to see where the fates will lead us. I'll be here waiting for you to return to me my mate."

"The glow is getting weaker," Doc Houston remarked. "I don't think we have much time to get this young man back."

"You're right doctor," Artemus answered. "If we're lucky, a dose of Atropine will increase the heart rate and bring the young man back to us once we remove the collar."

Alpha Grant stood up while he pushed aside a stray lock of hair from Ricky's face. "I can break the lock, but how do we destroy the collar?"

"That's where I come in." The Magi glanced at Dakota. "Do you have the things you took from me?"

Dakota looked at Alpha Grant who simply nodded his agreement. "Yes, I can get them for you and bring them here."

Artemus shook his head. "No, that will take too long, I can feel the life thread getting thinner and his aura is almost gone. Once the Alpha removes the collar, I'll take it and follow you. In fact, it would be better if it's destroyed away from the human."

Grant didn't need any further instruction. He reached forward and gently turned the collar until the lock was in the front. He studied it for a moment before he placed his hands on either side of the lock and pulled. He knew he had to be careful as his shifter strength could easily break his mate's neck. He continued to pull at the thick metal until he heard a click and the collar dropped from Ricky's neck.

Artemus reached over and grabbed the cursed object and quickly followed Dakota from the room. Grant watched as Doc Houston quickly placed the large needle over his mate's heart. The needle was plunged directly into the heart muscle as the medicine was dispensed. Grant stepped back as Ricky gasped and sat up clutching his chest before he fell back on to the bed.

"Ricky!" Grant cried as looked up at the doctor.

"His heart rate is a bit fast and his breathing a bit rapid but assuming there is no other damage, he should recover Alpha." Doc Houston shook his head. "I was sure he was gone—"

"Why isn't my brother awake?" Sandy demanded as he crawled onto the bed and lay down beside his sibling. His slim arms slipped around Ricky's chest as tears fell from the young shifter's eyes. "Artie said he would get better, but this isn't better. Ricky? Wake up, Ricky, I'm sorry about before, I didn't mean it."

Grant looked at the doctor who shrugged. "It's up to him now. I'm sure part of the reason he's not awake is because he's just tired, Sandy. We need to leave him alone and let him get some rest. Why don't we go to the kitchen and see what Vicky is making for dinner?"

"But I wanna stay with Ricky—he needs me!" Sandy argued.

Sparky stepped forward and pulled the young pup from the bed. "I'm sure Alpha Grant will let you know as soon as he wakes up. In the meantime, I just brought home the latest racing game—I bet you a plate of Vicky's cookies that you can't beat me."

Sandy glared at Sparky. "Can too! I beat you last time."

Sparky winked. "Ah, young Jedi, but that was because I didn't unleash my secret weapon. This time I can't lose!" Sandy began to follow Sparky towards the door. Grant chuckled as he listened to the shifters banter. "No cheating!" Sandy's voice echoed in the hall before the door closed.

"It's good to see Sparky with Sandy. The boy obviously missed his friend," Doc Houston said as he started an IV and inserted the needle into Ricky's vein. At Grant's look the doctor explained, "It's just fluids to keep him hydrated. We don't need any other complications. If he doesn't wake soon, I'll add something to give him the nutrients he'll need to recover."

"Will he be okay, Doc?" Grant asked as he pulled the chair in the room closer to the bed.

The doctor looked down at Ricky for a moment before he answered, "Normally I would be worried about the amount of time his brain went without oxygen. But somehow, I get the feeling the goddess has better plans for this young man. I noticed that he already heals faster than normal humans. Between his bond with you and whatever gifts he's received from the goddess—I think he'll be just fine." The doctor placed a hand on Grant's shoulder. "Just give him time. His body has been through a lot, even for a Bellatorum.

"A what?" Grant asked, as he smoothed the blanket over his sleeping mate.

Doc Houston smiled. "Don't worry I'm sure Artemus will bring you up to speed as soon as Ricky recovers. In fact, I think both of you need to talk to the Magi. Did you know his father died trying to protect the last Omega and his Bellatorum?"

Grant glanced back up. "So he knows all about Omegas?"

"Yep, and he's willing to help young Sandy, as well. Considering where you found the Magi, I'd say fate was smiling on you and your mate." The doctor gathered his things and walked towards the door to the room. "I'll check back later to see how he's doing; in the meantime, congratulations on finding your *Semme*, Alpha."

• • ❖ • •

Ricky blinked at the white fog that surrounded him. He had no idea where he was and it frightened him. The last thing he remembered was Alpha Grant's bite and an orgasm that had made him see stars—then nothing. "You have nothing to fear young one," a soft voice seemed to surround him. But he couldn't see the source.

"Who are—where am I?" Ricky asked.

"The 'who' in your question will become clear to you some day as to the where, you are neither here nor there. This is the place of decisions and it is time you made yours Bellatorum." Ricky shook his head. He should be afraid and yet the voice calmed him. For the first time in his life he felt truly at peace.

"Am I dead?" Ricky whispered.

A soft chuckle surrounded him. "No, young one, it is still not your time. I have much planned for you and your friends. However, even I have my limits. I cannot overcome free will. So the choice is now yours, return to your life along with all it entails, or remain here where nothing will touch you until your time to move on arrives."

"It is peaceful here." Ricky sat down and pulled his knees up to his chest. He sighed as he reached up to feel the slightly raised skin on his neck. The place where Grant had bit him still throbbed slightly. He rubbed at it absently as he continued to think out loud. "I made a promise to Grant and my brother. I know Grant thinks I'm strong and Sandy." Ricky chuckled. "Well Sandy thinks I'm Superman. But I'm not strong—"

"And that would be where you're wrong, my young warrior. Many before you have felt the same and yet they have found their way. You will too. Strength does not only come from muscle and bone but also from the heart and soul. Besides, I have provided you with someone to help you bear the weight you carry. Allow him to take over when the responsibility you carry becomes too heavy for one person." The voice seemed to flow over him, caressing him as it spoke. Ricky swore he could feel a gentle hand rest on his shoulders for a brief moment.

"I don't know how to protect Sandy. I don't even know what I'm supposed to protect him from. I mean, I know letting Alpha Clifton get his hands on him would be bad, but how am I to help him when I don't understand myself?" Ricky glanced around but still there was nothing but a gentle breeze in the white mist.

"I have provided you with one who will guide you and your brother. You will soon learn that you are more than capable to handle any challenge. In fact you and your friends have to succeed or all will be lost." Ricky looked deeper into the mist and though he could make out a vague feminine form, but before he could focus it was gone again.

"You're starting to sound like a bad impression of Yoda. Are you trying to tell me that the fate of the world depends on me? Because I gotta say, if that's the case—you and the world are royally screwed. I can't even handle my own life much less protect the rest of the planet." Ricky shook his head as he tried to understand what was happening to him.

Suddenly the peaceful feeling he'd had since he woke up disappeared and was replaced with a sense of foreboding. The mist was no longer a soft white but had begun to turn ominously dark. The voice was no longer calming, but threatening as it responded.

"How dare you question me?" The voice thundered while lightening streaked through the sky. Ricky could feel the anger as it surrounded him. He dropped his eyes and hunched into himself, waiting for a blow that never seemed to land. He stayed curled into himself with his eyes closed until a light touch on his shoulder caused him to look up cautiously. The mist was back to the peaceful white from before. "I apologize, young human; it is hard to remember that your society no longer understands who or what I am." In place

176

of the anger he'd felt before, a deep sadness surrounded him. He felt the need to comfort the unseen being.

"I'm sorry, I'm just trying to understand what it is you think I can do to help you? As you said, I'm just human and you're—well you are obviously some kind of god right?" Ricky stood and looked around before he sighed and sat back down. It was obvious the being wasn't going to show itself to him. In fact, he figured whoever it was had gone because there was nothing but silence for what seemed like a long time. Just as he was beginning to think this was all some kind of weird dream, the voice returned.

"I am not allowed to explain everything to you. Some things must just be accepted without true understanding. However, I can tell you that the reason we now must follow these rules is because in our superiority we allowed one to unleash the unforgivable power. A force that will mean the end to all that is good in the universe, in other words the balance between good and evil will be permanently tilted to the darkness. You, your brother, your friends and your children are the answer to keep the delicate balance."

Ricky shook his head before he stood and wiped at the knees of his pants. He now knew this wouldn't be possible.

"You said 'my children'? I hate to break the news to you, but I'm gay and I'm mated to a male wolf shifter. There won't be any biological children." A soft chuckle filled the air around him.

"There is more than one way to have a biological child, human. In fact, your seeds will be sown and begin to produce before you know it. Just remember, there is always a reason for what happens, even if you might not understand it at the time. Through adversity some of the world's greatest leaders have emerged. You are no different my young warrior."

Ricky couldn't believe what he was hearing. But as he was preparing to object, the voice interrupted him.

"But enough with the questions, I must have your decision."

Ricky sighed as he rubbed the tattoo on his arm. He swore he could hear Grant's voice pleading with him to remember his promise to give their mating a chance. While he still felt the Alpha had only acted out of sympathy, he had promised him he'd at least try. Maria's words also echoed in his head—he'd promised to take care of Sandy. There was no way he could keep his promises if he stayed here. He glanced around at the white mist one last time. It would be so easy to just stay here and yet, his heart had already made the decision. The wind began to swirl around him as he took his first step forward since arriving in this strange place.

"I will keep my promise. I choose my mate and my brother."

CHAPTER NINETEEN

GRANT STOOD AND STRETCHED AS HE WALKED TOWARDS THE window. The ground was brushed with a layer of snow while small flakes kissed the windowpanes, only to swirl away. Lake Serenity was frozen over now and the mountains that framed it now wore permanent caps of white. It was beautiful and yet the one who would make this moment perfect still lay quietly in the bed behind him. A soft knock at the door caused him to turn around.

"Come in."

David walked in and glanced at the bed before he returned his attention to his older brother. "I just wanted to let you know that the last of the Willow Creek Pack members have arrived and been given temporary housing. Luckily we had enough space for now, but we'll need to build more homes in the spring."

Grant nodded as he walked to the bed and sat down in the chair that now felt as if it had become a part of him. "How are the hired mercenaries doing?"

"Blaze has them under control." David sighed as he ran a weary hand through his short-cropped hair. "I hope we never have to do something like that again. Even Dad was affected by the number we had to kill. I just don't understand why more of them didn't join us; it was almost like they feared something more than death." The Beta shrugged. "But then I guess it's fewer we have to keep an eye on."

"Those who agreed to join us are still under guard, right?" Grant gently traced the faded scar on his mate's arm as he spoke. It had been almost three weeks and still there had been no change. In that time the Willow Creek Pack had been disbanded. There was no sign of Alpha Clifton and the hunt for their missing pack mates was still underway.

David winked. "Don't worry, big brother, they are wearing a special ankle bracelet. Not to mention we've finished installing the new surveillance cameras throughout the Alpha compound as well as throughout the pack lands. The bird and animal population has grown significantly after our latest success with the drones. Nothing happens without Jason and I knowing about it." The middle brother walked towards the bed and looked down at the quiet human. "He'll come back to you, Grant."

"He has to—" Grant said softly as he pulled the blanket up higher. "I can still feel him you know." Grant touched his head. "The connection is weak, but he's still here. Doc says he will wake up once his body is ready, but I wonder if it's not something more."

"You think he doesn't want to wake up?" David asked.

"Would you?" Grant glared up at his brother. "All he's known is pain and fear. Hell, from what I've learned, we are lucky that he is still with us at all. I never should have left him alone—"

David growled as he glared at his brother. "So what are you going to do? Lock him up or chain him to your bed? Get real big brother. No one could have stopped what happened. You sitting here day after day, avoiding the pack, your friends and even your family won't bring Ricky back and it certainly won't prevent bad things from happening to him again in the future. Give it a break, big brother, and face facts, even you can't control everything."

"That's my job damn it! I'm responsible for every member of this pack, for their safety and well being. How will it look if I can't even protect my own mate!"

Grant could feel the hair on his arms begin to sprout as he faced off against his brother. The stress of the past weeks was finally getting to him. His wolf had been fighting for control ever since the threat to his mate had been discovered. He knew he should have given his animal a chance to run free but he was afraid if he left his mate, the human would once again be gone when he returned.

"So this isn't about Ricky then is it, Alpha," David snarled. "This is about you not being as all powerful as you want to believe. Well let me tell you something—"

A soft groan from the bed was followed by a raspy voice, "You two are loud enough to wake the dead!"

Grant rushed to the side of the bed. Two hazel eyes blinked up at him. "You're awake, my mate." The Alpha couldn't keep the smile from his face or the feelings of relief that surged through him. Even his wolf was howling with joy. His mate had come back to him.

Suddenly the argument he had with his sibling no longer mattered; nothing mattered except for the slight human who lay in the bed looking up at him with confused eyes. The realization shocked the Alpha.

For years he told himself he couldn't have a true mate because it wouldn't be fair to his mate or his pack. How could he provide each with the care and focus required to be a good mate and a good leader to his pack? It was the main reason he had avoided any kind of emotional relationship. He'd seen the strain it has placed on his father and mother's relationship. They had come out stronger, but all had not always been good between them. However now he realized he could have both—he would have both and he dared anyone who tried to argue differently.

"Just relax, Ricky. You are safe. Nothing and no one will hurt you any longer, I promise."

Ricky swallowed and grimaced. He tried to reach up with has hand to rub his throat but was stopped by the IV attached to his arm. He glanced down and frowned before looking back toward the Alpha for an explanation. Grant gently pushed his mate's arm back to the bed. He grabbed the glass of water from the nightstand and helped Ricky sip from the cup.

He glanced up at his brother and ordered, "Get Doc Houston and let Sandy know his brother is awake."

"I can't tell you how happy I am that you're back with us," David replied as he gently patted Ricky's knee. "Maybe you can get my stubborn brother to at least take a shower now." David wrinkled his nose. "Pretty soon we'll have to call in a hazmat team to fumigate the place."

Grant growled. "Okay, okay, big brother," David said as he held his hands up and slowly backed towards the door. However before he left his sibling he couldn't resist one last jab. "Are you sure you're not a bear shifter? 'Cause I gotta say you got the grouchy part down pat!"

181

The Alpha stood to his full height as he glared at his soon to be extinct sibling, "Doc Houston—Now!"

David tilted his head in a sign of submission but a grin remained on his handsome face. He gave Grant a two finger salute before walking calmly through the door. Grant took a deep breath and tried to calm himself. Normally his brother's antics were just annoying and unfortunately today was no different. He sighed but then smiled as he heard a soft chuckle from the bed. It was a sound he didn't often hear from his mate but one he would make sure he heard more of in the future. As his eyes followed the gaze of his *Semme'*, Grant noticed that the water glass he had been holding for Ricky was now empty. Unfortunately, a large portion of it had splashed down the front of his mate's chest and onto the bed.

Grant groaned as he quickly placed the now empty glass back on the nightstand. "I'm so sorry; let me get something to clean you up."

Before Ricky could even form a word or make a move, Grant was on the phone asking for fresh bedding. He raced toward the ensuite bathroom and quickly returned with a large fluffy towel that he used to wipe down the human's chest. The whole time Ricky stared up at him, his eyes crinkled at the corners and a grin lit his face. It wasn't the first impression he'd wanted to make with his *Semme'* upon awakening, but at least the hazel eyes were no longer filled with fear or confusion.

"How are you feeling, my mate?"

The humor left the man's eyes as he shrugged and looked down at his clasped hands. There was a slight blush to the still too pale cheeks. "M'kay I guess," Ricky croaked.

The Alpha sat on the edge of the bed. He could feel the unease, the doubt and yes, even some shame coming through their newly formed link. But he refused to press further. He wanted his *Semme'* to trust him enough to actually tell him what was wrong.

Grant gently tilted the man's head upward until he could see his mate's eyes. "Talk to me, Ricky. I can't help if I don't know what is wrong."

Ricky reached up with his free hand to once again feel where the collar had been. The skin had healed while he had been in a coma. Grant remembered the reddened skin from what appeared to be some kind of contact burns. Even now he could feel his own anger return over what had been done to the human. No being should have been forced to wear the cursed device. One of Grant's first orders had been to make sure that there were no more slave collars at the Willow Creek Pack. He would not stand for them to be used for any reason. No being had the right to own another, regardless of their status. He was brought from his musing when Ricky moved his fingers to trace the mating mark on his neck.

"So it worked," Ricky said softly.

Grant smiled as he gently traced the scar with his own fingers. He watched as Ricky actually shivered at the touch, a small moan escaped from his lips. The mating mark would be an erogenous zone for the human from now on; one that the Alpha intended to explore often.

"Yes it did, my mate."

However before he could continue the discussion, there was a sharp knock on the door followed by a white blur as the doorway opened to reveal not only the doctor, but one of the female wolves who helped keep the Alpha's home clean and of course Sandy, who for some reason was in his wolf form.

"Sandy was outside going for a run with Jason when David gave him the news," Doc Houston said with a chuckle. "Apparently our young wolf couldn't wait to get dressed before coming to see his brother. Good thing Elaina here stopped to grab his clothes while she was getting the clean bedding you requested, Alpha."

Grant felt his hackles rise as he watched the Omega wolf begin to rub his face in the crook of Ricky's neck.

A calming hand on his arm brought his attention back to the Doctor. "Give them a moment, Alpha, no one doubts who the human belongs to now that you've mated."

Ricky must have heard the remark as his eyes widened for a moment before he gently pushed his brother down onto the bed. Grant could feel the fear from his mate. Taking a deep breath he managed to calm his wolf as he watched Sandy continue to try to crawl into his brother's lap. Logically he knew the two were siblings and his wolf would eventually get used to seeing another wolf getting affection from his mate. Unfortunately, his wolf wasn't on board at this moment and was pushing to reclaim his mate.

"Sandy?" Grant managed to keep the growl out of his voice as the young pup turned to look at him. "We need to get your brother into some dry clothes,

Elaina has to change the bedding and Doc Houston needs to take a quick look at him to make sure everything is okay. You need to shift and get dressed while we get your brother situated."

Sandy looked at his brother and whined softly. Ricky smiled and scratched between his brother's ears. "I'm okay, little brother. A little wet and tired, but I'll be just fine. Now do what your Alpha has commanded."

Grant couldn't help but grin as the young wolf actually managed to huff and roll his eyes before he jumped from the bed and grabbed his clothes from Elaina in his mouth. His tail swished as he stalked from the room but not before he glanced back one more time at his brother.

"Go on, get changed, pup. Before you come back, run down and ask my mother to put together a tray for Ricky too," Alpha Grant made the comment sound like a suggestion but even Sandy recognized it as an order from his Alpha. The Omega dropped his head slightly in acknowledgement and with a final swish of his tail left the room. Doc Houston moved towards the bed and glanced at Grant briefly before beginning his examination. The Alpha wanted to kick himself, not only was his mate afraid of him again but now everyone was walking on eggshells around him. He should have better control of his wolf.

"Wow, who died in here?" Sparky entered the room and stopped at the foot of the bed. A large smile covered his face as he watched the doctor remove the IV from Ricky's arm. "Obviously it isn't our young human friend here, although I have to say it is the first time I've actually seen someone actually look half drowned from a wet dream." The wolf turned to wink at the Alpha. "Of course if the heat between you two got any hotter, I can see why you'd want to douse the flames just a bit." Before Grant could respond Sparky continued, "Your mother sent me up here to find out what young Ricky can eat."

Doc Houston stood and patted the human on the shoulder. "I think clear broth for now and maybe some tea with honey to soothe his throat a bit. We'll see how he keeps that down and gradually work him up to solids." The doctor looked at Grant and smiled. "I actually expected him to be in worse shape, but from what I can see all he needs now is a little more rest, plenty of fluids and some good food. I've never seen a human heal this quickly—maybe it has something to do with that strange tattoo. But whatever the cause, he should be able to be up and around in a day or so."

Grant noticed Ricky was shivering slightly. It was time to get him into dry clothes and a dry bed. He still couldn't believe he'd spilled the water all over his mate. Ricky put his legs over the side of the bed and slowly began to sit up. The Alpha reached over to steady his mate. He didn't want to frighten the man further by making any quick moves. He could still feel fear from his mate and his wolf didn't like it. The human had to know that being mated meant he couldn't be anywhere safer.

"Let me help you, Sunshine," Grant said softly as he placed a steadying hand on the human's shoulder.

Ricky sighed as he pushed back a stray lock of his long hair behind his ear. "I guess I could use some help."

Hazel eyes looked warily up at Grant from beneath his mate's wispy bangs. Grant would do anything to get the mischievous light back in them but he had no idea how to go about it. The human stood but his knees quickly buckled. Without saying a word, Grant picked his mate up and carried him towards the bathroom.

"Well it's about time you carried him over the threshold—seriously, you have this whole wooing, mating and bringing home your forever someone kind of backwards," Sparky remarked as he moved to open the door to the bathroom. "Of course, when I find my mate I plan to do it up right."

Doc Houston chuckled. "Son, if you find your mate a room full of scantily clad men won't get your motor running."

"Who said I'd have a room full?" Sparky winked at Ricky. "I plan to be the star of the show." The flamboyant shifter swayed as if he was holding onto a pole while grinding his hips. "After seeing all this—my mate would surely skip the wooing and go right to hot monkey sex."

Grant shook his head but smiled at the chuckle he heard from his mate. The man was relaxed in his arms. His *Semme'* even had his arms looped around his neck and rested his head against his shoulder. The Alpha didn't mind the ribbing, especially if it put the twinkle back in his mate's eyes. As he entered the bathroom, he gently placed his precious cargo on the closed toilet seat.

He glanced back at Sparky. "I think I can take it from here."

Sparky cocked his head and placed a hand on his hip. "You sure you don't need a few tips? After all, Alpha, you are a bit rusty—"

185

"Out!" Grant ordered but made sure he didn't put much heat into the order. He'd noticed his *Semme'* was sensitive to his growl. Sparky winked as he turned and grabbed the doctor's arm. The two quickly exited the room followed shortly after by Elaina. The sudden quiet in the room should have felt uncomfortable, but it didn't. In fact, Grant noticed Ricky still appeared relaxed, although he shivered harder now.

The Alpha turned and started the shower. The large stall was big enough for two which would come in handy for what he had planned. He turned and knelt in front of his mate who seemed to find a loose string fascinating on his sleeping pants.

Grant smiled as he took the hand into his own. "We need to get you warmed up, Sunshine, and then we'll get you fed."

Ricky nodded but as he tried to stand, his legs wobbled. Before he could fall, Grant gently pulled the loose pants down and helped his mate get out of the wet garment. He lowered his mate back down on to the toilet seat before he stepped back and began to slowly remove his own clothing. He remembered the chuckle Sparky had gotten and wondered if he could get the same response. Normally he would have been mortified at doing something like this, but he knew if he wanted to win the human's heart, he needed to let him see another side to his personality.

He tossed his shirt to the side and began to swivel his hips as his fingers released the top button of his jeans. As he began to lower them, he turned and pulled down one side briefly showing his cheek before he pulled it back up. He glanced back and saw a smile on his mate's face. Grant knew he didn't have much time as his wolf was urging him to care for his mate but the need to see those hazel eyes sparkle drove him to continue his impromptu strip tease.

The Alpha turned and slowly lowered his jeans, allowing his member to spring up and slap his abs. He smiled as he saw the humor in his mate's eyes begin to change. The scent of lust filled the room as he continued to sway to his own internal music. He watched as Ricky's tongue came out to play, wetting his chapped lips before quickly disappearing. With a final flourish he managed to kick his jeans aside. He moved slowly towards the human, stalking his prey in a way his wolf fully approved. As he lowered his head to press his lips against Ricky's, he couldn't help the soft groan that joined with his mate's. For a moment he allowed himself to explore the delicious cavern before he pulled

186

back. He smiled again as his mate tried to follow him but he had noticed the shivers running through the man's slight frame. "As much as I'd love to continue, we need to get you warmed up." Grant held up his hand as he heard his *Semme'* begin to object.

He gathered his mate into his arms and stepped into the now warm spray of the shower. "But, I didn't say I'd stop exploring—"

Ricky groaned softly as the Alpha began to wash his mate. He worked his way down the man's body, keeping a steadying arm around his waist. Hazel eyes were half-mast as the man leaned into him. Grant pulled his mate against his chest and let the water run over them both to finish rinsing the soap from their bodies. He reached down and grasped Ricky's engorged cock in his hand and began to slowly stroke the velvety skin. He could feel the organ pulse in his hand.

"Oh god," Ricky moaned as he pushed his hips forward to get more friction.

Grant sped up the strokes while using his other hand to tweak first one nipple and then the other. He could feel his mate's need as his own weeping cock rubbed between Ricky's slippery ass cheeks. It would be so easy to slip inside but he wouldn't do anything to hurt his mate. Not only did he need more than just soap to ease his way, he knew his mate was tiring. It was time. Grant leaned forward and nipped lightly over his mark on Ricky's shoulder.

As the human shuddered he whispered, "Come for me Sunshine."

Ricky cried out as his seed painted the tiled walls. His own knees felt weak as his own orgasm ripped through him.

Grant grabbed his mate tighter as he felt the man's knees begin to give way. "Time to get dried off and get you back to bed my mate," Grant said softly as he quickly finished cleaning them both up before he picked the man up in his arms.

A short time later they both lay in the bed. The Alpha had gotten clean pajama bottoms for each of them, although he had to roll up the legs on the pair he'd given his smaller mate. It was obvious one of the first things they needed to do when Ricky felt better was to go shopping for some clothes. The meager offerings that came from the battered duffle bag wouldn't last the man more than a few days and while Grant wouldn't mind if his *Semme'* never wore clothes again—he had to admit it would be counterproductive to kill off anyone who looked at what was now his.

"I should probably go see what is keeping your brother with the food," Grant said as he began to get up from the bed. A hand on his arm stopped him.

"Don't go," Ricky said softly. He quickly glanced down as a blush rose on his cheeks. For a moment Grant thought the man would withdraw but his mate surprised him once again as he continued, "I—I feel safe when you are near me." His *Semme'* chewed on his lower lip. "Why is that? I've just met you and yet part of me feels as if I've known you my whole life. Sometimes I can even feel…" Ricky looked up "…I sense what you're thinking. It's kind of like I know when Sandy is upset."

Grant nodded as he lay back down and drew his mate against his chest. He shuddered slightly as his mate's hand slowly traced the muscles on his chest. "It is part of the mating bond between true Semme'. The first time I met you, I knew you were the missing part of my soul and once we completed the bond our connection simply confirmed it. As our bond grows stronger, you and I will be able to share our thoughts as well. I like to think it's because we really are one, two parts to the same whole."

"You mean telepathically?" Ricky asked in an awestruck voice.

"That is what I've been told," Grant replied.

Ricky was silent for a moment before he shook his head and sighed. "Well that would have come in handy when Beta Biff decided to grab me." The human looked up, his hazel eyes were filled with sadness. "I'm sorry, Grant—I know I should have trusted you but…"

"…you had only known one other Alpha and he didn't keep his promises," Grant finished. He ran a hand through the soft golden waves of hair before he kissed the top of his mate's head. "There is nothing to forgive. All I ask is that in the future, we talk about what upsets you—no more running, Sunshine. This is now your home and I'd kill anyone who tried to take you from me again."

"Sandy has already moved in." Ricky chuckled. "When I talked about leaving, he was your biggest supporter you know. Of course, it could have something to do with the fantastic bedroom you put together for him." His mate glared up at Grant for a moment and used his finger to push into his chest. "Which we need to discuss as well; you need to learn the word 'no' or my little brother will run right over you."

Grant sighed. "I know I should have asked you but in my defense, things have been a little hectic around here."

"True and I understand. But going forward, we need to talk about things and put up a united front—" Ricky stammered and looked back down quickly. "I'm sorry, I forgot he's one of your pack now and you can do what you want."

Grant refused to let his mate hide from him again. He gently tilted his mate's face up until he could see the man's face. Using his finger, he traced the light spatter of freckles on the bridge of his mate's nose. The need to kiss his *Semme'* was strong, but he knew he needed to make Ricky understand his role.

"It is true that Sandy is one of my pack, as are you now. As the Alpha of the pack, it is my job to take care of all the members. However, make no mistake Ricky." Grant tapped the tip of the man's nose. "We are partners not just in bed, but in all things. That includes raising Sandy as well as any decisions that affect our lives. There will be times when you will have to follow my lead, but I will always listen to what you have to say."

Grant traced the tattoo on his mate's arm. "And this means you were chosen to be Sandy's protector and his guide. Even an Alpha cannot take that role away from you."

Before Ricky could respond, Grant could hear the rattle of dishes. He grinned as he heard the object of their discussion complain to Sparky. "Why do I have to carry the heavy one?"

"Because young Padawan, you must learn balance—now pay attention or you'll drop the tray," Sparky replied. Grant sat up with his back against the headboard and helped Ricky to lean against him. At the questioning look in his mate's eyes he chuckled, "We're about to be invaded."

He no more than finished speaking than a light knock at the door sounded before it slowly opened.

Grant couldn't help the laugh that bubbled up when Sparky entered one hand over Sandy's eyes and the other over his own. "Let me know when you two love birds are decent—we have young eyes here and I wouldn't want him to be scarred for life!" Sparky split his fingers and brazenly gazed between the gaps. Sandy struggled against the hand over his face but stilled when he heard his brother's laughter. The sound was music to Grant's ears.

"Get in here, you two. Ricky is going to starve at the rate you are bringing his lunch," Grant growled but there was no heat in his voice. Sandy squirmed

189

out of Sparky's reach and raced towards the bed, the tray in his hands wobbled precariously but at the last moment the young pup managed to keep the food from spilling. Sparky took the loaded tray from Sandy.

"Compliments of your mother." Sparky's voice rose to a slightly higher pitch as he wagged his finger at the pair in the bed while he mimicked the woman. "Now you make sure both of those boys eat everything on this tray or else!" The shifter shuddered slightly as he placed the tray on the bed. "So please, Alpha—Sandy and I want to live to see the next sunrise. For our sakes, lick the plates clean!"

Grant glanced sideways as Ricky ruffled his brother's hair. "Hey squirt! What did you bring me?" The young Omega began to name off everything on the tray, "There's chicken soup, but it don't have any noodles or anything so I'm not sure why they call it chicken soup and Grandma Vicky made fresh bread this morning so you could have some toast, there's bacon and eggs for Alpha Grant and I guess he can have some of the toast too; oh and she let me squeeze the oranges which was kind of messy but also fun; she didn't even complain when I got some of it on my new shirt although she made me change but it's okay because I have more than two shirts now—can you believe it. Oh and she told me to tell you if you eat everything she might let you have some of her special cookies later—of course, she said she'd need my help with that too…"

As Grant listened to the young wolf continue to ramble, he realized for the first time in a long time, he was finally home and his family was now complete. He knew everything wasn't settled between them, but as long as he had Ricky by his side and his new son, anything else would be handled. The only thing he really wondered about right now was—how did that boy managed to talk so long without taking a single breath?

CHAPTER TWENTY
Epilogue

RICKY WALKED QUIETLY DOWN THE STAIRS, PAUSING HALF-way down to listen before he moved. It had been three days since he'd been out of the bedroom upstairs and this was the first morning he'd woken to find the room empty of a certain over protective mate. A slow smile crossed the human's face as he once again realized it hadn't been a dream; he was the mate of the Alpha of the Windy River Pack. Still while he appreciated Grant's need to make sure he took things slow, he didn't think he could take one more day of being waited on. His stomach growled slightly to remind him why he was making his escape.

It was strange that he didn't hear anyone else in the house though. Of course it was after ten o'clock, which was something else he wasn't used to; sleeping past the crack of dawn. He figured that the Alpha and his brothers were doing whatever they had done before he and his brother had arrived. With luck he could grab a cup of coffee and a quick breakfast before he was found and forced to return back to his bed. The truth was he felt fine, better than fine actually which meant it was time for him get off his ass and do something other than playing the damsel in distress. The problem was he had absolutely no idea what he could do or what his new role would entail. At least in his previous pack he'd known where he stood and what was expected, now not so much. Grant had been pretty tight lipped whenever he asked.

He paused outside the door to the kitchen and smiled when he saw Vicky Walker kneading dough on a floured board. Her braided light brown hair had streaks of silver-gray and yet even though she appeared to be in her sixties, she was still a beautiful woman. His smile grew as he saw the smudge of flour on her forehead. For a moment he wondered if he should just go back upstairs, but before he could move the she-wolf turned and wiped her hands on the apron she was wearing. "Well I wondered how long it would be before you made your escape. Come on in and sit down, I'll make you something to eat. Lord knows you need to put some more meat on those skinny bones of yours," Vicky said warmly.

Ricky looked down at the loose fitting t-shirt he wore and realized the woman was right. He'd lost even more weight during his recent visit with his old Alpha. Sometimes he wondered how Grant could find him attractive. Between the scars he bore on his body and his loss of muscle tone, no one in their right mind would see him as being sexy, and yet Grant couldn't seem to keep from touching Ricky. He jumped slightly as a light hand rested on his shoulder before he was directed to a chair at the kitchen table.

"Come, sit down, son. You know I've been waiting for a long time for my Grant to find the one who could help him with the load he carries." She paused before she moved toward the fridge to remove a carton of eggs and some bacon from inside. "I'm glad he found the right person."

"Me?" Ricky squeaked.

Vicky began to crack the eggs into a bowl while she waited for the pan to heat for the bacon. Without losing a beat she continued, "You don't see it now, young man, but I can already see a warrior who will stand beside my son and provide him with the support he needs to finally become the man he was meant to be."

Ricky shook his head. "Your son doesn't need my help. In fact, from what I've seen so far, he's pretty amazing."

He had listened in while Grant held meetings with his brothers and some of the other pack members. His mate had refused to leave the bedroom, so when something required his attention; he handled it in the room while keeping an eye on Ricky. The shifter never tired and always seemed to know what to do to solve the problem.

Yesterday he'd handled hiring some contractors to begin building more homes on pack lands. Even though they couldn't break ground until spring, there was much that needed to be done to ensure there would not only be a place for the new enforcers and others who may be seeking sanctuary due to the actions of Alpha Clifton, but to put in a new training facility as well. He also had talked to his brothers about changing the gym room in the basement to a war room. Their offices weren't big enough to accommodate the number of people who had been added recently. Apparently they had used the formal dining room to plan his rescue.

Grant had introduced him to the head school master, Beauregard Sheridan. At first Ricky had wondered how someone who reminded him vaguely of Mr. Kotter from the old sitcom on TV had become the Principal. But after being reminded that even though he looked to be in his thirties—in fact the shifter had actually been a teacher for more than seventy years before he'd been hired to run the school in Sugar Creek. Because the town was still fairly small, all the children attended the same school. Ricky was just glad there was one since the last pack he'd belonged to relied on the parents to teach the children to read and write.

Mr. Sheridan had agreed to provide a tutor to help his younger brother make up for any gaps in his learning so that Sandy could begin attending classes. He also understood that Sandy would have his own security guard. In fact, there had been discussion about providing some additional security to the school including a safe room to be built in the basement of the facility. Until they knew for sure what Alpha Clifton had planned and who else may be involved, Grant wanted to ensure their children and others who weren't able to fight would have a safe place to go to in the event of an attack. Other 'safe havens' were being built throughout the pack lands as well but it would all take time—time that Ricky had a feeling they were running out of.

The high-light of the meeting with the schoolmaster was Sandy's enthusiasm to finally be able to attend a real school. He smiled as he remembered how excited his little brother had been when Mr. Sheridan had provided him with a list of things he'd need to bring to school. To say his brother was excited was an understatement. Sandy had wanted to start today, but Mr. Sheridan thought it would be better if his brother started on Monday of the following week. That would give the tutor time to meet with Sandy and set up a plan to get him on track. Grant had arranged for Sparky to take the young shifter on another shopping trip, which is where his younger brother was this morning.

It had been a full three days and even better nights. While they hadn't done anything too strenuous, Ricky had learned more ways to be brought to orgasm than he'd ever thought possible. While it was wonderful, he still couldn't wait for Grant to take him again. His hole clenched and his dick hardened at just the thought of how wonderful it had felt when he'd been claimed. After years of being used, to look forward to the pleasure he'd discovered with Grant had been surprising. The old fears, no longer paralyzed him as they had before but he still couldn't orgasm without permission. Yet for the first time in his life, he actually thought about initiating sex with his mate.

He had planned on trying to coax his mate into doing more than just rubbing off this morning but Grant had been gone. The bed had been cold when Ricky woke, which meant his mate had been gone for some time. It must have been something important to force his mate from his duty of ensuring Ricky didn't exhaust himself—thank heavens. Yet he still felt disappointed to find his mate gone when he woke. Of course, maybe it was for the best since he had no idea how to entice his new lover; he'd spent too many years being told what to do.

He was brought out of his musings when Vicky placed a plate of scrambled eggs and bacon on the table in front of him. She added a couple pieces of toast and a cup of coffee to complete the meal. She grabbed a cup for herself and sat down across from Ricky.

Grant's mother waited a few moments for him to start eating before she continued her conversation. "You know, shortly after Forest and I met, things began to change for our pack." She took a sip of her coffee and looked past Ricky. "We aren't Semme' mates like you and Grant, but when I first saw Forest standing in that clearing…" A soft smile graced the woman's face "…well let's just say I couldn't imagine fate would find anyone who could make my heart sing the same way. But even feeling as I did, when Forest asked me to be his mate, I almost walked away."

"Why?" Ricky found himself entranced by Vicky's story.

Vicky shrugged. "He was Alpha and I was simply a shifter whose family had sought safety with his pack. I didn't see what I could offer. But Forest wouldn't take no for an answer and before I knew it, I was mated and a short time later I was pregnant with Grant."

The female wolf shifter stood and grabbed the coffee pot to refill both their cups. She glanced back at Ricky and smiled. "So I figured that was my job, to help raise the next in line to be Alpha and for a while, that is the role I played. We had two more sons and our pack continued to grow in size."

"Sounds nice," Ricky replied as he took a sip of the coffee she had poured. For a moment he wondered what it would have been like to be raised by two parents who had wanted him. Grant and his brothers obviously had been cherished; which is probably why they were the men they were today.

"It was," Vicky continued. "However the one thing about life is, just when you think you have everything, it throws you a curve ball. Did you know that when the humans learned about paranormals, Forest was the one who negotiated with the human government and paranormal counsels to have sanctuary packs across the country?" Ricky could hear the pride in the woman's voice.

"He must have been a powerful Alpha," Ricky responded.

Vicky nodded. "He still is. Yet even though he's retired, most shifters still look to him as being the leader of them all. You see shifters don't have a counsel of leaders like the other paranormal cultures do; they have always been independent."

"I know, Alpha Clifton told me more than once that he could do whatever he wanted to with me and my brother because no one would stop him." The human shuddered as he remembered the conversation; it had been just before he'd received punishment for the first time. Some of the scars on his back came from that particular lesson.

Vicky tapped his arm. "Everyone answers to someone, Ricky—even Alpha Clifton."

Ricky unclenched the fingers that surrounded the coffee cup. "I'm sorry, you were saying?"

Grant's mother patted his arm one last time before she continued, "Anyway, at first only a few like my family joined us, but as the cultures began to mix, more problems cropped up. As with any culture, most simply wanted to live peacefully but there were a few who felt they were superior to the others. The 'Purists' sought to either dominate or eliminate those they felt were beneath them."

"I remember reading about the Great War in school. No one knows how it really started although some believed it was rogue shifters. It's why the final peace agreement included an automatic death sentence for any shifter who was declared rogue by an Alpha." Ricky sat back in his chair. "Of course, the fact that just any Alpha can declare someone rogue without any kind of a trial is kind of stupid if you ask me."

Vicky laughed. "I can see your point and after what happened to you, Forest is planning to talk to the other leaders to try to come up with something better. However, we have gotten off the reason for this discussion, my young friend." Grant's mother winked as she took another sip from her cup. "The reason I started this history lesson was to help you understand that being the mate to the Alpha can be difficult. Goddess knows that I was ready to kill that wolf more than once during our life and there were times when I'm sure he wanted to do the same to me. Do you know the hardest part?"

Ricky shook his head.

"Knowing when to push and when to simply support him; I tried to never let him know when I was giving him a gentle shove." Vicky giggled. "It was always best to let him think it was his idea to begin with." Grant's mother stood and began to collect the dishes. "And of course we need to be the one to catch them when they fall, as all good leaders will do from time to time."

Ricky rubbed the tattoo on his arm. "I want to be there for him but I can't just stand by and let him fight all my battles. I'm supposed to be a warrior according to the shaman who put this mark on my arm. How am I going to protect Sandy and Grant when I can't fight my way out of a paper bag?"

"You learn to fight." Ricky jumped as Tank entered the room. He still was trying to figure out the man's name because he was small compared to all the other shifters and didn't have as much muscle mass. Yet he could tell from looking at the shifter that he was deadly, it was in the way he carried himself.

Tank smiled at Grant's mother. "The rest of the guys will be here shortly. Is there any coffee left?"

"Just take a seat, it won't take more than a couple of minutes to make another pot," Vicky replied.

Tank sat across from Ricky but remained silent. Ricky looked around for a moment but decided maybe he should return to the bedroom before Grant showed up. While he was pretty sure his mate wouldn't hurt him, a part of him still didn't want to take a chance. Before he could stand Tank gently grabbed his wrist. "You should come and train with the new Sentries."

196

"Me?" Ricky exclaimed as he pulled his arm free. "You want me to fight with shifters?"

Tank shrugged. "You mentioned your need to protect your brother and your mate. From what I've seen, you are strong for a human—just unskilled."

"How can I fight a shifter?" Ricky stood and motioned at his skinny frame with his hands. "Believe me I've tried to fight, but all I ever got for my efforts was severe punishment."

Vicky placed a cup of coffee on the table in front of Tank who nodded his thanks. He took a sip and calmly glanced up at Ricky. "So you think I cannot fight a shifter who is bigger than me?"

Ricky took a step back and wrapped his arms around his middle. Logically he knew the answer because the man wouldn't be part of the special enforcer group if he couldn't fight. "It's not the same thing—you're a shifter and I'm—I'm just a human."

Tank chuckled. "In my experience it isn't size that matters but rather your lack of skills and confidence. Look, I can show you ways to fight and win against almost any adversary; anyone can learn to fight. But you have another skill that is much more prized than the ability to injure or kill someone."

"What's that?" Ricky was intrigued as he sat back down in the chair.

The shifter leaned forward and tapped Ricky's forehead gently. "You, my young friend, have the wisdom to know when to fight and when to bend. You were untrained and yet you bided your time until you could get both you and your brother to safety. That takes courage and wisdom." Tank sat back and smiled. "When you want to seek training, I would be honored to be the one to work with you—but first you should ask your mate."

"Of course, I'd never do anything without getting permission from my mas—er—I mean my mate," Ricky stuttered. Tank looked like he wanted to reply but before he could do so, Grant walked into the kitchen.

"Get my permission for what?" Grant asked with a raised brow.

Ricky wanted to escape but the door was blocked by Sparky and his younger brother. The last thing he wanted to do was make a scene. He quickly looked down, unwilling to meet the eyes of the Alpha as he shrugged. "Nothing important, Alpha Grant." As he continued to keep his hands folded and eyes down, the only sound in the room was the sound of the coffee pot percolate. He should have stayed in the bedroom, why did he disobey? Ricky felt the panic begin to build, his breath caught in his throat as his lungs strained to bring in air.

A strong hand gently lifted his chin until he found himself looking into the dark brown eyes of his mate.

A soft smile was on the Alpha's face as he used his finger to slowly stroke the side of Ricky's face. "There you are." He paused but didn't remove his hand. Ricky couldn't help the slight shudder that ran through his body. A frown appeared on Grant's face but his voice remained soft, "You have nothing to fear from me, my mate. I thought…" the Alpha sighed, "…never mind, just tell me what you want Ricky and I'll do what I can to make it happen."

Ricky swallowed a couple of times before he finally managed to whisper, "I want to learn to fight…"

Grant stepped back, the frown on his face deepened. He shook his head before he spoke, "I'm sorry, Ricky, but the answer is no."

There was a sharp indrawn breath from Vicky, but otherwise there was no other sound from any of the people in the room. Ricky glanced back down at his fisted hands as he tried to quell the unexpected anger the Alpha's response had woken in him. How was he supposed to protect his brother if he couldn't learn to fight? Not to mention Ricky was tired of being someone else's punching bag. If he'd known how to fight, he might have been able to avoid being captured by Beta Biff. Suddenly he just couldn't stay in the too quiet room any longer.

He nodded at the Alpha before he turned to see his brother. Even Sandy seemed affected by the mood as he remained quiet. Years of being a slave is what allowed Ricky to swallow his anger as he put a smile on his face. "Come on, Sandy, why don't you show me what you bought today?"

Sandy looked to the Alpha who simply nodded. Great, it appeared he also needed permission to be with his brother. Things hadn't changed after all, which left Ricky feeling hollow inside. For a short time, he'd allowed himself to believe Grant when he'd told him he was no longer a slave. While his mate hadn't hurt him physically, it would only be a matter of time. He'd traded one master for another.

"Are you okay, Ricky?" Sandy's voice trembled slightly.

Ricky squared his shoulders and allowed the smile to reach his eyes. "I'm fine, squirt, now why don't we go out to the porch. I'll get some fresh air and you can show me the treasures you and Sparky found in town." He turned to Grant. "That is if it's okay with you, Alpha?"

The Alpha growled. "Of course you can go outside, this isn't a prison!"

"Could have fooled me," Ricky muttered softly as he quickly turned and followed his brother towards the front of the house. He paused for a moment when he heard the sound of someone being slapped followed by Grant's voice, "What did you do that for, Mother?"

"You deserve more than a slap to the back of the head, young man. You may be Alpha but you're still my son!" Vicky said forcefully.

Not wanting to hear anymore, Ricky continued to walk to the front door. This time he couldn't help the small chuckle that bubbled up and escaped. It seemed he had at least one person on his side in this house and he would place bets on who would win. Suddenly the darkness that had begun to swallow him seemed a little lighter. He'd deal with his mate later, for now he just wanted to relax and enjoy a few minutes with his brother.

Sandy had just finished telling Ricky about the tour he'd taken of the school with Sparky and the headmaster when the sound of motorcycles filled the air. A moment later the front door opened and Alpha Grant exited followed by Sparky and Tank. For a moment Ricky glanced up at his mate through his bangs; he had to admit the man was walking sex on a stick. Too bad he felt so intimidated by the shifter. Grant walked over and stood behind him.

He placed his finger under Ricky's chin and forced him once again to look up. "You and I need to talk, my mate."

"Yes, sir," Ricky replied softly.

Grant sighed and Ricky could see sadness in his mate's dark brown eyes. Before they could continue, three motorcycles pulled up in front of the wrap around porch. Blaze dismounted and walked closer. "We're ready to go, Alpha Grant."

"Good. I hope Shadow's Intel is accurate," Alpha Grant replied.

"He's good at what he does—we all are." Blaze winked at Sandy who for once was quiet.

Ricky chuckled at the look of awe on the youngster's face. Of course, the three large black bikes were impressive.

The lighthearted banter stopped, as Blaze's eyes appeared to glow with anger. "We have never lost a man and I don't intend to start now. We'll find Radar and Samantha, you can bet on it."

Sparky stepped down and walked towards Dove's bike. "What on earth? Is that—it is! You're taking Nutcruncher with you?"

Ricky glanced back towards the motorcycles and noticed that there was a small bucket seat settled between the handlebars on Dove's motorcycle. Sure enough, sitting up in the special seat was the robotic squirrel they had used to rescue him. He'd never seen the squirrel in action, but he'd heard about how the animal got its name. Even now he felt like crossing his legs. He couldn't help laughing though when he realized not only was the squirrel sitting in the small seat, but it was wearing leather chaps, a leather jacket and a small black helmet—did they even make helmets that small?

Sparky took a closer look but then clapped his hands and exclaimed, "Wait—wait, I have something for Nutcruncher! I'll be right back." Ricky wondered what the crazy shifter was up to. His question was answered as Sparky returned a moment later with a small piece of sparkling purple cloth in his hands.

"You can't have a mascot without giving him his own scarf," Sparky exclaimed, as he wrapped the vibrant purple cloth around the squirrel's neck. For a moment Dove looked like he was going to deck the shifter, but Falcon simply laughed. "Well at least you'll be able to find him if he jumps off and goes to find some nuts along the way."

"Keep it up and I'll let him check out yours," Dove growled.

Blaze chuckled. "I think we better get going before Dove decides to let Nutcruncher loose on Sparky or Falcon."

Alpha Grant shook his head. "Sparky get up here and leave the squirrel alone." He walked down the steps and watched as Blaze mounted his bike and started the engine. "Stay safe and make sure you let us know when you find them. Don't engage on your own," Alpha Grant ordered.

"Yes Sir!" Blaze tipped his head before he put on his helmet and signaled for the other two to follow. Ricky watched as the three men disappeared into the afternoon sun. He wrapped his arms around his middle and couldn't help the small shudder that shook his frame. There was something evil going on and

Alpha Clifton was in the center of whatever it was. He only hoped that when they discovered the crazy Alpha's plans, they wouldn't be too late to stop it.

About The Author

Raven lives in a small town in northern Illinois. She has been writing for years, but after discovering the world of paranormal romance, her muse and a few close friends finally prodded her to delve into this genre of writing. There is nothing better than a good romance filled with werewolves, hot men and other paranormal creatures to pass the time.

Most evenings you can find her reading, writing or cuddling up with her menagerie of cats and dogs.

You can find her on Facebook, Twitter or her website: www.darkwingpublications.com and of course you can always email her at darkwing.publications@gmail.com

Stay tuned for Book 2 of The Guardian Pack series: Battle for a Mates Heart